High of Heart

Also by Emilie Loring
in Large Print:

Lighted Windows
With Banners
Give Me One Summer
As Long as I Live
Stars in Your Eyes
Rainbow at Dusk
Bright Skies
I Hear Adventure Calling
Behind the Cloud
A Candle in Her Heart
The Key to Many Doors
Throw Wide the Door

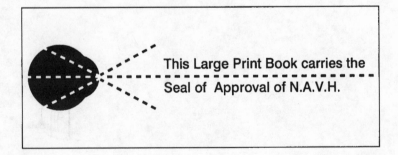

This Large Print Book carries the
Seal of Approval of N.A.V.H.

High of Heart

Emilie Loring

Thorndike Press • Thorndike, Maine

Large print ed.

Published in 2000 by arrangement with
Little, Brown & Co., Inc.

Thorndike Press Large Print Candlelight Series.

The tree indicium is a trademark of Thorndike Press.

The text of this Large Print edition is unabridged.
Other aspects of the book may vary from the original edition.

Set in 16 pt. Plantin by Elena Picard.

Printed in the United States on permanent paper.

ISBN 0-7862-2658-7 (lg. print: hc: alk. paper)

To my friend
BETH KERLEY
whose middle name is
Loyalty

I

Peter Corey stood on the hilltop in a world transfused with enchantment by the magic glow of a late winter sunset. He thoughtfully regarded the mouth of the girl who faced him. Her arm was slipped through the rein of a bay horse whose satin skin rippled with every movement of the muscles under it. It could be lovely, that mouth, but during the months of their engagement he had learned that its present tightness forboded trouble. Something was coming. It came.

"I won't play second fiddle to Constance Trent, Peter. Either put her out of your life entirely or our engagement ends here and now," Lydia Austen threatened.

Two sharp lines cut between his dark brows as he met the challenge in her angry green eyes. Beautiful but hard. He caught back the thought as disloyalty to his future wife. Behind her the sky was a crimson field patched with purple and lavender clouds, threaded by horizontal paths of topaz, jade and turquoise. High up rode a single star like the light at a masthead. Her brown riding costume was the perfection of tailoring, the green ascot accentuated the fairness of her skin, every ash-blond hair on her uncovered head which the sunset had turned to red silver, was in place.

He had a sudden vision of Con's dark hair fluffing and lifting in this light breeze. He clicked the shutter of memory. Better keep his mind on the present. He had come to a moment of decision which required his entire attention. His hand in its string glove which matched the hunting yellow of his riding jersey, tightened on the rein of his roan who was nudging his arm with a sleek nose.

"You are unfair about Con, Lydia," he protested gravely. "Her father, Gordon Trent, who was a business associate of my father's, brought her to us ten years ago when he learned that his number was up. She was thirteen and he made Mother her guardian. He lived for five years after that. I'm sure that his sense of security about his child lengthened his life. She's a grand person. She has been daughter and sister in our home. Ours is the only family she has."

"The only family which acknowledges her, you mean. Everyone knows that her mother deserted her husband when the child was three years old and ran off with another man. Her father was the younger son of an English baron, wasn't he? She'd better live on that family for a while."

"Con is not living on the Coreys, if that's what is troubling you, Lydia." Peter's voice was sharp with impatience. "The property her father left yields a fair income. She fitted herself to be a private secretary, but she won't even look for a job because she thinks there are dozens of women, to say nothing of boys and men, who need the work and she doesn't, except for extras." He smiled. "She's so full of energy and ideas that she has to be absorbed in something, so she's visiting all the older people, collecting their reminiscences and the stories they remember of happenings in our town, particularly of the World War. You know, she's got something worth while there."

"Patriotic, isn't she, for an alien!"

"Con! An alien!" He chuckled. "I would hate to have her hear you say that. She is one of those fierce 'Right or wrong, my country' patriots. She was born in the United States. She is an American citizen. I doubt if her father's family knows of her existence. He married an American after he came to this country. Even if it means losing you, I will not stop managing Con's business as you have hinted so many times of late, nor will I put her out of my life. Just to complete the record, you might as well know that should she lose her money and be unable to find a job she would be welcome to anything the Coreys have."

Lydia Austen's eyes sparked with anger as they met his steady gray ones. She shrugged, removed her left glove and drew off a ring. A round-cut diamond flashed like a sinister eye in her pink palm.

"That settles it! Take it. You have made your choice between Constance Trent and me."

He disregarded the outstretched hand. His eyes held hers.

"Sure you want it this way, Lydia?" he asked. "You promised to set the date for our marriage today. I have adjusted my business that I may be away three months on a wedding trip. Now you wreck all our plans by your silly jealousy."

"It isn't silly and it isn't jealousy. It's commonsense. There are hurdles enough along the rocky road of matrimony without facing a big one at the start. If you really loved me you would throw Con over in a minute. For the last time, will you do it?"

"No."

"In spite of your irresistible smile and your charm I've suspected that you are streaked with New England granite, Peter. Now I know it. I don't care for granite."

She dropped the ring into the pocket of his brown home-spun riding jacket.

"That's that! It's through. Finished. I'm going."

She adjusted a soft green hat at a smart angle. Without comment Peter Corey helped her mount. Swung into his saddle. Led the way down the hill. Click of pebbles against hoofs, creak of leather, the far, faint throb of an engine were the only sounds which stirred the brooding silence of the pungent, conifer-scented air. They entered the highway. Lydia Austen reined in the bay horse.

"Far as we go together, Peter," she announced jauntily. "Being engaged to you has been a liberal education — in restraint. If you should change your mind, should decide that you prefer me to Constance Trent, I mean," her eyes and lips flashed an alluring smile — "better let me know at once, I'm thinking of joining my sister Gertie, Lady Coswell, at her country home in England. *Au revoir.*"

Motionless as a bronze rider on a bronze horse Peter Corey watched her out of sight.

Was this just one more of the bitter arguments which had been recurring of late between Lydia and himself or was it the final crack-up of their engagement?

He visualized her small, tight mouth, which could be so sweet, her angry eyes, felt for the ring she had dropped into his pocket and answered his own question.

"Final!"

At the sound of his voice the roan turned his head and whinnied. Peter patted the sleek mane.

"I get you, Big Brother. You are thinking of home and the grain bin while I sit here wondering why I asked Lydia to marry me. Get going, stout fella."

Why did I? He followed that train of thought as the horse trotted toward Red Maples. Smoke in my eyes? I never felt the rapture I thought went with love. It needed something, less allure, perhaps, and a red-blooded transfusion of sympathetic understanding. We don't even enjoy the same things. Must have been an emotional brainstorm blown up by the feeling of emptiness in the house while Mother and Con were in South America last summer.

He thought of the long, unbearably hot days in the city when he had worked as he had never worked before and of the evenings when he had plunged into the swift current of unceasing gaiety whipped up by Lydia Austen and her friends. It had meant escape for a few hours from the maze of racketeer investigation into which his work had led him with the result that he hadn't taken a vacation in four years. Looked now as if the one he had planned had gone blooey.

Apparently this is just one of those days, his thoughts trooped on. This morning news comes that Dafter, the blackmailing, bank-robbing expert who is in the upper brackets of the Bad Man class, once more has slipped through the net FBI men had thought unbreakable and now Lydia gives me my *congé*. Why don't I feel defeated and jilted, instead of having a sense of emerging from fog into sunshine?

He faced the question squarely and knew that lately, deep in his consciousness, he had been aware that when he proposed marriage to Lydia Austen he had taken the most important step in a man's life impulsively, thoughtlessly — he, who had been privileged to see the close and stimulating partnership of his mother and father grow more beautiful as the years passed. That Lydia could be sweet and sympathetic and provocative was no excuse for him. He would have put on the wise-older-brother act to Tim if he had done such a fool thing. He didn't deserve this easy release from a tragic mistake.

Deserve it or not, he was free. He knew now how a man felt who had been subconsciously aware that he was approaching the edge of a precipice and had been snatched back. He squared his shoulders and drew a long breath. March was going out. Already there was a faint scent of spring in the air. What would he do with a three months' vacation?

What would his mother say? He remembered her consternation when he had told her of his engagement, her exclamation, "To Lydia Austen!" and her haste to attribute her shocked voice to surprise.

And he remembered how Con had sprung from the corner of the living-room sofa in which she had been curled reading. He even remembered how Whiskers, the wire-haired terrier, squatting beside her, had regarded her with his white head tipped and a black ear cocked as she exclaimed:

"Engaged to that poisonous girl, Peter! You're crazy! Her PQ is one hundred per cent., she's all smiles and charm when a man's in sight, but you should see her with the female of the species, it's minus, then. Besides, she's silly about Lady Somebody or other, that sister of hers who married an English baronet. 'Twouldn't be long before she threw you over for a Lord Whosis. She's —"

"Connie, my *dear,*" Angela Corey's vibrant voice had stemmed the passionate torrent of protest, but only for an instant.

"I can't help it, Angel. You, his mother, and I can't sit on the side lines and see Peter mess up his life, without protesting, can we?"

"After all, it is my life, Con," he had reminded caustically, hurt to the soul by her lack of sympathy in what he had felt then was his Big Moment.

Little flames leaped in her dark eyes. She was white as she flared:

"Sure it's your life, Peter Corey, but I'll remind you that my life is mine the next time you turn thumbs down on some of my boy friends. Because Angel laps up everything you say as gospel truth and I don't want to worry her, I've been dumb enough to refuse to go out with those of whom you don't approve. Never again. If you can't do better with your own life you can't manage mine."

Since then there had been a chill in her manner to him, faint as the first frost on a windowpane, but it was there. She had been such an adoring youngster while she was growing up. College hadn't diminished her devotion to him. The change had been like a cold wind against his heart. Would the breaking of his engagement melt the frost?

Whiskers charged down the stairs when Peter entered the hall at Red Maples. He jumped and quivered in welcome as he ran ahead into the softly lighted living room. The pearl lamp shades lined with soft pink gave the effect of glowing sea shells. His mother was at the tea table. There was always an aura of exquisiteness about her. The pale gray of her frock, her prematurely white hair, her lovely patrician face, were tinted by the rosy reflection of the fire which leaped and licked as if eager to see its tonguelike flames in the massive silver kettle.

Angela Corey looked up at her son with the smile and the light in her dark eyes he thought the most heartwarming sight in the world.

"You are early, Peter. Where is Lydia? I thought you were to ride with her and bring her here for tea."

He backed up to the fire and rested an arm on the mantel. Better get it over, he decided.

"I was riding with Lydia. I didn't bring her here because we parted at the foot of

Shootflying Hill. *She* says — forever."

"And what do you say, Peter?" Angela Corey's voice was tense with anxiety.

"I? I agree with her. I think she has the right idea."

"Peter! My dear! Thank God! With her you never would have had the rich and splendid life marriage should bring to you! I knew it and I've been as helpless as that eternally smiling woman on the Chinese screen at the garden-room door. I have been terrified for fear that sometime you would wake up and realize that you love —" she broke off the sentence sharply. "I am so glad! So hap—"

The word ended in a choked sob. Peter couldn't remember that he had seen tears in his mother's eyes since the death of his father ten years ago. Two great crystal drops rolled down her cheeks. She dabbed at them hastily. Her voice was shaken music as she apologized:

"Sorry, Peter. I should have thought of your pain and disappointment, before I rejoiced, my dear."

"That's all right, Mother. I'm not heartbroken. Of course, I may still be numb from the shock. Lydia was to set the date of our marriage today."

"Why did she break with you?"

"She put it to me straight. Would I give up handling Con's business affairs? If not she would give me up."

"You wouldn't consent?"

"The engagement is broken. There's your answer. Something tells me that Con was the occasion, not the real reason of the break. Fee, fi, fo, fum, I smell the blood of an Englishman. She is planning to visit her sister, Lady Coswell. She may see a title in the offing."

> " 'Oh, when I think of what I am
> And what I useter was
> I think I've thrown myself away
> Without sufficient cause.' "

The words floated down from the hall above. The sweet husky voice died away in a theatrical trill. The wire-haired terrier cocked a drooping ear.

"Con acquired that song shortly after she heard of my engagement," Peter Corey observed dryly. "I presume she thinks it fits my case to a T."

"Don't be bitter, Peter. Connie is modern — I don't like that word in connection with her, it is used to excuse so much that is cheap and shoddy — but she is modern, in the best sense of the word. She knows what

18

marriage means, that it is a fifty-fifty proposition, and she was convinced that in short order Lydia would smash yours on the rocks. That is her expression, not mine. Now that your engagement is broken I can tell you that your fiancée never lost a chance to plant barbs in Connie's heart. Sly references to the mother who deserted her, who never has tried to find her, thrusts about her father's family which has ignored her. Connie's a thoroughbred. In spite of the way she has been treating you — I've noticed her frostiness — she is sweet and sound and loyal to the core. I couldn't love a daughter of my own more than I love her. I've seen her face whiten and her lips compress but she never shot back at Lydia. She told me once that if she did it might react and hurt you."

"Why haven't I been told this before?"

"Because I have hoped and prayed you would find it out for yourself. You might have thought I was jealous."

"You, jealous! You're too big for that. Pity there aren't more mothers like you." He cleared his voice of emotion. "Speaking of mothers and Lydia's thrusts, it is curious we've never heard a word of Con's."

"Gordon Trent never tried to trace her. As you know, he wouldn't start action for divorce. I think to the day of his death he hoped she would come back to him. He loved her and knew that his one-time friend with whom she ran away would not marry her. He argued that if she wanted to be legally free she would appeal to him. She did not. Just dropped completely out of sight. Perhaps she changed her name, perhaps she died. Whatever happened, the child was well rid of her. You tried to trace her, didn't you, Peter?"

"Yes. I knew that the uncertainty of her fate was like a thunderhead low on the horizon to Con. I wanted to make sure that the woman would not appear to threaten her or make her unhappy. I didn't get hold of even a thread of clue as to what had happened to her, not surprising when all I had to start with was a faded, tinted photograph and her maiden name. Gordon Trent gave me those scraps of information. He would talk by the hour about his old home but if I mentioned his wife he would shut up like a clam. When Tim was all excited about that detective correspondence course he was taking, I turned over the picture and the sparse information I had to him and told him to go to it, *cherchez la femme,* but he didn't get anywhere either."

"Here's Connie. As usual pelting downstairs like a mountain torrent. Will you tell her your engagement is broken, Peter?"

"Not here. Not now. Pour my tea, will you, Angel?"

" 'Lo Peter! Aren't you home early?" Constance Trent asked as she entered the room. With a yelp of joy the dog rushed at her.

"Whiskers, you make me think of a bunch of fur strung on wires. You know you'd desert me like a flash if you sensed Peter in the offing. Cultivate poise, my lad. Where's Lydia, Peter? She phoned that she would drop in this afternoon to ask me to be one of her bridesmaids. I didn't know the happy date was set. She said her attendants would wear green. That lets me out. Green is frightfully unbecoming to me, she knew it, brings out the yellow in my skin. That's the Voice of Experience speaking, in case you care. Watch your step, Angel. That cup's running over!"

Peter's eyes were on her as she dropped a kiss on the top of his mother's head, an apology for her flippant voice, he knew, and dexterously replaced the brimming cup with an empty one. His heart felt as if it would expand to bursting point, his throat tightened. He understood now Con's coldness toward him. Why had Lydia wanted to hurt her? His mother was right, she was sweet and sound to the core and loyalty was her middle name.

He tried to appraise her with the eyes of a stranger. The line of satin-black hair about her forehead was beautiful. Her brows, which had been left in their natural silky line, slanted ever so little. When she lifted heavily fringed lids her eyes were as dark as her hair, a rich, velvety black with a luminous glow when she was excited. Her skin, smooth as the petal of a gardenia, was slightly pink now from the reflection of her rose-color frock. Her nose was straight and adorable. Her mouth was generous and her vivid lips tipped up slightly at the corners; there was a dimple in her chin. "Exotic type," a fashion reporter had described her.

"Is it your custom to glare at a witness as you are glaring at Connie, Peter?" his mother inquired with a lilt in her voice he hadn't heard for months, not since the day he had told her of his engagement, to be exact. "Because if it is, I don't wonder they call you Man-eating Corey, that you convict eighty per cent. of the criminals brought into your court."

"Angel! What has happened to switch your spirit to high?" Constance demanded before Peter could answer. Her smooth throat contracted as if she were swallowing a sob before she added unsteadily:

"It's — it's wonderful to have your old self back."

"Connie dear, have I been so selfish —"

A black-frocked rosy-cheeked maid with a white cap on her blond head entered and presented a card on a silver tray.

"The gentleman says it's most important. He must see you and Mr. Peter, Madam."

Angela Corey frowned at the card.

" 'Mr. Clive Neale; Neale, Bridgers and Bridgers, Solicitors, London,' " she read aloud. "Is he one of your British clients, Peter? Here's something else — 'Representing Major General Lord Vandemere Trent-Gowan, Retired.' "

She looked up.

"Gowan! Trent-Gowan!" she exclaimed in a startled voice. "He's your grandfather, Connie!"

23

II

Clive Neale, of Neale, Bridgers and Bridgers, was not the type of English solicitor representing a family whose titles and estates dated back to the fifteenth century that motion pictures, plus imagination, had prepared her to expect, Constance Trent reflected, as from under her fringe of black lashes she regarded the man talking earnestly to Angela Corey. According to fictional tradition he should be spare and gray and stooped. Instead he was tall. He might be in the late thirties, but not a year older. His dark eyes were in startling contrast to his hair and slight mustache, which were almost yellow.

He had set saucer and cup on the floor beside his chair and with the thumb and forefinger of his finely shaped hand was tenderly massaging the lapel of his black morning coat.

As he talked he cast an occasional glance of appeal at Peter Corey who stood before the fire as still and about as responsive as the terrier, who squatted motionless as a graven

24

image, beside him. The man was good-looking and a snappy dresser, Constance admitted. Of course, he hadn't Peter's air of distinction, nor his engaging smile, nor his wonderful gray eyes which had a way of lighting as if flames had leaped in them for an instant, and of turning one's mind inside out till he knew exactly what one was thinking, nor his clean-cut firm chin, but —

"You should talk to Miss Trent, not to me, Mr. Neale."

Angela Corey's voice roused Constance from the coma of surprise into which the Englishman's announcement that he was an emissary from her father's father had plunged her.

With a sudden instinctive need for something strong and impregnable to grip she rose and slipped her arm within Peter's. She saw his face flush with dark color, saw the twitch of a muscle in his cheek before he encouraged:

"Here we are, judge and jury prepared to listen to your argument, Mr. Solicitor."

As the maid left the room with the tea tray Clive Neale replied to the challenge.

"What I have been saying during the last fifteen minutes — Miss Trent has heard little of it, I am sure — sums up to this:

"Lord Gowan wants his granddaughter,

his only remaining descendant, to come to Trentmere Towers. A year ago, after the death of his elder son who left no heir, he set agents on the trail of his son, Gordon; Trent is the family name. The search ended in this house."

"For a good many years he didn't care to know whether that younger son starved or prospered," Constance reminded bitterly.

"Your grandfather has given superb service to his country, Miss Trent. He has the heart of a lion, the temper of a wildcat and the obstinacy of, I know of no adequate comparison, it's colossal. Also, he's a dashed fine Greek scholar. He came from generations of soldier barons whose loyalty was rewarded by kings who settled on them great estates. The family history is woven into Britain's. It was a bitter disappointment when his younger son left home rather than continue in the army, a commissioned officer in his father's old regiment. Failing male issue, the title, which does not descend through the female line, will go to a son of a cousin, Captain Ivor Hardwick." Neale's eyes and voice hardened as he spoke the name. "He is one of the popular bachelor hosts in London. Eventually he doubtless would have come into the estate, though it is not entailed, if your father had left no child.

You are Lord Gowan's direct heir. To his friends he is 'Lord Van.' "

"Present the 'direct heir's' compliments to Major General Lord Vandemere Trent-Gowan, Retired, and tell him that she is interested neither in him nor in his estate, that she belongs to another family." She looked up. "I do belong to the Coreys, don't I, Peter?"

"You do indeed, my dear, utterly, but I think you should go to your grandfather."

"Peter! You can't mean it! You don't think I should, do you, Angel?"

"I do, Connie."

"You would. Peter's word is law to you."

"Don't make me out to be *quite* so spineless, my dear."

"I'm sorry, Angel. Of course you're not spineless, don't you rule us all? Iron hand in velvet glove stuff. I'm not spineless, either. I will decide this on my own. I won't go to Trentmere Towers. I am engaged in important historical research here. Besides, we like our life as it is, don't we, Whiskers?" The dog planted his forefeet on her frock and gazed up at her with his soul in his eyes.

"What are you getting all steamed up about, Slim? I heard you laying down the law as I came in."

Constance made a little face at the tall,

blond young man who followed his voice into the room. Her heart tightened. He still showed the results of the attack of flu which had pulled him out of his last year at law school and made the doctors warn him gravely to keep away from study for a while. He was too thin, his skin was too white, his blue eyes too translucent. At twenty-four he should be stocky and bronzed. If anything happened to Tim she couldn't bear it, that's all, she just couldn't bear it. To camouflage the sudden surge of terror she said:

"This is Timothy, my other brother, Mr. Neale."

As he grinned and extended his hand to the solicitor with the cordial charm so like Peter's she added flippantly:

"Tim, you have arrived just in time for a preview of Little Lord Fauntleroy brought up to date. English Baron graciously forgives runaway son and sends the family solicitor to America to bring long-lost grand-daughter to the ancestral home that she may be given a screen-test for the role of heir to the estate. Can't you hear a voice shout 'Camera!'?"

"Well, what do you know about that! Stop and get your breath, Slim. Is that straight goods?"

"It is quite true, Mr. Timothy," Clive

Neale assured before Constance could answer. "But Miss Trent has left out the setting of her cinema. The house, Trentmere Towers, a large part of which dates back to the sixteenth century, is very beautiful, set in its famous gardens, with farmhouses, stables and garages. From the top of a hill it overlooks its own villages, streams and valleys. It has been modernized in keeping with its architecture and, unlike many of our old homes, has been kept in perfect repair. The estate covers 30,000 acres. It is one hour from London by express and forty-five miles by good motoring road."

He drew a folder from the breast pocket of his coat with the assured manner of one about to play the ace of trumps.

"I have photographs of it here."

"Not interested," Constance declared indifferently. She freed her arm from Peter's, turned her back, rested her forehead against the edge of the mantel and stared unseeingly down into the leaping, writhing, scarlet and gold flames. With a deep-drawn sigh the terrier dropped to the rug and laid his nose on her shoe.

As if *she* needed to be shown photographs of her father's old home, she thought bitterly. Hadn't pictures of it been etched deep into her memory by the keen, merciless point of his heartsick longing for it? Her throat ached, her lids stung from hot, repressed tears as she remembered his wistful eyes, his unsteady voice when he had tried to make her visualize the deeply carved, richly painted ceiling of the great vaulted hall, the Spanish leather of its walls, the gallery along its western end from the long, narrow windows of which one could watch the white border in the fountain garden slowly dyed to crimson beauty by the slanting sun.

Had only five years passed since his death? It seemed a century ago. He had been so tender. His passion had been music. Life had hurt him cruelly. He had been little more than a boy when he was hurled into the bloody vortex of war. He had loved the wife who had run away with his friend. He had loved England. He never had lost the feeling that he was an exile but he never had regretted in the darkest hours that he had refused to spend the best years of his life in the army. He hated war. It was such a tragic waste. Nothing ever was gained by it.

"Don't misunderstand me, Connie," he would say. "Of course armies must be maintained, adequate provision for defense must be made, and there are thousands to whom that life appeals. If ever Britain again needs me, my life is hers. I would die willingly in defense of the honor of my country, but I refuse to spend it in garrisons in distant lands or parading to the rhythm and martial music of bands. I don't want to kill or cripple my fellow man. There must be other ways to adjust international quarrels. I have a deep, abiding belief that sometime some great mind and heart will work out the solution."

And because he refused to spend the rest of his life in a profession for which he was totally unsuited his father had let him go, never had tried to find him. Had this man, Neale, who had spoken so casually of tracing Gordon Trent, learned that there had been weeks and months at a time when he and his small daughter had not had enough to eat? When they had shaken with cold? When the child had been taunted by other children in the poor neighborhood with the fact that her mother, her own mother, had run away and left her?

Probably he had ferreted that out too, but he couldn't know that for months, after her father had begun to prosper, and for years after she came to Red Maples she had felt that her mother had left a dark stain on her heart which one who looked close enough could see. Angel had comforted and loved that inferiority complex away until now it was a mere wraith of memory.

To the accompaniment of the murmur of voices behind her her thoughts drifted back to the day on which her father had brought her to this mellow old house set against a background of maples which flamed crimson and scarlet and gold in the late afternoon sunlight. She saw herself a thin child of thirteen, so thin and scrawny that later Tim had nicknamed her "Slim," seated stiffly on the edge of a chair in this very room which had been softly lighted by shaded lamps and the flickering fire and scented by a great bowl of yellow roses whose velvety petals were reflected in the shining mahogany of the piecrust table. She remembered how she had pleated and unpleated a fold of her red tweed coat with unsteady cold fingers while in another room her father conferred with recently widowed Angela Corey and her elder son Peter, who was twenty-four and just starting in the practice of law.

That had been ten years ago but she remembered as clearly as if it were yesterday the constriction of her throat as she asked herself, "Will they want me? It would be heavenly to live in a home like this after the years I've traveled with Dad, though since he has been in business with Mr. Corey we've had money enough to live in nice places." And she remembered how she had jumped to her feet and how her nails had bitten into the palms of her clenched hands and how her eyes had flown to her father's lined, white face as the three had entered the room. He was smiling. Her heart had spread wings. Angela Corey had welcomed tenderly:

"Your father has loaned you to us, Connie, dear. Gordon, you must have been divinely inspired to bring her here. We lost the two little girls who came between Peter and Timothy. You boys and I need a daughter and sister in the house, don't we, Peter?"

She thought of the glow which had stolen through her veins as her anxious eyes met Peter Corey's clear, amused gray ones and of his smile so like his mother's and felt again the surge of passionate adoration of the two which had flooded her heart. The passing years had but intensified her love for them.

A hand touched her shoulder.

"You're unfair to Mr. Neale, not to listen to him, Con," Peter Corey protested. "And darned rude, too," he added in a low voice.

The color scorched her face as she turned.

She must have been putting on a spoiled-child act to have Peter speak in that tone.

"I'm sorry, Mr. Neale," she apologized. The unexpected warmth of her voice and the charm of her smile sent a sudden tinge of color to the Britisher's face. "I was thinking of the past, which is an extravagant waste of the precious present, isn't it? I'll be good now."

The depth of Clive Neale's sigh of relief expressed even more than the eagerness of his voice.

"Thanks for giving me a hearing, at least, Miss Trent. Our firm has administered the affairs of your family for generations. I should hate to fail in my errand." As Constance impulsively opened her lips, he held up his hand.

"Give me a minute, please, let me explain. Your grandfather has no intention or desire to separate you from your foster family. He earnestly hopes that you, Mrs. Corey, and your two sons will accept his hospitality and will with his granddaughter, occupy Cherry-tree Farm during your stay in England. It is a jolly old stone house, with oak-paneled drawing rooms, dining rooms, six bedrooms, tennis courts and garages, and a garden which is the show place of the county. It is fully staffed with servants. He thought that Miss Trent would be happier to have that arrangement at first."

"Very considerate of him," Constance countered quickly, "but his proposition leaves me cold."

"But, I say, Miss Trent, your father never became naturalized in the United States. You are a British subject."

"Your mistake, Mr. Neale. Quote. 'Persons born in the United States, though of alien parents, are citizens.' Unquote. That's the law, isn't it, Peter?"

"It is. I am sure that Mr. Neale is aware of it. But being an American citizen doesn't change the fact that you are the granddaughter and heir of Lord Gowan."

"Even if I am, I shan't —"

"Suppose you give us time to think over the invitation, Mr. Neale," Angela Corey interposed. "That old stone house fully staffed with servants has an alluring sound to me."

"Do you mean you'd consider going to England, Angel, and leave Peter and Tim?" Constance demanded incredulously.

"But your grandfather wants you all," Clive Neale reminded. He laughed as the terrier hitched forward and looked directly up into his face. "That goes for the dog, too; he appears frightfully interested. Apparently he doesn't intend to be left behind. Lord Gowan wants to know the family with whom you have grown up. He hopes that you will come to him at once. I have been instructed to arrange for all expenses; and —"

"Skip it!" Peter Corey interrupted curtly. He smiled. "Better accept my mother's suggestion, Neale. Give us twenty-four hours in which to consider."

"If you think twenty-four hours will change my mind, you have another think coming to you, Peter Corey. I hate England," Constance declared hotly.

With no further attempt at argument Clive Neale bowed himself out. Angela Corey and Tim accompanied him to the hall. Con curled up in a corner of the sofa. With a "whoof" of content the dog snuggled down beside her. . . . She glanced furtively at Peter in the deep chair beside the fire. . . . Head tipped back he was thoughtfully blowing smoke rings. . . . With a rosy-nailed finger she drew an intricate pattern on her tweed skirt.

"I presume that Mr. Neale will return to England and report that the Xanthippe female has nothing on Constance Trent for a nasty temper," she announced aggressively.

"You'll have to admit that you weren't at your sweetest and sunniest, won't you?"

"I know. I was horrid. But when I thought of all Dad went through and of this chance to return to his home coming five years too late —" her voice broke.

"He loved that home, didn't he?"

"He did. He would talk about it for hours. I know every crack and cranny of it, though according to the family solicitor it has been kept in too perfect repair to crack. I could see 'Bunny' the round and rosy housekeeper who, apparently, adored him. I can describe the crest enameled on the window through which the ghost of the Spanish Bride appears and disappears before the marriage of an heir."

"Wouldn't your father want you to go to Trentmere Towers?"

"Not if he knew how I would loathe it. That closes the subject, forever. I'm not going."

"It's up to you. It will be quite a blow to Angel. Didn't you notice the sparkle in her eyes when Neale spoke of that garden? She's a little mad on the subject of gardens. Tim's expression was positively beatific when the stables and garages were mentioned. Do you know, Con, I believe that a few months in England would make that boy over. But, why think of it? You don't want to go. That ends it."

Constance stirred restlessly.

"You make me out a selfish beast, Peter."

"Not at all. Why should you do something you hate?"

"Even if I did consent to go, Angel wouldn't leave home before your marriage and Mr. Neale said my grand — Lord Gowan — wanted me to come at once, didn't he?"

Peter watched a smoke ring ascend, curl and uncurl, before he said:

"But, I'm not going to be married, Con."

She was on her feet, looking down at him unbelievingly.

"Not going to be *married!* So that's why Angel's spirit is riding the crest of the wave! Why? When — how?"

"Lydia threw me over today, if that's what you're trying to ask?"

"Oh Peter! Are you terribly hurt? Are you —" the sentence broke on a sob.

"I'll weather the gale. If you don't mind I'd rather not talk about it. The evening paper must have come. I will get it."

"Don't move! Sit there and rest. I'll bring it to you."

He rose with a laugh which disclosed a flash of perfect teeth.

"I'll get it myself. A broken engagement doesn't automatically make a man an invalid, Con." He caught her hand.

"Like me again?" he asked with sudden, deep tenderness in his voice.

"Love you!" she declared passionately. She flung her arm about his neck and pressed her lips to his.

She stepped back and looked at him with horrified eyes.

"I shouldn't have done that. You haven't kissed me since I went away to college, perhaps you thought I didn't notice it. I don't wonder your face is a deep, dark, dangerous red. But I was so happy to think you were free. Now, perhaps you'll sing again. Do you realize that you haven't sung since you became engaged to that —"

"Forget it, Con. Let's talk of something else. I'm a little disappointed that you won't accept your grandfather's invitation. I had planned to take three months' vacation and now that my wedding trip has gone blooey, Trentmere Towers sounded inviting after four years devoted to trial and conviction and smashing Rackets with a capital R."

She caught the lapels of his riding jacket and administered a slight shake.

"Peter Corey! Do you mean that you'll go with us? Of course I'll go! I'll go anywhere on earth you want me to."

"I may remind you of that sometime.

Come on. Let's tell Angel we're all set to cross the pond."

" 'A life on the ocean wave!
   A home on the rolling deep!' "

he sang in a rich baritone. Con's sweet, husky voice joined in the refrain as together they left the room with the hitch and roll of the sailor's hornpipe, the terrier barking and nipping at their heels.

In the hall she squeezed his arm and said with a sob in her voice:

"Petey, isn't it heavenly to be friends again?"

III

Soundlessly, as if touched by a magician's wand, not by human hands, the great oak doors of Trentmere Towers swung open. Con's heart mounted to her throat and beat its wings. Somewhere inside the house her father's father was waiting. He had asked her to come alone. Little he suspected that wild horses couldn't have dragged a member of the Corey family with her to this, their first meeting. She had refused Tim's offer to drive her, thinking that the walk from Cherrytree Farm would give her time to plan what she would say to her grandfather, something casual with a light touch to break the ice which would be wide as a pond, deep as a well, between them. Just as if she had thought of much else since she had set sail for England on a fast ship a week ago, she derided herself. Then it had been March. Now it was April.

The walk hadn't helped. All the way she had felt as if she were moving in a dream, that she would waken and find herself in her own white-canopied bed at Red Maples. If it were a dream she wouldn't feel jittery inside and her mind wouldn't seem like a great empty room without even the echo of the footstep of an idea, would it? She lingered on the terrace trying to get her emotions under control.

Above her the historic house wrought of limestone and granite reared massive turrets slitted by narrow windows, which frowned like battlements against the turquoise and white of an April sky. Round and round the tallest towers, ivy-covered to their finials, rooks were circling. Below her lay the gardens. The warm sun sucked the breath from the box hedges till it scented the air. The yellow centers of narcissus in the white flower border shone like gold coins. A fountain shot up thousands of glittering diamond drops to shimmer down into a glinting sapphire pool. Great oaks spreading low their mighty branches, tall elms faintly green and gold tipped, the more slender larches, cast drifts and pools of purple shadow on emerald velvet lawns.

The distant river curved like a silver sash trailing from a woman's frock through fields which had the lovely warm tint of green gold. A slim Wren steeple in dramatic contrast to the belt of dark firs above which it loomed pointed the way to the azure sky and

Heaven. Gray stone farmhouses with mossy roofs napped in the mellow sunshine. Cream-colored cattle lazily chewing their cuds in the lulling shade dotted a smooth pasture. The faint haze above the river through which she could see the sloping hills, soft green at the base, purple-blue at the top, made Con think of a gossamer screen hung before *tableaux vivant* to soften the effect.

The peace and scented quiet stilled the tumult in her heart. She must go in. She would trust to luck to say the right thing when she faced her grandfather.

She took a reluctant step forward. Stopped. What was that sound? She turned. A black and white head with brilliant bead-like eyes was poked above the upper step to the terrace.

"Whiskers! You bad dog! Have you followed me all the way?" The terrier stood on his hind feet and laid dusty forepaws on her skirt in answer.

"Down! Down!" As he sat back on his haunches and gazed up at her in quivering expectancy, she regarded him thoughtfully.

"You trail me every minute now that Peter isn't here, don't you, young fella? I miss him too. Perhaps you are the ice-breaker-answer to a maiden's prayer, Whiskers. If Lord

43

Gowan happens to like dogs, he'll recognize you as a Best of Show and remarks about you will get conversation away to a good start. Come on! Remember, you are to be a perfect gentleman. A credit to the house of Corey."

Smiling a little, head high, pulses fairly steady, feeling reinforced for her foray into the enemy's country by the presence of the dog trotting behind her, she entered the house. Crossing the threshold was like opening a long-locked door in her life from which she would fare forth into unknown country, on an unknown road which might prove adventurous, exciting, perhaps dangerous. Whatever it was, she could take it. She had been longing for a change, for a break which would give her a new and broader outlook on life. And here it was. A footman in maroon livery appeared as if by magic. He bowed almost to the silver buckles on his shoes.

"His lordship is waiting for you in the hall, my lady," he said. "This way."

As Constance followed him she caught a reassuring glimpse of her slim self in a huge mirror at the foot of the historic white marble staircase, its wall hung with Romneys and Gainsboroughs, upon which, her father had told her, the great of centuries had passed up and down. To switch her thoughts from him and the meeting ahead she told herself she was glad she had worn the rose-color linen frock, matching shoes and large hat of fine straw. The triple strand of silver beads and broad bracelet were perfect accents. Her eggshell-color bag and gloves gave the last perfect touch to her costume. The servant paused:

"The Honorable Miss Trent, your lordship." She had been so absorbed in thought that his voice startled her.

In the still moment which followed the announcement, through Con's mind echoed Tim's teasing admonition as she left Cherrytree Farm:

"Keep your chin up, Slim. Wait till you see the whites of his eyes before you shoot. The Major General at the Towers won't gobble you even if you do look good enough to eat. You're a knockout in that rig."

The memory of his words braced her spirit. There was a hint of a smile on her vivid lips as she entered the great hall. She had seen it all before through her father's eyes; the richly blended gold and crimson of the vaulted carved ceiling; the rays of color slanting down from the jeweled tops of the narrow windows in the gallery; the Spanish-leather walls, the portraits of knights in plume and armor, of lords and ladies, dead and forgotten these many years, the rich oak and walnut furniture, the Trent-Gowan crest surrounded by a wreath of oak leaves carved above the huge mantel.

But, she had had no adequate picture of the gray-haired man who stood straight and tall in front of the fire. Not so old as she had imagined him. A hawkish nose was the dominating feature in a face which was alert, powerful, austere. A monocle was screwed in one eye. His attitude was that of an aristocrat convinced of his superiority.

For an instant only she saw him. With a snarl and a fierce growl something hulking, something with rolls of fat about its short neck, with a jaw like a heavyweight champ in defense of his title, shot past the man in front of the fire and presto! something white and black and furry shot from behind her. The two forces met with an impact which bounced each one back, then plunged forward and clinched.

"Whiskers! Whiskers!" Con cried and grabbed the terrier's upright tail.

"Let him go! Keep out of the fight!" roared a voice. Even in the excitement Con wondered if that were the tone in which a Major General shouted orders. "Sacks! Gore!"

A man in maroon livery and one in the smart black of a butler rushed in. The footman grabbed the bull dog's collar and choked him till his hold broke. The butler danced around the edge of the melee like a referee at a prize fight. Con still gripped the terrier's tail. Shaking with excitement she sank into a large chair while he growled and snarled and tugged for freedom. Blood was trickling from his right ear and red spots were oozing from his breast.

"Sacks. Send the vet here at once."

"Very good, your lordship." The butler left the room in quickstep time. The footman dragged away the growling, straining bulldog by the collar. As the two disappeared Con struggled to keep down the rising storm within her. One second she wanted to cry, the next she felt she must shout with laughter. Hysterics? She never had had even a touch of them in her life. She wouldn't disgrace herself before the stern man looking down at her with piercing blue eyes which made her think of hunks of aquamarine.

"Those dogs broke the ice for the return of the Prodigal, didn't they?" she asked unsteadily and sternly swallowed something in her throat which was a cross between a sob and a giggle.

Lord Gowan did not answer. He dropped the monocle and readjusted it. He stood immovable before the fire as somewhere a clock ticked off the minutes. The terrier whined and began to lick his breast.

"Oh, Whiskers, did that brute hurt you terribly?" Con crooned and dropped to her knees beside him, while not for a second relaxing her hold on his tail. "Why did you fight? Do you call that being a perfect gentleman?"

"Don't put your face so close to the dog," Lord Gowan warned. "He may snap at you."

"He wouldn't hurt me, he's so friendly and gentle-hearted."

"He gave every indication of it," Lord Gowan observed sarcastically.

"You wouldn't have had him roll over and paw the air while John Bull attacked him, would you? Americans don't knuckle." Her eyes burned with indignation and her cheeks felt like the red spots on a clown's chalked face.

"I begin to believe you. Here's the vet. Jaggers," he spoke to the horsy-looking man, with a rubicund face, attired in a suit whose design was a steal from a checkerboard, who trotted into the room at the heels of the butler. "Take out this dog, dress

48

his wounds, and see that he is returned to Cherrytree Farm. Then take a look at Roustabout."

"Yes, your lordship." The vet regarded Con with a kindly understanding smile. "Better let go 'is tail, my lady. 'E'll come along with me, all right, won't you, boy?"

Whiskers sniffed at the hand he extended, then laid his nose against the checked sleeve with a sigh like that of a tired child. The man picked him up.

" 'E'll be all right, in a day or two, my lady. Don't you worry none."

He talked in a soothing undertone as he carried the dog from the hall. Con's eyes which had been following him came back to the man before the fire.

"I suppose you are my grandfather?" She had difficulty in keeping the inquiry steady. "I really didn't have a chance to introduce myself formally."

"Quite so. Quite so. And you are my son's daughter, Constance. Your voice is still shaking from nervousness. I don't wonder. Take off your hat. Lean back in that chair. Sacks, serve tea at once."

"Very good, your lordship."

Lord Gowan's eyes followed the butler until he left the hall, came back to the girl.

"I apologize for Roustabout, Constance.

Usually he is a peaceful citizen, but in years past the bulldog was bred to be the prize fighter of the canine world and sometimes he reverts to type. Fortunes changed hands because of him until 1835 when dog fighting became illegal in England."

She realized that he was talking to give her a chance to calm down. Her nerves still tingled as if they were in contact with an electric battery.

"How can you endure anything as ugly as that creature about this adorable place?" she asked.

"I am glad that you like Trentmere Towers — at least."

"Did you expect me to like you?" There was no bitterness in her voice, only surprised inquiry.

"You are frank. Dash it all, that word 'expect' would be better changed to 'hope.'"

He was frowning at her from beneath heavy iron-gray brows. She noticed the deep radiating lines about the corners of his blue eyes, the hard set of his mouth which bespoke an embittered man. She remembered what her father had told her of the dissipations and extravagances of his elder son. Through the corridor of memory echoed Gordon Trent's regretful voice admitting:

"Perhaps I should have stayed at home,

Connie. Maybe had I had patience Father might have come to see things my way, but I was young and could see only one side of my fight for freedom."

He hadn't stayed at home, if he had she wouldn't be sitting here, with her heart shaking like jelly and her hands thoroughly iced and a perfectly insane feeling that she had been here before, that she belonged, was a part of it, that she had returned home from a far country.

"I hope Mrs. Corey and her sons have found Cherrytree Farm comfortable?" Lord Gowan inquired with chill courtesy.

Con forgot her bitterness, forgot that in a way she was the stand-in for a Prodigal who had not returned. She remembered only the original oak-timbered first floor in the stone house, the fireplace in the great lounge blazing with logs the day of their arrival; the flowers everywhere, the charm of the chintz-hung bedrooms, the clockwork smoothness of the service rendered by the welcoming staff, the unbelievable beauty of the garden.

"It's perfection!" With the exclamation went all her fear and embarrassment. It was like breaking through a tough skin in which her real self had been sealed.

The butler entered. Behind him, Gore,

the footman, propelled a laden tea wagon.

"My granddaughter will pour the tea, Sacks," Lord Gowan instructed and seated himself in a massive carved chair near the fire.

"Very good, your lordship."

Con was not so preoccupied with the manner of her presentation to the servants that she did not note the richness and heaviness of the Georgian tea service. She had thought Angel's wedding silver fit to adorn the home of a multimillionaire but this fairly shouted of pomp and ermine, empires, kings, queens, palaces, and cloth of gold.

"That will be all, Sacks." Lord Gowan dismissed, after the butler and footman had solicitously served him.

"Very good, m'lord. The bailiff would like to see you when you are at liberty. Important, he says."

"As 'faultily faultless, icily regular, splendidly null' as if you hadn't pulled a fierce dog out of a fight," Con thought.

It frightened her a little that the line from Tennyson's "Maud" should flash through her memory as she watched the wooden-faced footman depart. She hoped her mind hadn't split to run on two tracks, for she thought it had been entirely occupied with the problem of what to say next. Try as she might, she couldn't keep the shuttlecock of conversation in the air.

"I don't like the publicity the American newspapers gave your coming to your father's people. Here, only Ivor and my solicitors knew you had been found, until after you had sailed," Lord Gowan declared irascibly. "They even played up the fact that your mother left you before you were old enough to know her. Dangerous. Very dangerous!"

"Dangerous! Why?"

"Blackmail. Some woman may come forward and claim she is your mother."

"Perhaps she would be telling the truth."

"Nonsense. She is dead. I have proof." He attempted to smooth his corrugated brow and lighten his voice. "Are you music-mad, too?"

"If you mean have I my father's gift for conjuring pure beauty of sound from the piano, no. Men who know, have said that he would have been a great artist had he had a chance." Realizing from Lord Gowan's expression that she was on skiddy ground she added hurriedly, "Of course I play, enough to accompany Tim and Peter. Peter has a marvelous voice. Not big but oh so — so heart-stirring."

"He has, eh? Peter is Mrs. Corey's son, isn't he? Why didn't he sail with you?"

Con was quite unaware of her little sigh of relief. Peter was a subject about which she could talk for hours. She observed her fingers as they picked up a slice of the richest, darkest, most delectable fruit cake she ever had seen — thank goodness, the shakes had left them.

"Peter is arriving tonight. He is a lawyer. Business came up at the last minute to detain him. He hasn't had a vacation for years. He was all set to take three months for his wedding —" she bit off the sentence. She had no right to chatter of his personal affairs.

"Wedding!" Lord Gowan blustered and Con could imagine him roaring commands in the army, if a Major General gave commands except through a staff officer.

"Whom was he planning to marry? You?"

"Marry *me! Peter!* Don't be foolish! He is my foster brother!"

She saw his color rise before he growled:

"I've heard that American girls had no respect for rank or age or —"

Con's flash of temper had evaporated. Perhaps a perfect lady didn't tell a baron of the realm not to be foolish. She smiled and apologized:

"Sorry I was rude, but your question was

54

so ridiculous. You haven't picked up the age germ, have you? We Americans," she imitated his inflection of the word to a nicety, "think that a man who looks and stands and walks as you do, is in the very prime of life. What's more, we consider references to our advancing years to be in as poor taste as wailing about a diminishing bank account."

He rose, squared his shoulders as if casting off a burden and adjusted his monocle more to his liking. There was a twinkle like her father's in his eyes.

"By Jove, I can see that the possession of an Americanized granddaughter will prove a liberal education."

That brought Con to her feet. With difficulty she kept her tone light and slightly amused.

"You may be surprised but I don't care for that word 'possession.' I belong to myself and the Coreys. I am not 'Americanized,' but, to use a hackneyed expression, 'one hundred per cent. American.'"

"Stuff and nonsense! You're an Englishwoman and my granddaughter," he contradicted in high-tempered protest.

His tone was maddeningly dictatorial, his face was a choleric red, his blue eyes emitted sparks. She knew now what her father had been up against when he made his fight for freedom.

"I'm not and what's more —"

"Did you ring, m'lord?" a soft voice interrupted.

IV

The plump, short, white-haired woman in creaking black taffeta, snowy collar and cuffs of incredible fineness, who had spoken, was halfway between the door and the fireplace. Her cheeks, crisscrossed with wrinkles like a waffle, burned with the color of a red Mackintosh apple, her brown eyes were worried. This must be "Bunny" the beloved housekeeper of whom her father had spoken, Con decided. It must have been ESP, that "extra-sensory perception," which had brought her into the room at the critical moment to prevent a battle of wills.

"You know I didn't ring." Lord Gowan's voice had lost its aggressiveness as if the woman's presence had been a reminder. "Constance, this is Mrs. Bunthorne, who came to the Towers when your father was a little boy."

"And he never forgot her. He told me how wonderful she had been to him."

Tears flooded the housekeeper's eyes in response to the warmth of Con's smile and

57

the unsteadiness of her voice.

"Did he? Did he really, my lady? Master Gordon was the darling of my heart and you're as bonny as I knew his child would be." She brushed away a tear with a plump hand.

"Tut! Tut! No crying," Lord Gowan interrupted testily. "Bunthorne, show my granddaughter about the Towers while I talk with the bailiff. Tell Sacks to send him here. Come back to the hall before you go, Constance."

Mrs. Bunthorne led the way from room to room chattering ceaselessly. "His lordship's very proud of that word granddaughter, I can see, my lady. This is the gold salon with the famous Fragonard panels. Many's the time I've lingered outside when your father was playing on that very piano. Often it seemed to me I could feel the brush of angels' wings as they bent down from heaven to listen. He would have been a great musician had he been given the chance.

"Behind this door are iron stairs descending to a dungeon and a tunneled outlet in the stone wall.

"That ceiling painting was discovered under lath and plaster only fifty years ago."

She led the way up the marble stairway, along a broad corridor, and opened a door.

"And here, my dear, is where the Spanish Bride appears."

Her hushed voice and the caution with which she tiptoed into the room whose ceilings were adorned with figures and inscriptions painted in raw colors, whose walls were hung with faded shell-pink brocade into which had been woven the family crest, set Con's nerves a-tingle. The sense of unreality persisted as she looked at the great four-poster bed with the crest carved in the headboard and embroidered in gold on the pink satin spread.

"And who is the Spanish Bride?" she asked in a voice designed to break the magic web which an unseen force seemed to be weaving close about her.

"Didn't your father tell you, my lady? Didn't he tell you of the ghost of a woman in gauzy silver draperies who appears at that long window with our coat of arms enameled in colors on the glass, when the waning moon is visible from this room? She comes before the marriage of an heir to the Trent-Gowan title and estates. There is a legend that she loved an untitled man of her own country when in obedience to her father she married one of your ancestors. She brought him a fortune but died. She returns to remind bride or groom to be true to the loved one."

"She must have skipped a personal appearance when my father — m-married across the ocean," Con said in a tone she had intended to be sophisticatedly amused but which was punctuated by a nervous gulp.

"I saw her, child. It's only those who are loyal and true of heart who see her. I thought then we would hear of Master Ernest's marriage, he was your father's elder brother. I set down the date in my diary, I have a day by day record of what's happened at the Towers since I came here forty years ago and photographs of the family at all ages, but since his lordship had his son Gordon traced I've learned that the ghost of the Spanish Bride appeared to me the week before his wedding day."

Con incredulously regarded the woman's flushed face and excited brown eyes. How could she believe that stuff? She slipped an arm about her ample waist.

"Sometime I'll sleep in this room, maybe the lady in silver gauze will drop in on me," she teased. "Oh, come on, Bunny, let's call it a day about the ghost. You don't mind if I call you Bunny, do you? That was Dad's name for you. You needn't call me 'my lady,' either."

"It makes me proud and happy, my la—

dearie, to know that Master Gordon thought of me in exile. I still think of them as 'Master' as I called them when they were little boys. He was the darling of my heart." Mrs. Bunthorne sniffed and swallowed hard. "The Lord was good to us when He sent you to carry on at Trentmere Towers instead of Captain Ivor Hardwick, after his lordship passes on."

They were descending the white marble stairway, when the housekeeper made the startling statement. Con stopped and regarded her in amazement.

"You don't think for a minute that I intend to stay here? To live in England, do you?"

"Why of course, my lady." It was Mrs. Bunthorne's turn to register surprise. "You couldn't let his lordship grow old and die without anyone of his own about him, could you?"

"I not only could, but I will." Sudden tears scalded Con's eyes. "He let my father die without any of his own family near him, didn't he?"

"There, dearie, there," the plump hand patted the girl's shoulder. "I didn't mean to tear open an old wound. His lordship loved his younger son, he was his favorite."

"He took a grand way of showing it, to

61

turn him out of his house and never try to find him. Do you call that love?"

"It's a part of love, my lady. It's a twist disappointment gives to love sometimes. The deeper the love the deeper the hurt. Have you never felt bitter toward one you love?"

"I? *No.* I —"

Con's indignant denial broke in the middle as into her mind flashed the memory of the unbearable hurt of Peter's engagement. She remembered the bitter things she had said to him, remembered her repentance after she had put out the light at night, her resolve never again to hurt him and she remembered how the very next day, perhaps, her certainty that he was wrecking his life would get the better of her and her tongue would slip its leash. She loved him more than anyone in the world, he had taken her father's place, and she had been hateful to him. Who was she to judge her grandfather?

She pressed her lips impulsively to the housekeeper's wrinkled cheek.

"I'll remember what you have said, Bunny, dear. Now let's go back to the hall and I will say good-bye. Peter is arriving tonight and I must be at Cherrytree Farm to welcome him. I shudder to think of his reaction when he sees the battered wreck which once was the cocky Whiskers. That dog adores him. I believe he senses Peter's presence when he is miles away."

She was smiling at the thought of Peter's coming as with her free, graceful walk she crossed the jewel-toned rugs toward Lord Gowan who sat in the carved chair near the fireplace. She hesitated as the man seated opposite him demanded:

"You want me to marry her? No money for me, only the empty title, if I don't? I say, that's frightfully unfair. But you've got me. This debt must be paid. Settle it for me and I will —" He left the sentence dangling as he saw Con and rose.

As if drawn and held by a powerful magnet her eyes met and clung to his. Her heart seemed to drop. It was too fleeting a sensation to be a premonition, too formless to be a warning. His eyes were brown with topaz lights. They were compelling eyes. His features were the most perfect she had ever seen on a man's face. His skin, now darkly red as if from anger, made his light brown hair and small mustache seem blond. His clothes were perfection. When he smiled and disclosed teeth almost as even and white as Peter's, she liked him, liked him tremendously. He came forward with out-stretched hand.

"So this is the long-lost heir," he said in a voice which set her heart beating queerly. As she continued to took at him in puzzled questioning, he added gaily:

"I say, I'm the man you've pushed out. I am your cousin, Ivor Hardwick."

He turned to her grandfather who was standing before the fire glowering from beneath bushy brows.

"By Jove, I withdraw my objections to your plan, Lord Van. I'm awfully keen for it. Now will the Honorable Constance Trent pour a cup of tea for an abject admirer?"

Con looked at her grandfather's frowning face and then back to the man who was twisting an infinitesimal mustache as he regarded her with intent eyes. She laughed.

"And I had always heard that the British were slow. You're the fastest worker I've ever met, Cousin Ivor. Lemon or milk?"

Half an hour later as she passed between the lacy iron entrance gates of Trentmere Towers into the road which led to Cherrytree Farm she looked back. Against a shrimp-pink sky the house towered tall and forbidding like a grim overlord frowning down upon the farms and light-suffused fields, upon the slim white spires of parish churches, upon ranks of trees standing stiff and immovable as a regiment of soldiers on parade and upon the silver ribbon of river and the faraway blue hills.

She walked on and the vision of the great house went with her. She thought of the man, her father's father, who ruled there and of her curious feeling in the hall that after many years she had come home from a far country. She remembered the flicker in Ivor Hardwick's eyes, the hint of earnestness in his laughing voice as he said:

"By Jove, I withdraw my objection to your plan, Lord Van."

What had he meant by that? Had the plan concerned her? She felt a sudden inner conviction that it had. Was it her grandfather's intention to force her life into a pattern of his choosing? Little chills rilled through her veins.

Don't be foolish, she rebuked herself sternly. We are not living in the Middle Ages. Besides, Peter is coming and if Peter isn't a match for "his lordship" I've missed my guess.

Peter is coming! The words ran like a refrain beneath the surface of her thought which was occupied with the summing up of the events of the last hour. She tried to bring order out of the chaos of impressions.

Her grandfather was as hard, as stalwart, as tough of resistance as one of his own oaks.

Apparently he had learned nothing from his experience with his younger son. Would he attempt to break her to his will as he had tried to break her father? Let him try. He would find that she didn't break.

She smiled as she visualized tender-hearted Bunny and her belief in the visitation of the ghost. She was just the type to be such a goose. Her father's description of the housekeeper's dovelike personality had been perfect. So the Spanish Bride had appeared before his marriage? Pity she hadn't warned, "Stop! Don't do it!" in a whisper which would have been heard by him across the water.

Curious that she had never seen a picture of her mother. By the time she was old enough to realize that she had run away, all photographs of her had disappeared. When once she had asked about her Gordon Trent had answered, sharply for him:

"That's behind us, Connie. Forget it."

She thought of her grandfather's suggestion that a woman might appear and falsely claim to be her mother. How could he prove that her claim wasn't just? But, if she were alive, wouldn't she have appealed to her husband for a divorce long ago? Lord Gowan might be right, maybe she was dead but how could one be sure? Peter and Tim had tried to trace her. If they couldn't no one could.

It would be interesting to know what the girl whom her father married had looked like. Not like me apparently, she reflected. Dad used to say that I was all Trent-Gowan, except the nose. Allah be praised that I wasn't endowed with that Romanesque feature.

It was quite evident from the tone in which Mrs. Bunthorne pronounced his name that she had no use for Captain Ivor Hardwick. After that first queer sensation as if her heart had dropped down a dark and dangerous elevator well, she, herself, had liked him. He was breath-takingly good-looking. He had a sense of humor, if slightly imbedded, not the American brand, but it was there. He was carefree and debonair, apparently. There had been a caressing friendliness in his voice which had set her pulses quick-stepping and her mind tingling with repartee. In short, in a moment they had been friends. She couldn't remember ever before having felt such a quick response to a stranger's personality.

Wonder if Peter will like him, she asked herself and had a prompt conviction that he wouldn't. She was glad she had firmly refused Ivor's suggestion that he walk back to

Cherrytree Farm with her. She had told him she wanted to be alone, that she might catalogue her impressions, to which he had replied with a quick look at Lord Gowan:

"Right ho. While you're doing that frightful lot of thinking remember to put me in number-one place in your heart and jolly old England second."

The word England switched her thoughts to the present. She had been moving like a sleepwalker through this late-afternoon world. And what a beautiful world!

She filled her lungs with the fragrant air cooled by the approach of evening and opened wide the eyes of her mind and senses to the beauty about her. She passed a low stone farmhouse from beside which stole the faint perfume from a row of magnolias. Their boles and boughs glistened like bronze. A million shell-like petals shone mother-of-pearl. A woman's face peered from behind a lattice window, quite in the manner of a neighborhood busybody in a movie. A little girl in blue-checked gingham swinging on a creaking gate jumped off and bobbed a funny curtsy. She stuck a finger in her mouth and regarded Con with black, saucerlike eyes. The bleat of sheep came from behind the house, with the smell of a barnyard.

A man approached driving loitering black-and-white cows across the road. He was big and ruddy and had a spatulate nose. Con had seen only one like it and that had been in a motion picture. She had wondered then if noses really grew that way or if it were a product of the make-up man. His cotton clothing was as clean as the child's gingham frock. He touched his red hair in lieu of a cap.

"Welcome home to yer ladyship. I'm farmer Chettle, my missus' brother is butler up h'at the Towers."

His voice was courteous, but she didn't like his eyes. They were small eyes, secrets peered from behind them. She felt the same queer drop of her heart she had experienced when hers had met Ivor Hardwick's for the first time. As if he felt her distrust he pointed to the cottage garden where early tulips, crimson, white, pink, bronze, yellow and purple, jostled daffodils and narcissus, which, in turn, crowded the polyanthus and the stiff crown imperials. The hum of bees above them sounded like the purr of a faraway plane.

"It tykes a dye like this to bring the posies and the bees h'out proper, ye ladyship."

He pulled at his hair again and herded the lowing cows through the broad gate of the farmyard.

Con's eyes followed him until he was out of sight. Was he a Trentmere tenant? He had said, "Welcome home!" Was he, like the occupants of the house towering on top of the slope, taking it for granted that she had come to stay? Could they make her? She had an instant's panicky sense of futility.

As she approached the stone house, its upper story half-timbered old oak, which sprawled within a frame of yew hedges at Cherrytree Farm, her mind was exclusively preoccupied with a plan for firmly, but politely, impressing upon Major General Lord Vandemere Trent-Gowan, Retired, the fact that she did not intend to remain in England. She was so preoccupied that not until she was almost upon it did she see the shining limousine with two men in green livery before the gate, the posts of which were topped with huge balls.

One of the footmen sprang to the ground and stood rigidly with finger-tips at his hat. She noticed the crest blazoned in colors on the car door. Must be at least a marchioness, calling, she decided.

The afternoon had had such a fairylike quality that she wouldn't have been surprised to see the footman turn into a fish, like the footman in *Alice in Wonderland*, see him produce a great letter, hear him declare solemnly:

"For the Duchess. An invitation from the Queen to play croquet."

As she stepped into the hall, something held her motionless for a second. She had the curious sense that she was on the threshold of a mystery, a mystery which reached far, far back into the past, that she had but to wrench open a tightly locked door in her memory and she would find the truth for which she had been searching confronting her in a blaze of blinding light.

"Silly," she said under her breath. "Silly. You are not searching for anything, are you? Doubtless you're having an attack of jitters from the hang-over of a previous incarnation. Perhaps once you lived in this very house. That Spanish Bride stuff got under your skin. Forward, Miss Trent, to meet the Duchess, if it is a Duchess."

V

Con was smiling at her own absurdity as she entered the great lounge furnished with rich oak and walnut, hung with family portraits. There were mullioned windows at each end and a large stone fireplace. Angela Corey, in a frock the color of wood violets, was presiding at a silver-laden tea table. She was talking to a guest. Who was the woman? Did the pomp and glitter outside belong to her? She was beautiful, as a work of art is beautiful, with evidence that plumpness was lurking round the corner ready to pounce if she increased her intake by so much as one calorie. Her black costume, which accentuated the rose-leaf perfection of her skin and the size and luster of three strands of pearls, was chic to a degree. Her smart hat revealed hair that was a metallic red. She looked to be in the early thirties, if one didn't notice the hardness of her eyes and her expression of discontent. Those eyes knew the world from A to Z, Con decided, and felt a little shiver of aversion.

She looked at Angela Corey whose lovely

face reflected the inner radiance of her spirit. She was so poised, yet determined, so worldy-wise and yet so tender. She had such deep-rooted convictions as to morals and manners, such a firmly grounded code of conduct that just looking at her was like feeling the security of a rock under one's feet in a heaving sea of uncertainty.

"Oh, here you are, Connie," Angela Corey greeted. "Lady Hanford has been waiting to see you."

The violet eyes of the woman on the Sheraton sofa stared at Con. She's about as responsive to my smile as a face on a postage-stamp, the girl thought. Did she go white under her rouge, or did I imagine it? Have I insulted her high position by keeping her waiting?

"But, the Honorable Miss Trent is so worth waiting for. She is so lovely," purred Lady Hanford. Her voice and inflection out-Britished the British. "Really my dear, the rotogravures which followed the announcement of your arrival in the Court Circular, haven't done you justice."

"Rotos!" Con exclaimed.

"Oh, we have such things in our tight little isle. Did you think that the granddaughter of Major General Lord Vandermere Trent-Gowan could materialize out of space without attracting the attention of the world of society?"

"But, I didn't come out of space. It was the United States, in case you care. That's enough tea, Angel, you know I like my brew strong of hot water."

"Do sit here beside me, my dear, and tell me whom you saw at the Towers?" Lady Hanford urged.

Con took the seat she indicated on the sofa. "Lord Gowan, of course and — and others —" She swallowed a ripple of laughter as the close-up of the butler and footman dancing madly round the fighting dogs, flashed on the screen of memory.

"Oh, here you are, Tim!" Angela Corey exclaimed, as her son entered looking like a fair-haired young god in white tennis flannels, if young gods ever wear tennis flannels. She presented him to the guest who held out her hand and looked up with half-closed eyes.

"Nice boy. I adore boys — like this one," she said in a voice that brought the color to Tim's pale face. "Really, my dear Mrs. Corey, what a charming family you have. I hear that there is still another son?"

"Yes. We expect Peter to arrive at any moment. He brought over his car and is motoring from London."

74

One would think from her eyes and honeyed voice as she smiles up at him that Tim had swept her off her feet, and he looks as stunned as if a ghost from his past had popped up, if ghosts pop, Con thought, with a queer sense of panic. He dropped into that chair as if his knees had given way. Oh, dear, has he tired himself over lawn tennis?

"Mr. Timothy, do use the courts at my home, Fordham Manor," Lady Hanford invited. "My husband was awfully much older than I and now that he is gone, I find I crave the companionship of youth." Her sigh expressed a wife who had been in chains, misunderstood. It was a masterpiece. "I shall plan for you to meet some of the young people of the county, Miss Trent, and a dinner for you, Mrs. Corey. Really, my dear, aren't you thrilled to have this charming house put at your disposal? It must seem luxurious to you," she added as she rose.

"It is delightful but we're not absolutely grubby at home," Angela Corey replied coolly. "Must you go? Good afternoon."

Lady Hanford left the room in a wave of perfume and the whisper of taffeta with Tim in attendance. Con seated herself at the piano. Under her fingers the keys gave forth a soft accompaniment to her voice.

" 'If it's love you're after, perfume's your

silken snare,' not original in case you care, Angel. I'm quoting an ad which seemed to fit our departed guest to a T. Hasn't this instrument a marvelous tone? The boys will love singing to it." She chuckled, " 'Really, my dear,' you certainly put that red-haired glamour-woman in her place, plenty hard."

Angela Corey's cheeks burned bright pink.

"I couldn't help it. Her tone was so patronizing, so maddeningly superior that when I thought of our perfect Red Maples —"

"You drew your trusty blade and stabbed her through the heart," supplied Tim who had returned to the room. "She's pretty darn fascinating, isn't she?"

It wasn't like Tim to fall for a girl at once, to say nothing of an older woman. With a panicky attempt to curb his enthusiasm Con responded quickly:

"If you like that sort of fascination she has the sort of fascination you'll like. I'll wager the aforementioned blade couldn't penetrate that woman's heart, it would turn the point. It's marble. I wonder why she was so anxious to know whom I saw at Trentmere Towers." She left the piano and perched on an arm of the sofa. "I could feel her tenseness as she asked the question."

"Whom did you see?" Angela Corey

asked and picked up a mass of rose-color wool she was knitting into a cardigan.

"First a footman in maroon livery. Then Major General Lord Vandemere Trent-Gowan, and then, 'Listen my children and you shall hear.' Whiskers had followed me, so I foolishly allowed him to enter the house. I had caught my first glimpse of Lord Gowan standing like a stone image before the fire when, before we had a chance to introduce ourselves, whiz-bang, an ugly bulldog shot from somewhere and met Whiskers head-on in the middle of that baronial hall. A footman pulled off the bulldog — while I hung onto the terrier's tail, thinking all the while 'Suppose it comes off! Suppose it comes off!' Looked at in retrospect it was terri—bly funny." Her laugh was like music.

"You think it's funny that you mixed into a dog fight, don't you? You might have been horribly bitten. I call it darn foolishness, Slim. You're a terribly reckless person. You dash into a situation without stopping to think where it's coming out."

"Perhaps that's what makes me so nice."

"All right, treat it as a joke, some day you'll find it's a pretty grim one. Ever heard that one about millions of the living being already dead?" Tim tapped his forehead significantly. "That's you? Why did you take the dog into the house?"

"I thought he would break the ice."

"And here he is," Tim exclaimed as the terrier slunk into the room, bearing the marks of the fight in a torn ear, a half-closed eye and a bandaged breast. "Looks to me as if the ice wasn't the only thing which broke. What did you do to the bull, poor little fella?" he asked tenderly as the dog jumped to the window seat and looked out.

"Peter must be within fifty miles, Whiskers is watching for him," Con said. "To continue the saga of the first visit to my ancestral acres, after the smoke and din of battle had cleared, I introduced myself to my grandfather, served tea, then Mrs. Bunthorne, the housekeeper, made a timely entrance and personally conducted me through some of the rooms. Last but not least, Captain Ivor Hardwick appeared. Sounds like the personages of a play in order of their appearance, as printed in a theatre program, doesn't it?"

Tim helped himself liberally to plum cake.

"Ivor Hardwick. He's the guy who will have the title and would have had the estate if you hadn't stopped playing with the angels, isn't he, Con?"

"He is. As far as I am concerned he may

still have it. How long had Lady Hanford been here, when I came in, Angel?"

"Perhaps half an hour."

"She's a knockout isn't she?" Tim observed with a faraway look that brought back Con's apprehension. "She's got the come-hither eye. But you didn't like her, did you, Mother? I wish we had a record of your voice when you said, 'We're not absolutely grubby at home.' It dripped icicles."

The color of Angela Corey's face deepened.

"I'm sorry I was so gauche as to show my feelings, Tim, but the woman irritated me. Before you two children came in I felt as if I were on the witness stand being cross-examined."

The terrier dashed for the door.

"And who had the temerity to cross-examine you, Mrs. Corey?" inquired a voice.

"Peter! Peter! You've come!" Con rejoiced.

As his mother met him at the threshold he bent his head and kissed her. He looked down at Con who had slipped an arm under his. As his eyes met hers something in them seemed to overflow into her heart and surge up in tears.

"How's everything, Con?" he asked quickly.

"Everything's fine, now that you are here. Sit down and I'll bring your tea. You must be tired."

"Tired! I feel like the World Champ on the eve of defending his title. I'm in the pink of condition. I slept all the way over on the ship, almost all the way. That's what one gets from going four years without a vacation while dynamiting the underworld."

He settled back in a deep chair near the fire. The terrier whined and tried to climb into his lap. "What the dickens happened to you, Whiskers?"

"The British Lion and the American Eagle staged a showdown," Con explained. "Nothing serious." As she met Tim's accusing eyes she asked before he could reveal her part in the fight, "Isn't this an adorable old house?"

"It is. This lounge is great. I like that portrait of the woman in white satin and yellow rose above the mantel, if there is more rose than satin. And a piano! All the comforts of home. The place lives up to Neale's description. By the way, he motored from London with me. He'd had a summons from Trentmere Towers. Something to do with the man who had expected to inherit. He'll get the title anyway; Neale anticipates a fight with him about money."

"With Ivor Hardwick. He won't make trouble!"

"What do you know about Captain Hardwick, Con?"

Tim chuckled.

"When man-eating Corey speaks in that tone, step right up on the witness stand, gal, and swear you will tell the truth the whole truth and nothing but."

Peter ignored his brother's teasing.

"Have you met Hardwick, Con?"

Con bit her lips to steady them. Peter hadn't seen her for two weeks and instead of seeming glad to be here he was cross-examining her.

"I have and I like him. Like him better than any man I've ever met. Something tells me that my dream prince has come at last! Stop me if I'm wrong," she added flippantly.

"So that's the way it is. After turning hangers-on away in squads, at long last she meets the man she's been waiting for," Tim proclaimed theatrically. "Curtain on act one!"

"Pipe down, Tim. So you like Ivor Hardwick, Con? All right, you like him. Now what?" Peter demanded.

"Now, if your problem child may step down from the witness stand, she will dress for dinner."

She flashed out of the room before Peter could reach the threshold and stop her. His eyes followed her flight up the stairway before he returned to back up against the mantel.

"Whew!" Tim exclaimed, "what started the fireworks? You ask a question. Fuse to a bunch of rockets. You don't suppose she really fell for that Hardwick guy? That it's some of that love-at-first-sight film stuff, do you? I'll nip that in the bud, quick. Can't have her going British on us. Hi, Slim!" He took the broad stairs two at a time.

"Peter, what is wrong with Captain Hardwick?" Angela Corey asked anxiously.

"Everything, Mother. Neale told me coming up that although Lord Gowan makes his cousin once removed a generous allowance he's always in debt. That's why Neale was sent for today; Lord Gowan refuses to settle up for him again. I gathered that Captain Ivor is one of those men who has put nothing into the world and has tried to beat it at every turn. His reputation for financial fair dealing is decidedly frayed around the edges, and he's deep in an affair with a widow — in fact, a double widow — whose husbands come under the head of late, not former, and each of whom left her a substantial fortune. She's stuffy rich, that's

Neale's word, not mine, and besides being infatuated with the man she covets the position that being mistress of Trentmere Towers would give her. Con's coming must have put a crimp in that possibility, because Lord Gowan is planning a marriage between Ivor Hardwick and his granddaughter which will consolidate title and estate."

"Peter! Did Clive Neale tell you all that on the way from London?"

"He did. I had a hunch he was warning me. That's why I was too troubled to be politic when Con said she had met her 'dream prince.' "

"But, you know Connie well enough to know that if she had met her 'dream prince' she wouldn't talk about it."

"I know, Mother, but Neale told me a lot of stuff that won't bear repeating, so when Con said she liked the Captain I went haywire. Can we stand by and let her marry a man who will break her heart? It's such a loyal heart."

He rested an arm on the mantel and looked down into the fire.

"How does she fit into the life here?" he asked.

"Apparently she is thrilled by it."

He turned, hands thrust hard into his pockets.

"And she belongs to it and it belongs to her. Remember the sentence you left unfinished when I told you that my engagement to Lydia was broken? You said 'I've been terrified for fear that sometime you'd wake up and realize that you really love —' you meant that even then I loved Con, would want her for my wife, didn't you? Well, I waked up with a bang when she kissed me that epoch-making day at Red Maples when Lydia broke our engagement and Clive Neale appeared. I knew that after ten years of brotherly affection I was desperately in love with her. I want her. But, how can I ask her to give up this life of luxury and pomp to which she really belongs?"

Angela Corey slipped her hand under her son's arm.

"Try not to think of it at present, Peter. I suppose I might as well tell the west wind to stop blowing. We must leave Connie uninfluenced to make her choice between the home of her father and the home of her adoption. If she suspects that you love her—"

"She might choose me out of gratitude, you mean? Looks as if it would be nice going, doesn't it? If I let her know I love her, I may ruin her life. If I don't she may fall for that rounder, then it is sure to be ruined."

"She will know, Peter. Try as you may to conceal your emotions, your eyes will carry messages and open a line of communication between her heart and yours and if she finds she loves you, all the titles and estates in the world won't hold her on this side of the Atlantic, unless you decide to make her interests here yours and become a British subject. We all make compromises with life."

"A British subject! You mean live *here?* You're crazy! Give up my work at home? I'm committed to it."

"It is such dangerous work, Peter. You wouldn't let me know, but I've heard that certain members of the underworld have threatened to 'get' you."

"Who told you that stuff? Those racketeers are out to 'get' anyone who opposes them. If you stop to figure up the number of them there are in the United States and the number whom they put on the spot, the figures are not startling. Sometimes I get so boiling mad at the way they slip through the nets spread by the Intelligence department that I fairly ache to get after them myself. I have views on how they might be caught. But conviction, not detection, is my work. You wouldn't want me to shirk a job for which I'm really fitted, would you?"

"N—no, Peter."

He put his arm about her shoulders and drew her close.

"That-a-girl! Don't worry about me. Carry on, Mother. I haven't told you before, but it's as sure as anything can be in the world of politics, that I'm to be District Attorney next autumn. Not even for Con would I let down the men who have worked for me nor give up the chance to do something constructive for first, my state, and then the country at large, which I know I can do."

"As long as you are you, it does sound impossible to renounce your citizenship, doesn't it? Whatever the outcome, we want Connie to make the choice which will lead to the happiest, richest life for her, we are agreed on that, aren't we, Peter?"

"We are. But if she chooses Ivor Hardwick there will be darned little happiness for her. As I told you, he's up to his neck in a messy affair with a widow. A Lady Hanford."

"Lady Hanford! She was here this afternoon. When Connie came into the room the woman's eyes were so cold and calculating that I was startled. Her 'affair' with Captain Hardwick explains her antagonism. She's afraid she will lose him and Trentmere Towers to our lovely girl."

"She's not half so afraid as I am, Mother. The title which might have been her father's may make a powerful appeal to Con."

VI

The river crooned against the canoe. The shadows of snowy cloud galleons sailing majestically across a turquoise sky changed the colors of the pink and amber and white washed houses along the banks like the shifting patterns of a kaleidoscope. As he dipped his paddle Peter Corey smiled at the girl facing him.

"Do you realize that this is the first chance you and I have had for a heart-to-heart since I arrived, Con? Wouldn't have secured you now had I not discovered this canoe a couple of days ago and sold you the beauty of the country as seen from the river, would I, Miss Trent?"

Constance laughed, settled deeper into the crimson pillows and clasped her hands behind her head, covered with a fantastically designed blue and red linen kerchief which tied under her chin.

"You didn't say enough for it. I love the mellow old farmhouses, the stone villages and the wooded hills we've passed. It's the first time I've had a chance to really see the country. The river is so soft and blue. Smell the lilacs, the sun is baking the fragrance from those purple plumes. The men and horses in that field are black cut-outs against the sky. Look at that old mill standing in tall rough grass. It sets my imagination racing."

She stretched outspread hands high above her head.

"Peter, when I see a world as beautiful as this I feel I must give thanks." She flushed brilliantly as her eyes met his. "Can you bear it if I get sentimental?"

"Go as far as you like as long as you confine sentiment to places, not persons," Peter replied and knew as he said it that he was voicing the uneasiness which had pricked in his mind like a nettle since the moment she had said, "Something tells me my dream prince has come at last."

"Little chance I've had to go sentimental about persons. I've met scads of them. They've said 'How do you do?' in beautifully cadenced voices — I love their clear enunciation, their 'howevahs' and 'hereaftahs' — and gone on as if they were whisked by on a moving platform. I've been teaed and lunched and dined until I fairly loathe the sight of food. I have danced my shoes thin with young officers from the nearby garrison town. I've walked out on a reception this afternoon; it wasn't for me, I wouldn't be quite so crude. Tomorrow evening Major General Lord Vandemere Trent-Gowan presents his granddaughter to the county at a ball. I begged him to wear his uniform, but he won't. Petey —"

"Look out! You know better than to jerk up like that, Con." He steadied the canoe with a quick stroke of the paddle.

"Sorry! Excitement got the better of caution." She settled back among the crimson cushions. "As I was about to observe when so rudely interrupted, I was glad to escape, glad of this chance to be alone with you. I've something very special to consult you about. My faith in my own judgment has dropped to an all-time low. I wonder if life begins to be complex for everyone at twenty-three?"

Peter's heart turned over. Had it come? The moment he had been fearing when she would tell him that she was in love with Ivor Hardwick?

"All right, let's have it. There is nothing in the world you can't talk over with me, remember. Must be a terrific problem to make you sigh like that. What's on your mind?"

"It's nothing to make you turn white,

90

Peter. I haven't hit-and-run, though I'm having a nervous breakdown trying to remember to keep on the left when I drive the snappy green roadster my grandfather has given me. I have learned to figure in pounds, shillings and pence, to ask for 'petrol' and the 'sugar basin' instead of bowl, to use the words 'lift' and 'cinema,' so I'm getting on. I haven't stolen, or fallen in love with my best friend's husband or any trifle like that; it's only that I don't feel honest."

"Honest?" he repeated and felt his color surge back. She wasn't in love with Hardwick, thank the Lord.

"Yes. It's like this. My grandfather has planned the huge ball for me. He has deposited a thousand pounds to my account, said he thought I would like a little spending money. Little! It is more than twice my income for one year. He has given me my grandmother's pearls, coronet and necklace. I am to be presented at Court. He is doing all this because he believes I will stay in this country and I won't, Peter, not for all the roadsters, money, pearls and diamonds in the world."

"Don't you feel any affection for the home of your ancestors, for the old and powerful family to which you belong?"

"I do and it frightens me. Sometimes Lord Gowan reminds me so much of Dad, the way he quirks his eyebrows when he is amused, the gestures of his fine hands and especially when I sit beside him in that adorable old chapel and the sun picks out the gold letters in the tablets devoted to the exploits of my remote forebears. I feel like resting my head against his arm and snuggling close, as I did to my father when I was a little girl. All my bitterness toward him melts away and instead of detesting him, as I was sure I would, I love him. I am not a very good hater, Peter, I can always see the other person's side. I feel as if I were being swept along on a tide of sentiment. I can't get a foothold to stop it."

"Why stop it? You belong here."

"I belong more at home. To you Coreys and the United States I owe all that I am."

Peter winced. That was old bogey Gratitude poking its mischievous head between them. How could he know if she really loved him when she felt such a sense of indebtedness?

"You're wrong about owing everything to the United States," he dissented. "Your character is rooted in the traditions and ideals of your father's house. You are quite a different person than you would be if they were not in the very marrow of your bones."

"Peter Corey, are you arguing that I should stay here? Don't you *want* me to go back to Red Maples?"

Her eyes were wide with hurt amazement. Peter remembered what his mother had said about lines of communication and looked off at the distant purple hills. Much as he loved her, and each day brought with it a keener realization of what she meant, had always meant to him, she must come to him with a love untinged with any sense of gratitude. He had mentally faced that decision an hundred times, hadn't he? And would doubtless have to face it an hundred more.

"Of course we want you, but the decision is entirely up to you," he answered gravely. "It is your life, Con. No one can live it for you."

"That's a shivery reminder. It makes me feel so, so alone."

"Each one of us walks alone, no matter how many who are dear to us are near. If you will be happier here —"

"I won't be! England is charming and peaceful and soaked in tradition, but sometimes I yearn for the vitality, the rush and tingle, the clang and crash of home, even for the fire sirens which howl like a Siberian wolfhound, home being the United States, in case you care. I'm an American. I wouldn't give up my citizenship and my family, you and Angel and Tim, for the grandest estate or the most fascinating man on earth."

"Wait till you meet the most fascinating man on earth. Then see what happens. Suppose you loved an Englishman who loved you wholly, desperately, wouldn't you marry him and make his country yours?"

"Having been brought up in the 'Thy country shall be my country' school of thought, doubtless I would."

"Then what's all the shootin' about? Relax, lady, relax."

She shook her head as she met his laughing eyes.

"But that isn't the situation. I am not in love with a man. I'm in love, colorlessly in love, with what my father's family and estate stand for and I am in love, wholly, desperately, with the country of my birth which still is mine, which gave me everything when England ignored me. I'll never forget that. It would be sheer sentimentality if I were to persuade myself that it was my duty to carry on here, that Major General Lord Vandemere Trent-Gowan needed me."

"Perhaps he does. Tim says you're a pretty darned nice person to have around.

There are times when I'm inclined to agree with him."

"Thanks for the lollipop. You're pretty darned nice yourself, Petey, you're a dear to let me talk out my doubts and perplexities. Perhaps my dream prince, an English dream prince, really will appear and that will settle the matter. I was merely wisecracking when I went sentimental about Ivor Hardwick the afternoon you arrived. He is fascinating and he does try to make me believe that his life was an empty shell before I came into it. His attitude is so amusing that I play up. I'm the wide-eyed, credulous ingénue. It's fun."

"You've been seeing him often, haven't you? What does your grandfather think of that?" Peter asked, as if he didn't know only too well what Lord Gowan thought of it.

"He hasn't commented on our friendship. He asked me to spare time for the Towers every day. I go usually in the morning and chatter about the persons I've met and where I have been. We ride together and call on the tenants. I've met them all now. I'm collecting their World War memories as I did from people at home, invaluable bits that will be lost if someone doesn't salvage them.

"Then he tells me of the affairs of the estate and has me read reports to him. I listen but at the same time I'm building up sales resistance. I keep trying to make him understand that I have no intention of living in England, but he always interrupts with the word, 'Wait!' and tells me what my father would want me to do, just as if he had understood Dad."

"Probably he understands him now that he has lost him. It happens that way sometimes."

" 'Too late.' Tragic words, aren't they? Curious how little my mother counts in my life. I presume I have inherited something from her. Perhaps it's my nose. That hawkish model, characteristic of the Trent-Gowan family, wouldn't look so well on a girl, would it? The first afternoon I went to the Towers my grandfather, I call him 'General,' I think he rather likes it, stormed about the publicity the American newspapers had given to my coming to England. He growled, 'Some woman may appear and claim she's your mother!' and then he said she was dead, he knew it."

"If Lord Gowan has that proof he has dug up something I could not find. As the years pass don't you remember anything of your mother, Con?"

"Nothing but what I have told you before. I was only three when she ran away but I remember seeing her in something white and shiny with her hair like spun gold. I remember feeling such a warm surge of love for her beauty that I stroked her frock with one sticky hand, in the other I clutched a slice of buttered, sugared bread which accounted for the stickiness. I'll never forget her sharp blow on my fingers nor her angry voice, 'Don't touch me, you dirty thing!' That memory is burnt into my mind. A choice one, isn't it?"

"I wish it might have helped trace her. Both Tim and I tried our best to find some clue to her after your father went, but too many years had passed since her disappearance. We had nothing but a faded, tinted photograph to go on."

"You never showed me that picture."

"Your father didn't want you to see it. He felt that it would be better to have the past remain a closed book to you in so far as she was concerned. While he lived he made no effort to trace her, he was sure that sometime she would come back to him of her own accord."

"Perhaps he was right, about the closed book, I mean. Her desertion fairly ate into my heart when I was a child. Couldn't seem to overcome it until I went to live with Angel. Perhaps she died. Perhaps she married. That's a thought. But how could she? She was not divorced."

"She could have pretended to be single. Could have lied about it. I presume it has been done," Peter responded dryly. "But if Lord Gowan has proof of her death, that settles that."

"Think of what she lost by stepping out? If she had remained with Dad he might not have died, she might have lived, and in time she would have been chatelaine of the Towers. Often, I pinch myself to make sure that I am the one-time unimportant Constance Trent. The servants call me 'my lady.' I discovered by looking in Burke's Peerage, that I am not entitled to be so addressed but they like it, so what? I'm living in a dream world. Everything, everybody is unreal except you and Angel and Tim and Whiskers — he isn't just a dog, he's a personality. Do you realize what a change it is for me from being a mere nobody?"

"You! A nobody! Where did you pick up the inferiority complex? You are the most beloved, admired, popular girl in your set at home!"

"Thanks for them kind words, mister. Don't scowl. I know you think they are true, if you are the only person in the world who does. If I was liked at home it was for myself.

Here all the tumult and the shouting is for the granddaughter of Major General Lord Vandemere Trent-Gowan who materialized out of the everywhere like the screen heroine of a mythical kingdom. Honestly, Peter, at times it seems so like a play that I feel as if I were standing in the wings of a stage waiting for the director's cue to go on with my part. Perhaps when I get over all this excitement, I'll settle down to being myself again. I feel positively guilty spending so much wrinkle-browed thought on my own problems when a large part of the world is heaving and writhing in turmoil."

"It is my belief that if a person doesn't first work out his own problems, he will be of mighty little use in solving those of the world. How often one sees a man or woman leading a party or a cause whose own life is in a terrible mess. I never feel great confidence in that person's judgment.

"There's nothing unreal about you in that white silk shirt and those sharkskin slacks. Tailored to perfection, aren't they? Some girls look so sloppy in them. You're a snappy dresser, Con. Your clothes always have dash and fling without being ultra," Peter commented matter-of-factly hoping to quiet the unsteadiness of her voice, while he thought that her beauty and tender charm had done more than her grandfather's position to make her reception by the county families cordial and enthusiastic. To divert her thoughts he asked:

"What are you wearing tomorrow night?"

"White. The skirt is all long glittering crystal fringes which go 'klish!' 'klish!' when I move. I adore the sound."

"Sort of 'the Campbells are coming' motif. As has been said before, I like you in white, it brings out a tint of gold in your skin. Excited about the ball?"

"As jittery inside as I was the night of my coming-out party at home. Remember my speechlessness when you and Angel gave me this ring?" She held up her right hand to show the large star sapphire set in diamonds on the little finger.

"May I engage you for a dance, that is, if the granddaughter of Lord Gowan will be permitted to dance with a mere commoner?"

"Now you're talking what Cousin Ivor would call 'chawming nonsense,' Peter. Not dance with you! I'd like to see anyone try to stop me. I presume the Towers will swarm with the great and near-great. I hope I won't be overcome by the magnificence of it all. I'm to dress there and stay overnight. I have asked Bunny to give me the Spanish Bride's room. I have a deep, abiding belief in things unseen but I can't make that silver gauze apparition seem probable or possible. Thank goodness, I am to dine alone with my grandfather who decided not to entertain at a large dinner before the ball. Even Ivor won't be there."

"Ivor?"

"Why the raised-brow glare? Why shouldn't I call him by his first name? He is a cousin of sorts, isn't he? I forgot. You don't like him. Well, as I said before, I do. He amuses me.

"Why should the fact that I like a man set little flames in your eyes? Don't you *want* me to like people? Don't you *want* me to get some pleasure out of this visit which turns a knife in my heart every time I think of my father and of what all the beating of social tomtoms would have meant to him? Just remember that I didn't want to come to England, but you and Angel were all for it and here I am."

Her indignation was so like the little gusts of temper of the child Peter had seen grow up that the tension in his heart eased. Even if she thought him "fascinating," she couldn't love that rounder, Ivor Hardwick, something deep in her soul would take his measure and find him wanting.

"So, the only reason you came to view your ancestral acres is because Mother and I were for it?"

"Mostly that, but partly because I thought the change would be good for Tim. Now, I'm not so sure."

"What do you mean by that gloomy, prophetic tone?"

"Look out! You almost upset the canoe that time." She clasped her hands about one knee and confided. "I'm afraid Tim is falling for the glamour-woman. That's what Angel and I call our neighbor at Fordham Manor."

"You mean Lady Hanford?"

"Yes. I had forgotten you haven't met her. You will be knocked in a heap when you see her. *She* knows plenty about clothes. You and Angel and Tim are dining with her before the ball tomorrow evening, aren't you? Better watch your step. She is a trapper of men. I've met her type before. That's why I am troubled about Tim."

"Don't worry about him. In spite of his boyishness he is twenty-four and mentally older than his years. He's too much his mother's son not to have acquired a sense of human values. He may lose his head for a while but not his footing."

"You may be right, but something, plus

fiction, tells me that love and a glamorous lady can give a terrible tripping to the afore-mentioned footing. He has been to Fordham Manor almost every day for lawn tennis and yesterday when I came upon him suddenly in our garden, he was nodding his head like a mandarin and smiling like a cat who has fooled a mouse. Was it what I've said or what I left unsaid that sent your eyes boring into my brain and brought on your legal look, Peter?"

A smile chased the gravity from his face.

"Let's drop problems and have ourselves a time, Con. Don't forget, I'm on vacation. If I were to hear even the soft swish of a crime wave approaching, I'd make a break for an island where radio and cable are unheard of. See that stone inn on the hillside? It was once a posting house. Famous because George IV stopped there and later Queen Victoria. I heard a rumor that some titled woman had re-established a coaching service, drives herself for the thrill of it. You may be living in a dream world, but I am prosaically hungry. What do you say to tea at the old posting house? I remember the place from four years ago when I was in England; you wouldn't come, remember, so you and Mother went to France. They serve honey, pots of it, and hot scones. Shall we try it?"

"I'm all for it. I have the queerest feeling, Peter. As if you were quite a different person from the man at Red Maples who brought me up in the way I should go. Perhaps it's your white clothes, though I've seen you in them plenty of times at home. You seem so, so young."

"*Young!* Why shouldn't I seem young? I'm not quite eighty, yet. It's a long time since you've seen me really on vacation. No knowing how I may cut loose now that I have left what you call my 'legal self' on the other side of the Atlantic. Better keep me on leash, Con, I'm likely to do some cockeyed thing."

"You have the nicest laugh in the world, Peter. Anyone would know to hear it that you sing divinely. You are on the crest of the wave, aren't you? I hope this vacation will be perfect."

"Nothing can spoil it." He brashly defied the Fates. "Here we are." He paddled close to the small rustic dock. "Hop out."

He made the canoe fast and slipped into a camel's-hair cardigan. They climbed a cobblestone lane, banked on each side with red earth crowned with a crop of young green, to the quaint inn with heavy timbers and leaded windows set in a garden pink with tall, late tulips. There was the waxy smell of beehives and box in the fresh warm air. By the side of the house white, woolly lambs were kicking up their heels. A tethered shaggy pony watched their antics in dour disdain.

Con lingered an instant at the door to view the sloping pastoral country, a steeple turned to rose gold by the slanting sun, the winding river, green and violet hills, a few of them scarred by mineral mines. Some were patterned by the shadows of drifting clouds. In the distance she caught a glint of white beach and beyond it the milky blue water of the Channel.

Peter opened the door of a low-raftered room. Through open windows on the front came the mellow music of horns, the stamping of hoofs, the jingle of silver-plated harness.

Con dashed to the window. A road coach drawn by six horses whose muscles rippled under coats of burnished bronze, drew up to the door. The woman who handled the ribbons was large and of the sporting type. Her checked tweeds fitted as if she had been poured into them. Her voice was loud, her laugh was coarse. She spoke to the passengers behind her:

"Well, here we are, on time to the minute." She flexed muscular hands. "I'm ready for tea. Those bally horses almost pulled my arms from their sockets."

As a liveried groom assisted her descent, Con said quickly:

"They're coming in, Peter. Let's not be caught staring at that outfit as if we were hicks who never had seen a coach and horses, though I'll admit I've never seen one like that in action before. We'll order."

A rosy-cheeked maid in a pink gingham so crisp that it rattled brought tea and scones and blue stone pots of honey. Con, who had thought she never could eat again, felt a sudden surge of appetite.

"I could die eating honey," she exclaimed. "Peter, here they come, the coaching party, I mean. Too bad you are back to the door. It's like something out of Dickens brought up to date. It's — why there's Lydia!"

VII

"Did — did you know she was coming, Peter?"

Angrily aware of the surge of color to his face Peter Corey snapped:

"No! Do you think I would have brought you here had I known?"

He rose as Miss Austen approached the table.

"Hello, Lydia! Where did you drop from?" he asked.

Her knit frock was no greener than the eyes with which she looked up at him.

"Your surprise is perfect, Peter." She transferred her emerald regard from him to his companion. "You wouldn't imagine from his expression that he and I were on the same ship when I came over to visit my sister Gertie, Lady Coswell, would you, Con?"

Peter was aware of Con's why-didn't-you-tell-me? glance. As his crossing had had a nightmare quality because of his attempts to dodge his ex-fiancée, he had tried to forget it.

"It's a wonder you remember that I was on shipboard, Lydia," he evaded lightly. "You and I met once. I was too dead to the world to be other than a boring companion so I kept out of the way."

"You boring — you couldn't be." She turned to the large woman who had covered the distance from door to table in two strides. "Gertie, you remember my fiancé, Peter Corey, don't you?" As Lady Coswell gripped his hand with a strength which made the bones crackle, she added:

"This is Constance Trent, the long-lost heir of Trentmere Towers, who broke our engagement."

"*Lydia!* What do you *mean?*" Con demanded.

"Steady!" Peter gripped her shoulder and pressed her gently back in her chair. Before he could speak Lady Coswell's coarse laugh jarred a tinkle from the burnished-copper saucepans hung around the fireplace. She extended her hand.

"After that dose of Lyd's poison tongue, Corey ought to be thanking God on bended knees that he is an ex," she observed in a deep voice which should have belonged to a man. "Glad to know you, Miss Trent, glad to know anyone who can checkmate my catty sister."

Crimson spots burned in Con's cheeks, her eyes were luminous with anger:

"But I —"

"Why try to explain, my girl? Grab what you can in this world and keep it. I've wangled an invitation to the ball for Lyd from your grandfather; we all call him Lord Van, you know. I'm preparing you that you may hold your shock troops in readiness to fire back tomorrow night."

"Thank you, Lady Coswell, for the warning. Won't you join us for tea?"

"No thanks. My passengers are waiting for me. See you tomorrow. Come, Lyd."

As the sisters turned their backs Peter resumed his seat. Con's eyes glowed like stars aflame.

"What did she mean that I broke your engagement?" she demanded.

"Forget it, dear. This is a party. Have one of these fresh scones. They're corking."

Con's eyes flashed into laughter though her mouth quivered at the corners.

"They are, and — and I hope Lydia's choke her. That's how much of a perfect lady I am."

It had been difficult to appear party-minded at tea with the words, "This is Constance Trent who broke our engagement," going round and round in her mind like a crowd in a skating rink, Con reflected, as she snuggled among the crimson cushions of the canoe for the return trip on the river where late afternoon sunshine steeped the houses and fields on its banks with rose and amber and patterned the rippling water with an hundred golden designs.

The loud voices and laughter of the members of the coaching party hadn't helped, neither had Lydia's cold eyes which hers had encountered as if drawn by a powerful magnet, each time she looked up from the table. She had been aware of anger seething beneath Peter's cool courtesy. She regarded him now from under a fringe of black lashes as he paddled with rhythmic monotony. A muscle in his cheek twitched faintly. She knew that symptom. He was still furious. Why hadn't he told her that Lydia was in England? Did it mean that he still loved her too much to talk about her?

His eyes met hers. A smile dispelled his gravity. It was like watching the sun drive away a cloud.

"Get it out of your system, Con," he advised. "You are fairly aching to know why I didn't tell you that Lydia and I crossed on the same ship, aren't you?"

His laughing indifference was like a cool compress applied to a stinging, smarting scratch. Her heart stopped hurting.

"You must be fifty per cent. radio activity if you can see into my mind and discern my thoughts like that, Peter. I did wonder."

"I didn't tell you because I didn't want a moment of my shining vacation tarnished by the memory of a period of darn foolishness."

"I presume you are referring to your engagement. You call it darn foolishness now, but if Lydia makes up her mind to get you back, then what? She has a lot on the ball."

"Skip it, Con. You can't tell me anything I don't know about Lydia. If there's truth in that hoary adage, 'A burnt child,' and so on, I'm safe. Believe me?"

Her eyes which had been on the dark line of hills against the crimson sky came back to his. She nodded.

"I believe you."

"Promise that you'll always believe me, Con, will trust me and believe that no matter what I do, it will be because I think it best for you."

His voice and eyes set a little pulse beating in her throat, sent a queer shivery tingle along her veins.

"I promise," she said huskily.

"Then that's settled for keeps. Who's

singing?" He stopped paddling. "It's the man in the punt who poled past a minute ago. Listen! *'Ich Liebe Dich'* The girl in the bow is strumming a guitar accompaniment."

> " 'I love thee dear,
> I love thee dear
> Now and forever more.' "

As the last note faded in the distance Con appraised:

"A musical but untrained voice. I wish he could hear you sing that, Peter. It's my favorite in your repertoire. My heart goes all soft and melty like a chocolate peppermint in the sun when you sing, 'I love thee dear, now and forever more.' "

He threw back his head and laughed.

"You are inimitable, Con. I get what you mean, though a chocolate peppermint never has a chance to melt with me. I love 'em. Two stately white swans are following the punt as if they had been hypnotized by the man's voice. See them?"

"Yes. Glamorous creatures, aren't they? They always seem fairylandish to me." She watched him thoughtfully, surreptitiously, as he paddled the rest of the way in silence. Of what was he thinking?

"Lady Hanford and Tim have just landed

from a punt. They are waiting for us," she whispered as they approached the Towers dock.

"You are just in time," Tim welcomed as he helped lift the canoe from the water. "I'm taking Lady Hanford to Cherrytree Farm for tea."

Two sharp little lines cut between Peter's brows as he looked at the woman in the white sports suit waiting for them. There was something familiar about her profile. Had he met her somewhere and forgotten her? Not probable. It was his business to remember faces.

"You don't need an introduction to Con, Lady Hanford. May I present my brother, Peter?" Tim's voice was drenched with pride.

Con noticed that the woman looked at Peter with the same stare with which she had regarded her that first afternoon at Cherrytree Farm. It was as if she had rallied all her forces, all her power to drain her eyes of expression. One could feel the tenseness of her body. Perhaps her phobia — psychologists claim that almost every person has one — was dread of meeting strangers. Peter was rather forbidding as he looked down at her with that crease between his brows. Now that he saw Tim with her, was he worried?

Lady Hanford purred an inanity and the frown vanished.

"Happy chance to meet like this," he said as he fell into step beside her.

Later in the flower-scented living room Con watched her. Angela Corey in an orchid crepe frock was her most gracious self and Lady Hanford responded with vivacious cordiality. She devoted her entire attention to Peter as she had to Tim that first afternoon. She was a woman who tried to absorb each man she met as a cat licks up cream to the last drop, quickly, greedily, before any other woman could get a chance at him, Con concluded. When she was not talking she assumed a Mona Lisa smile, baffling, enigmatic. Was it a trick to make the two men wonder of what she was thinking?

"Don't forget, Mr. Corey, that you are dining with me tomorrow, before the ball of the century," she reminded coyly as she rose to take her leave.

"How could I forget — now," he answered with just the right pause and accent on "now" as he bent over the hand she extended.

He and Con stood at the window as she and Tim passed through the garden.

"That woman worries me," he observed. "I had the most curious impression when I first saw her, that I had seen her before. And yet I'm sure I haven't, not as Lady Hanford. You and Mother had her number when you called her glamorous."

"She's like Lydia in her male approach. Watch your step, Peter. There was a charge of dynamite in that 'now' of yours. A breach of promise case has been started on less."

"Thanks for the warning, Con. I told you I was on vacation and might need watching. For me, Maggie?" he asked as a trim black-frocked maid entered with an envelope on a silver tray.

"Yes, sir. A man brought it. Said you was to 'ave it as soon as you came in, sir. I put your letter in your room, my lady."

"Thank you, Maggie."

Peter waited until the maid had left the room before he tore open the message. "Did I brag that I was on vacation, Con?"

"What is it, Peter? Sealed orders? Business? You haven't been called home, have you?"

"Can't tell yet. It's from Bill. In code. Don't mention the fact that I received this, please."

"Of course I won't. Do you think I could live ten years in the house of a lawyer without having it drilled into me that I must never chatter about anyone's business, particularly my own? I'm going up to dress for dinner. Thanks for a grand afternoon. I just can't bear it if you have to leave, Peter. What's the use having a partner like Bill if he can't manage the business when you are on vacation?"

In her room, the dark quaint room gay with the hollyhock chintz she loved, a ray of crimson light from the low sun shot through a lattice window and fell on the old broken-front desk. It illumined a squatty inkwell and turned to rosy pink a letter braced against it. It was postmarked London. Who would write to her from there?

She slit open the envelope and read the words on the sheet of paper. Caught her breath. Read again:

"If you want news of your mother, advertise 'Yes' in personal column of *Times*. Box XXZ. Keep this secret. If you tell even one person we shall know it and disappear."

Surprise suspended the beat of Con's heart for an instant. She reread the message and it was back on its job thumping like a trip hammer. There was no signature.

Who had written it? Did she want "news" of her mother, the mother who had deserted her? She did. Her grandfather had declared that he had proof of her death. It might be a mistake. She would like the uncertainty as to her whereabouts cleared up, then she would no longer wonder as she passed a woman on the street if it had been she who had deserted Gordon Trent. Until this moment she hadn't realized what a habit that had become. After all, a person could have but one real mother. Wasn't it natural to want to know if she were in the land of the living? Doubtless the note was a type of racket. Hadn't Lord Gowan growled, "Some woman may come forward and claim she's your mother?" That might be the explanation, then again there was a chance in a hundred that the writer was on the level.

Should she consult Peter? If this were a brazen attempt to extort money it would be right up his street. But that would mean that it had a criminal angle and hadn't he said this very afternoon that if he heard even the soft swish of an approaching crime wave he would make a break for an island where radio and cable were unheard of? She must not appeal to him nor to anyone else. The note had warned: "If you tell even one person we shall know it and disappear."

She would handle this crisis in her life herself, if it were a crisis. It was high time she grew up and stopped depending on Peter. "It is your life, Con. No one can live it for you." His words rang through her memory as clearly as if he, himself, had broadcast them. Whether she were making a right or a wrong decision this was a road she must walk alone. Suppose she secured information for which he and Tim had been searching for years? It would be a feather in her cap, wouldn't it?

The ray of sunlight vanished. Dusk settled into the corners of the quaint room. She leaned against a casement of the lattice window and looked down into the garden all soft rose and lavender, pale gold and opal in the afterglow. Leaves rippled in the soft breeze, clapping daintily together as if applauding the crimson glory of the sunset. Peter was pacing the flagged path, smoking. The light had turned his white clothes faintly pink. He was frowning. Was it because of the message he had received? Curious that he and she should have had one the same day.

Her glance traveled to the silver ribbon of river, on to the dusky purple hills, to the ivy-covered towers of Trentmere. It was all so like a picture in a story book and the mysterious writer of that note fitted perfectly into the fairy tale she was living. There should be a wicked witch or a malevolent magician in it to make it run true to form. If she followed the letter up it might lead to a series of amazing adventures.

So much the better. She could take it. Before Clive Neale had made the dramatic announcement in the living room at Red Maples which had turned her world topsy-turvy, hadn't she felt that she was so protected that she was merely nibbling at life, that nothing exciting ever could happen to her? That she was on a treadmill that never would get her anywhere? Not that she had had any definite ideas as to a destination. She was like Dickens' Arabella Allen. She didn't know what she did want but she did know what she didn't want, she didn't want to live a purely social existence. She was trained for a position, but how could she take one when so many men, boys and women were out of work?

Suppose she did land in a mess if she followed up this note? It couldn't be anything very serious. Who would dare harm the granddaughter of a man as high in the esteem of the government as Lord Gowan? She wouldn't appeal to Peter for advice. For once she would make a decision uninfluenced by another person's judgement. Tonight she would mail her answer "Yes" to

Box XXZ, Personal Column of the *Times*, and await results. That word "results" sent a little shiver along her nerves.

In the garden Peter was standing frowning into space. Had the cable been about business, perplexing business? If it had, all the more reason for her to follow up that mysterious note without troubling him.

As if attracted by her tense regard, he looked up, saw her, smiled and waved his hand. Her heart thumped, her cheeks burned with guilt. Suppose he found out what she was planning to do? He could be rather terrible when he was angry. He shouldn't find out. Couldn't she keep a secret as well as he?

As she vanished from the window Peter Corey's thoughts returned to the cable message which occupied them to the exclusion of all else. Translated it had read:

Bad hombre sailed same ship as your mother. Tourist class. One of three. Thomson. Barclay. Sacks. Letter. Bill.

He resumed his pacing of the cobble walk. "Bad hombre" was Dafter, of course. Bill wouldn't cable him about any lesser public enemy. It meant that he must get in touch with the officials of New Scotland Yard. It meant also that he would have to leave Con, for days at a time perhaps. He wouldn't do it. He'd be darned if he would. Wasn't he entitled to a vacation?

You know you'll go, he answered his own question. The FBI has been after that racketeer and blackmailer for years. You wouldn't leave a mad dog at large because you were on vacation, would you? The day after the ball, my boy, you head for London.

VIII

As Con stood on the broad landing halfway
up the white marble stairway and looked
down upon the gorgeous pageant of beauty
and color from which rose the blended scent
of many perfumes, the murmur of voices, the
sparkle of laughter, she thought that the
present chapter in her fairy story was even
more breathtakingly magnificent than she had
imagined it could be.

Footmen in white perukes, maroon livery
with satin knee breeches and buckled shoes
were everywhere. Women in exquisite
frocks, designed to accentuate the rose-leaf
or gardenia perfection of bare arms and
shoulders and backs, wearing unbelievably
sumptuous ropes of pearls, diamond tiaras,
necklaces, bracelets of incredible brilliance,
were mounting the stairs or talking and
walking with men in scarlet and gold uni-
forms, men in the austere black and white of
evening clothes decorated with stars and orders and ribbons. There were Scots in
tartan and a few jeweled Orientals. Many

were dancing in the great ballroom to the dreamy music of a Strauss waltz. She liked the mixture of all ages she had found characteristic of English social functions.

Pride in birth and family had been bred into these people for generations. She glanced at her grandfather beside her and felt a sudden overwhelming surge of that same pride. He didn't need a uniform, he was outstandingly distinguished in evening clothes. She was a Trent. She was a descendant of men who had won their lands and titles fighting for their kings. Only half of her, she remembered with a quick catch of her breath. What would she hear about the other half, her mother? The thought thrust itself into her awareness of surrounding beauty like a serpent rearing its fanged head in the midst of paradise.

She forced her attention back to the present. Being at Trentmere Towers still seemed like a dream, she told herself, even as she smiled and welcomed and returned greetings. She twirled a crystal fringe between her fingers. That was real. So was the rope of pearls on her neck and the low matching coronet on her head. So were her flowers, sprays of white orchids and feathery stephanotis which had come from Peter "With all our love" on the accompanying card. Ivor had sent her magnificent red roses. They were now in a tall crystal vase in the gold salon. There had been no question in her mind as to which she would carry.

She was awake, all right. How long would she be expected to stand here welcoming guests? Why hadn't Angel and Peter and Tim come? As if he had read her mind Lord Gowan growled:

"Where are your friends, the Coreys?"

"They dined with Lady Hanford."

"What do they mean dining with —"

"Mrs. Corey. Mr. Corey. Mr. Timothy Corey."

The names were passed from footman to footman who lined the stairs beneath the Gainsboroughs and Romneys on the wall.

A wave of loneliness swept over Constance as she watched the three figures leisurely mounting the broad stairs. They were notably distinguished even in this company of titled, political, military and social headliners. She felt as if she were in another, a strange world where her life would never again be a part of theirs. The concealed floodlight set every silver thread in Angela Corey's orchid satin gown to shimmering and every diamond in her magnificent necklace ablaze. This is an occasion, Con thought with an inner chuckle; Angel has brought out the family jewels; she so seldom wears them, thinks them too gorgeous for the ordinary social affairs at home.

"Holds up her head and mounts those stairs as if she were a queen and so few women walk upstairs gracefully," Lord Gowan growled under his breath, but Con heard him. Her eyes were luminous with love and pride:

"There never was a queen more beautiful. Why shouldn't she be proud with two such sons to —" Emotion choked off her voice as Peter smiled at her and Tim closed one eye in a prolonged wink.

"There are sons and sons," her grandfather retorted bitterly before he bent over Mrs. Corey's hand. "It is a privilege to see you here, Madam," he greeted with stiff formality.

"Lady Hanford. Captain Ivor Hardwick, Mr. —"

Con lost the rest of the footman's announcement.

"I'll be down to dance in a few minutes, Peter." For an instant her hand clung to his. "Angel, you're perfect! Tim, don't eat all the supper, leave some for me, I'm starving." Ivor Hardwick touched her arm.

"His Imperial Majesty, your grandfather, has given you permission to dance. I'm awfully keen for it. May I have the pleasure, Cousin?"

Con looked at Lady Hanford who in a gauzy, flounced black net with a strapless bodice breath-takingly off the shoulders, stood between Lord Gowan and a man in Gordon tartan. She was smiling but her smile was as stiff as if it had been stitched into shape. The atmosphere was suddenly charged with animosity.

"The Honorable Miss Trent is looking at me for permission, Ivor," she said in a tone which brought a tinge of color to his face. "Really, my dear, go with him. I'm all dated up with that fascinating 'brother Peter' of yours."

"Lady Hanford talks such chawming nonsense," Ivor Hardwick cut in smoothly. "A dance is beginning, Cousin. Come."

While she danced, and later, seated on the broad parapet of the terrace with her head tipped back against a rough stone column, Con couldn't rid herself of a feeling of hurt, as if she had taken a wrong turn. Was Lady Hanford really "all dated up" with Peter? It was heavenly out here in the star-spangled pageantry of night. The moon flooded the earth with silver. The soft wind laid satin fingers on her face, the fountain showered diamonds, she was in a fairyland of beauty, of dreams and romance, yet something had tarnished the glamour of the evening.

"By Jove, I believe you've forgotten I'm here, what? Why didn't you carry my roses?" Ivor Hardwick demanded in his most effective, spoiled-boy voice.

Constance transferred her attention from a meteor that had dropped like a star shell, to the flame of his cigarette lighter. Apparently her indifference to his flowers had touched his vanity nerve.

"Peter and Angel and Tim sent me the white ones," she answered gravely. "I wouldn't have carried any others if the King had presented them. I haven't forgotten you are among those present this minute. You are part of it."

"Of what?"

"The dream. The Towers. Major General Lord Vandemere Trent-Gowan. The ball. These pearls. Pretty soon I'll wake up and find myself at Red Maples with life going on as before."

His laugh was indulgent.

"The dream is that you think for a moment that you'll go back to those United States. It's jolly absurd. You couldn't leave all this grandeur and family background to return to a country, frightfully crime-infested, badly governed, where kidnaping is one of the bally industries, could you?"

"How British." Con's eyes were brilliant as black diamonds. "I'd like you to know that no other profession in America is moving to the top so swiftly as law enforcement. Go on, tell me some more outs about my country. That we haven't mastered the technique of living as the Europeans have is one, of course; that 'there was an America which died with Lincoln' — I've heard that since I came — and what is wrong with our art, our literature. You've already paid your respects to our government and politics, our m"anners, our voices —"

"Nothing the matter with your voice, Cousin, it's like velvet, perhaps at the present moment with the pile rubbed the wrong way, but *chawming* velvet."

Con refused to be mollified. "If our politics are corrupt in spots, is that a justifiable excuse for me to shake the dust of my country from my feet? All the more reason to work and work to make it better, to try to awaken the patriotic conscience of citizens who have been dozing while difficulties of the nation mounted, to make them realize that it is up to all of us with advantages of financial and social security to keep our own lives straight and by example bolster the weaker until they stand upright too. Women can do so much, if they will only wake up and insist upon thorough and unprejudiced investigation of some government procedures. Have you never heard the pledge to the Stars and Stripes? 'I pledge allegiance to the Flag of the United States of America and to the Republic for which it stands, one nation indivisible with liberty and justice for all.' "

"Bravo! Bravo, Miss America! *Such fervor!* Such *fire!*"

It was a perfect dramatic situation. So might the current male movie idol have clapped his hands, have stooped to flatter an awkward extra, Con thought angrily. His indulgent amusement brought a hot wave of color to her face. She must have seemed ridiculously young and unsophisticated to a hard-boiled man of the world like Ivor — and much as she liked him she recognized the fact that he was hard-boiled — to have recited the Pledge to the Flag in that impassioned way. Recognition of his point of view only served to increase her indignation.

"That's a moth-eaten trick, Ivor, to make fun of an argument when you can't answer it. Do you think I'll stand here like a dummy and let you criticize the United States when it has the highest standard of living in the world and our minimum wage and hours of work are far better than in your old England? When I left home high-minded men were coming into office and fearless young ones were becoming figures of national significance. Peter —"

"Peter! I say, that chap's a little higher than the angels in your estimation, what?"

The edge in his smooth voice, his hostile eyes warned Con. She'd better watch her step. This man and her grandfather might combine to make Peter's proposed stay in England unendurable.

"You and I couldn't agree in a thousand years," she countered lightly. "Our upbringing and environment have been so different. You've never been in my country, have you? What do you know of the stimulation and inspiration, the sparkle and dash and fun of life as it is lived there? It makes me homesick just to think of it. Let's forget it." She abruptly changed the subject. "Ivor, did you ever hear anything about my mother?"

He regarded her through half-closed eyes.

"What started you on that train of thought, Miss America?"

"Oh, nothing, nothing special. It's natural, isn't it, that on an occasion like this I should wonder what, if any, difference it would have made in my life, had she not deserted me?"

"Frightfully queer you should have asked

that question now, for last week while I was doing a spot of hunting through papers of my father's I came across a photograph of her that your father had sent him. They were cousins, rather keen for each other, you know. He had written on the back of it, 'My wife, Viola.' "

"Ivor! Did you bring it?"

"It's upstairs in my bag. I thought you might like to see it. I intended to tell you about it later."

"You dear! Get it, will you?"

"Meet me in the Tower room after supper. Be frightfully careful. Don't mention it to anyone. If Lord Van hears that I have showed it to you he will cut me off without even a shilling."

"Here they are, *Peter*."

It was Lady Hanford's voice. Lady Hanford's bare hand, glistening with gorgeous rings, slipped into Ivor Hardwick's. The facets of the diamonds surrounding the emeralds in her necklace, in the bracelets which encircled her left arm from wrist to elbow, were no more brilliant than the sparks in her eyes.

"Do take me back to the ballroom," she pleaded. "Really, my dear, Peter has been distracted looking for you, Miss Trent. He said —"

Con's gay laugh checked the purring voice.

"Peter distracted, Lady Hanford? Then you've seen him as opposing counsel in court would give their eyes to see him. I can't believe it, but perhaps he was. Who am I to attempt to probe the dark, hidden depths of the human mind?"

"Call it distraction or persistence, thanks to Lady Hanford, I've found you." Peter Corey's amused eyes met Con's. "Shall we dance?"

"I say, we'll continue our conversation later as *arranged*, Miss America." There was an ugly note in Ivor Hardwick's voice. "Of course the Duke will take you out to supper, he's tremendously keen on youth and beauty. I'll make you give up the fantastic idea of returning to those United States if it takes the rest of the year. Come, Celie."

Peter's eyes followed the man and woman till they stepped into the ballroom.

"Ever notice how some of the English persist in speaking of our country in the plural?" Con asked as lightly as she could with the prospect of securing a photograph of her mother when she met Ivor in the Tower room, tingling in her mind. "What knotty problem is knitting that classic brow of yours, Peter?"

132

"I'm thinking it is curious how the impression persists that somewhere I have met Lady Hanford. It annoys me not to remember. You and Mother were right when you called her a glamour-woman. What jewels! She glistens like a Christmas tree."

"What about Tim? Did he appear completely bowled over at dinner, as if she were his heartbeat?" Con inquired anxiously.

"Couldn't make the boy out. Couldn't decide whether he had really fallen for his hostess or whether he was putting on an act of devotion, though I can't conceive what his motive would be for that. Let's forget her. Will the Honorable Miss Trent do me the honor to —"

"Peter, don't call me that even in fun. It makes me feel so far away from you and Angel and Tim, I just can't bear it."

She pressed her face against his sleeve.

"When you turned away from me on the stair landing I felt as deserted as — as a foundling left on a strange doorstep."

He had to bend his head to hear the muffled words. His lips lightly brushed the satin softness of her hair.

"Than which there is nothing more deserted." His laughing agreement was unsteady. "Hey, you're not fading on this party, are you? I'll remind you, Miss Trent, that you are holding up a dance." He drew a handkerchief from his pocket. "You'd better dry those uselessly long lashes with this before we go in. I should hate to have anyone think I had made you cry on this sumptuous occasion."

"I'm not fading on the party and I don't need your handkerchief, thanks. But sometimes, Peter, I feel as if I were a wishbone being pulled two ways. I love this place and all it stands for and yet —"

"The Coreys are not pulling you, Con."

"That's the trouble. I wish they were and I wouldn't hesitate a minute. It's my love for home and you all that's doing the pulling one way and a sense of duty the other. What *is* duty, Peter?"

"Duty? I'd say about seven tenths of the time it is what the other fellow thinks you should do, the other three tenths is what that character scout who perches on the hillock of Conscience tells you you must do." He laughed. "Have I made it clear?"

"Clear that no one can help me, that I've got to work out the decision myself. You are always so decisive and sure, Peter. Do you ever feel pulled in two directions?"

"Do I? You're asking me!" His voice was grim. "Come on! Let's dance."

134

IX

From a balcony in the softly lighted, green-garlanded ballroom Lord Gowan saw Constance and Peter enter. He frowned when she smilingly shook her head at the young officers who swarmed from the champagne bar toward her like bees to a honey tree. As the two danced into the crowd of white, scarlet and black shoulders to the music of the current dance hit he said to Clive Neale beside him:

"My granddaughter is charming, she's so tender, so true, so fearless. She isn't afraid of me and dammit every other person on the place is. Whenever I see her, I think of Nausicaä, daughter of Alcinoüs, in the *Odyssey*, 'high of heart.' The characterization suits her, doesn't it?"

"It does." Neale's response was so fervent that Lord Gowan cast a quick look at him.

"Youth and audacity driven tandem make a great team," he declared. "Good fortune won't just happen to her, she'll make it happen. We made a mistake when we invited Corey here. He will interfere with my plan to marry Constance to Ivor."

"I wouldn't be too sure of that, Lord Van. Corey was engaged. The engagement was broken, but broken engagements have been patched up. The girl, Lydia Austen, is here tonight with her sister, your eccentric neighbor, Lady Coswell."

"That terrible woman who is driving a coach between the old posting house and London? If the sister is as masculine as she, I don't wonder Corey broke with her. Dash it all, I detest loud-voiced women who stride."

His attention returned to his granddaughter.

"Don't like the way Constance looks up at him as they dance. We must get Corey out of the way, make it worth his while to return to the United States. We'll put him to work on the titles of those New York business blocks we are transferring. Pay him well, of course."

"You can't influence the Coreys with money, Lord Van. I looked up their rating after I located your granddaughter. They belong to one of those New England families whose loyalty to their country, wealth and local influence has been a constructive force for generations, but whose tastes are simple, whose belief that living may be raised to a fine art, whose firmly grounded code of conduct which includes voluntary self-discipline, has been inherited."

"A sort of Corey tradition?"

"Yes. I was told that Peter has an uncanny flair for law enforcement, that he has brought some of the previously invincible racketeers to justice. I was assured he will be District Attorney next year. Since her husband's death Mrs. Corey has served as director on the board of some of the corporations in which the family has large interests. You owe it to her that your granddaughter has been brought up to be a lady and an intelligent human being with ideals and ideas and old-fashioned moral standards."

"By Jove, you do admire the Coreys, don't you? I wish you could say as much for Ivor as for Corey, but, except for his extravagance I presume he isn't any worse than the majority of his generation in the same social scale. I don't like the woman with whom he is running round at present."

"She is received by the Duchess, Lord Van. Invitations to Fordham Manor are sought by all the county families."

"Hmp! Hanford bought the Manor not quite five years ago. Never could understand why he settled in this part of England. He had an estate in the North whose grouse

137

moors are famous. Didn't live long after he bought the Manor. Died three years ago while I was out of the country, didn't he? Did he pick his wife off the cinema, a music hall or a night club?"

"Neither. Her first husband was a baronet, a rich totter with no relatives. She had been his widow two years when she married Lord Hanford."

"Dash it all, what does that prove? The woman's an adventuress. Think I don't recognize one when I see one? She's scheming to be mistress of Trentmere Towers. Thinks Ivor will get the estate as well as the title, I presume. He won't unless he marries Constance. It's a pity Corey isn't the heir to this title. The estate could use a man like that, a man who realizes that life can be amazing, thrilling, satisfying, although lived decently. Well, he isn't and we must get him out of the country. Ask him to come to the Tower room to have a smoke with me before supper is announced. I'd like to sound him out. If he is the type of man you claim he is, he has too fine manners to object to leaving the ballroom for a few moments with his elderly host. I'm tired. I'll drop out of the party for a while."

Con saw the two men leave the balcony.

"Exit grandfather and his man Friday. I

like Clive Neale. I have a feeling, Peter, that if I were in trouble of any sort I could tell him all, sob out my sorrow on his shoulder, figuratively speaking."

"What's the matter with mine, Miss Trent?"

She glanced up with the first hint of co-quetry she ever had used toward him.

"It looks fairly comfortable, but —"

He drew her close to avoid contact with a couple and stopped in a corner of the room.

"There are to be no buts, understand. You are to tell your troubles to me, Con. Begin now. Too late. Captain Ivor approaches."

"And see who is with him!"

"Hope you are enjoying the party, Lydia," she greeted Miss Austen who, in a glistening wave-green frock had tucked her hand under Peter Corey's arm with the air of a woman whose dearest wish has been granted.

"I'm having the time of my life, now," she said and pointed the last word with a smile that hardened his eyes.

"Jove, that makes me feel frightfully *de trop*. Shall we dance, Miss America, what?" Ivor Hardwick slipped his arm about Con. Clive Neale touched Peter's shoulder.

"Sorry to break up the party but Lord Gowan wants you to join him in the Tower room for a smoke, Corey. Miss Austen, may I pinch-hit for him? Jolly music. Shall we dance?"

Peter took in every detail of the Tower room as he entered in response to a gruff, "Come in."

Two perfectly lighted Rembrandts against walls of oak and walnut; ceiling with molded ribs which connected carved heraldic shields. Laden book shelves, a flat desk which looked as if it had served generations of Trent-Gowans; rich faded hangings drawn at long windows, and old rugs; a stag's head with twelve-pointed antlers, and a dim portrait; racks of guns, deep chairs and shaded lamps. A tall folding screen of embossed Spanish leather above which he could see the top of a door. A wagon service table with decanters, siphons and glasses, a stand with cigars and cigarettes. Six-foot logs blazing beneath the high chimney piece, in a chair before it a large man with a decoration in the buttonhole of his black evening coat; a bulldog on the floor beside him. The rhythmic tick of a clock. The scent of tobacco. The faint smell of liquor. All quite as he had imagined it as he had listened to Gordon Trent's nostalgic descriptions of his English home.

"Hope I'm not disturbing you, Lord

Gowan? Neale told me you wanted to see me."

"Come in, Corey. Sorry to take you away from the ballroom but I thought you'd be willing to spare me a few minutes. I wanted a chance to get acquainted with my granddaughter's friend. Shut the door. Help yourself." He waved a fine hand with its signet ring in the direction of the service wagon. "Smoke?"

"Nothing to drink, thanks. I'll take a cigarette."

His host would be surprised if he knew how little he regretted leaving the ballroom, Peter thought. He had been glad to sidestep the dance with Lydia. Was the remainder of his vacation to be haunted by the wraith of his late engagement in the person of his ex-fiancée? Not if he could escape her, and with the Dafter hunt on it ought not to be difficult.

He tried to brush away the annoying memory of her voice, possessive eyes and clinging hand, but it persisted. Why was she trying to get him back? Hadn't she found a title which she wanted, that wanted her? Had she heard of the probability of his becoming District Attorney? Did she think it would be a steppingstone to higher honors she might share with him? If she did she had another think coming to her.

He forced her from his mind and regarded the white-haired man who was looking up at him. He was vigorous, handsome, in spite of the fact that life had carved deep lines of disillusion and bitterness in his face. The dog rose, stretched, sniffed at the stranger's trousers and returned to lay his nose on his master's knee. Lord Gowan smoothed his coat.

"That means you are acceptable in this room, Corey. Roustabout has an unerring instinct for human values if he did fly at Constance's dog and take a few bites out of him. The vet told me later that the terrier gave as much as he took. You knew Gordon, well, did you not?" He dropped the monocle from his eye and polished it with a fine handkerchief.

"We were friends. After my father's death, he talked to me as he had once confided in him."

"Did he speak of me, of his home?"

"Rarely of you, sir, but often of Trentmere Towers. I could find my way round it in the dark. This room is familiar to me from his description. Talking about the place and describing the inside of the house seemed to ease his aching homesickness."

"If you knew him so well, you must know that he would want his daughter to take her rightful place as my heir."

"I knew him well enough to know that he would want Con to choose the way of life which would seem best to her."

"What could be better for her than to assume the high position she has inherited? She declares she won't stay. I pretend not to believe her but, dash it all, I'm troubled. You and your mother have great influence with her. I am depending upon you two to advise her to remain, to show her where her duty lies."

So, that's why I'm here, Peter thought. He tossed his cigarette into the fire. His steady eyes met the stern blue eyes looking up at him.

"Con must decide that for herself. It is a matter upon which no one should presume to advise her."

"You advised her to come to England, didn't you? Neale said that at first she refused."

Peter remembered the diplomacy he had used and smiled at the memory.

"I wouldn't call it advice, exactly, perhaps the power of suggestion."

"Advice or suggestion. Use it again. Persuade her to stay here."

"No. Con will make that decision uninfluenced by Mother or me."

"Does that mean that you won't tell her you love her? That you want to marry her?"

Lord Gowan was standing now. Peter felt the color surge to his hair and recede as his eyes met the demanding blue eyes on a level with his own.

"I repeat that I shall not influence her to stay or leave. Put any construction on that statement you like."

"Quite so! Quite so! I know you're a man of your word. I'll have to be content with that. It's jolly lucky I have only you to fight. No knowing what crazy ideas the girl's mother might put into her head were she alive."

"Are you sure she isn't?"

"Yes. Clive Neale found the tragic facts of her death in a small city in your New England. It took three detectives to trace her."

"May I see the report? We followed the few clues we had and landed in a blind alley."

"The papers are behind the panel beside the fireplace. I'll have Neale get them out for you. There is a copy of the marriage certificate and all other data except the place and time of the divorce."

"There was no divorce, I know that."

"What d'you mean? That Gordon held onto the woman after she ran off?"

"He told me that the man with whom she went away never would marry her. He didn't try to trace her after she left him. He was sure that sometime she would return to him and her child if he did not divorce her."

"Sounds like Gordon. Visionary, quixotic. Cut free from home rather than continue in His Majesty's service." Back in the chair Lord Gowan stared at the fire from tinder shaggy brows. "Why am I thinking of that? It's past. I have his daughter. I will keep her."

"If you can. Con is —"

"Did I hear my name?"

The girl's vivid face with a coronet of pearls on the dark hair which framed it appeared at the partially opened door. The music of an orchestra, the murmur of distant chatter and laughter drifted into the room.

"I missed you, General, and was quite sure you had escaped to your den," she accused. Peter smiled as he heard the "klish! klish!" of the crystal fringes as she approached her grandfather.

"I came to remind you that no one may go to supper until you take in the Duchess! I've learned that in my short stay in England. Your guests are beginning to look wistfully in the direction of the feast. Is this a council of war? You both appear so — so problem-logged."

"Not at all, my dear, not at all," Lord Trent disclaimed hastily. "Thank you for reminding me of the Duchess. You will go in with the Duke. Come back here after supper, Corey, and bring Neale. He will show you those papers."

X

The fire blazed and faded. The clock ticked off the seconds. The dog roused from a doze as Lord Gowan, Peter Corey and Clive Neale entered the Tower room. One of the hangings moved as if a breeze no stronger than a breath had stirred it, and was still.

Curious, Peter thought, and looked quickly at the screen. Had that moved too? The portion of the door above it was slightly ajar. It had been closed when he first noticed it.

With a sigh of relief Lord Gowan settled into a deep chair.

"By Jove, that's done! The voice of the Duchess flowed along as steadily as our river without the stream's small bubbling rapids to break the monotony. Dashed if I'm not half hypnotized. Neale, show Corey the data about Gordon's marriage and the woman's death. What the deuce is the matter with you, Roustabout?"

The bulldog's teeth snapped on a hanging. For an instant each person in the room seemed turned to stone. Lord Gowan sat rigid in his chair; Clive Neale's hands tightened on the papers he had taken from a drawer behind the panel. Peter, with lighter halfway to his cigarette, stood motionless. The three men might have been run-down mechanical toys waiting for the winding by a master key to loosen their metal joints.

Roustabout growled. Arrested motion was released. Lord Gowan rose. Neale flung the papers on the desk. Peter threw the cigarette into the fire and dashed for the hanging. He caught a rough sleeve and jerked a man into the room, a man who brought with him a strong barnyard smell, a man with a spatulate nose who pulled awkwardly at his forelock.

"So, it's you, Chettle? Quite so. Quite so. It would be you," Lord Gowan roared. "You needn't hold him, Corey. On guard, Roustabout."

As the bulldog with fangs glistening, eyes burning like red stop lights, crouched and growled, Peter folded his arms on top of the back of a tall chair opposite the screen.

"Who let you in?"

" 'Twasn't nobody, your lordship, I hope I sees you well." Chettle's eyes roamed from face to face. Oily was the word for his voice. "I was walkin' round outside quiet an' decentlike to get a look at the nobility an' gentry, an' I sees a crack of light at this 'ere window an' I ses, 'It's open. 'E forgot to lock it,' meanin' by 'e Mr. Sacks, your lordship's butler."

Sacks! The word clanged through Peter's memory. A man named Sacks had sailed on the ship on which Dafter had left the United States. Had the gangster he was hunting assumed that name? Perhaps it was his own. Would the hunt end here, in this house? Was Dafter a relative of the butler? Could it be as easy as that? The possibility set his imagination racing. He forced his attention back to the yokel who was shifting from one foot to the other.

" 'I'll tyke a look in,' I ses to meself," he rambled on. "I'll see if it's the syme as w'en I useter come 'ere to collect 'arf a crown fer carryin' a private letter fer young master Ernest to some of 'is lydies. I'm allus willin' to oblige, yer lordship. 'E was a great one with the lydies, 'e was."

His insolent implication suffused the face of Lord Gowan with deep color and deprived him of his voice.

"How long have you been behind that curtain, Chettle?" Clive Neale demanded.

"Law, sir. 'Ow do I know? It might be 'arf an hour, it might be 'arf a minute. I dessay the gentleman leanin' on the chair can tell. I 'eard in the pub that he's someun as ye might call special in a legal wye over in the States."

"Ring for Sacks, Neale. We'll have him remove Chettle. Chettle, this time I'll let you off. After this keep away from the Towers grounds, understand?"

"Ay, yer lordship. I'm allus willin' to oblige."

The door opened. The butler appeared on the threshold.

"Oh, there you are, Sacks," Lord Gowan fumed. "Take Chettle out through the billiard room. Hand him over to one of the village constables, there should be a number round the house tonight, and have it understood that he is to stay outside the grounds."

"Yes, my lord."

The face of the butler was livid and taut. Peter had a sudden conviction that Lord Gowan was inadvertently playing into his servant's hands by turning Chettle over to him.

"Let me personally conduct the man to the gate, Lord Gowan," he suggested. "Sacks must have all he can attend to in other directions with the house bulging with guests."

Peter had met many malevolent glances

but never one of quite the intensity that Sacks turned on him before he asserted:

"I can deliver Farmer Chettle to the constables without assistance, my lord."

"Cripes, 'e don't have to put me out, yer lordship. I'll go pleasant an' easy as 'arf a crown slippin' into me pocket. Perhaps ye think I come in to pinch somethin'. Lor, I didn't."

"Corey and I will escort him out together, Lord Van," Clive Neale suggested.

"Carry on. Go back to the dining room, Sacks."

"Very good, my lord."

As the butler closed the door the expression of the flat-nosed man was a blend of cunning and contempt.

" 'Ow Mr. Sacks do 'ate to lose the job of puttin' me h'out to be sure," he sneered. "Fair vexed, 'e was. 'E don't love me, if 'e is me missus' blood brother. I don't need nobody to put me h'out, leastwise nobody wot's 'ere. I'll go meself."

He slipped between the hangings. A latch clicked. Peter and Neale reached the window at the same instant. They saw a hand clutch the balcony. Loosen. Came the crash and crackle of shrubs.

"He's saved us a lot of trouble," Neale remarked as they turned away. "Now we'll take up the matter of those papers you asked me to show Corey, Lord Van."

"Let the papers wait. I want to know what the man was doing in this room? That's all poppycock about taking a look in to see if it was as it used to be."

"More likely he was here to meet someone. And if I'm not mistaken, the person is behind this." Peter stepped quickly to the screen, moved a fold and disclosed Captain Ivor Hardwick, who regarded him with hostile eyes.

Peter stared back in surprised concern. Had he known that a member of Lord Gowan's family was the eavesdropper he certainly would not have forced him into the open. For the second time that evening he appraised the man facing him. He was hard and crafty under a veneer of good looks, culture and breeding. In the early forties at least. Indubitably a man pursued by women, he had that type of man's insolent air of superiority. This was the husband Lord Gowan had selected for his granddaughter, for Con, who was so lovely, so tender, so loyal and sweet and gay, who was so excitingly unpredictable.

Hardwick stepped forward as nonchalantly as if it were as much a daily occurrence for him to be discovered behind a screen as for a magician to produce a rabbit from a hat. There was a hint of contemptuous indulgence in his smile.

"Rather a neat exposé, what? Awfully sorry to have intruded but I didn't expect to find the Tower room occupied while the guests are departing, Lord Van," he apologized and criticized in the same breath. "Leaving your chawming granddaughter to carry on alone, are you?"

Lord Gowan rose hurriedly.

"You're right, Ivor. You're right, I should be outside but I get so dashed bored with crowds." He glowered beneath bristling brows. "How like you to switch attention from yourself. Why were you hiding behind that screen?"

"Hiding is such a frightfully unpleasant word, Lord Van. I'd rather you would call it 'waiting,' if you don't mind."

" 'Waiting' then. Who the devil were you waiting for? Why don't you answer? This is my room, my private room. What d'you mean using it for a rendezvous? For whom were you waiting?"

"Beastly nuisance, I can't tell you — but as to the lady, here she is now." Hardwick cast an exultant glance at Peter as Constance entered the room.

The man was lying, Con had not come

here to meet him, Peter assured himself, then remembered the Captain's reminder to her in the ballroom, "We'll continue our conversation as *arranged.*" His heart turned to ice as the girl apologized somewhat breathlessly:

"Sorry, I'm late, Ivor. General, I came for Peter. The Duchess has heard that you sing, Peter, and awaits you in the gold salon."

"I haven't any music here. Besides, I'm not in the mood for singing," he protested.

"You'd better go, Corey. A request by Her Grace is almost equal to a royal command," Lord Gowan advised.

"Oh, all right. Let's get it over. Come on, Con. You'll have to accompany me. I'll sing something we both know without notes. You're not all coming, are you?" he demanded, as he stood aside for the girl to precede him from the room.

"Only to say good night to my guests, not to hear you sing," Lord Gowan answered with a twinkle in his eyes which vividly reminded Peter of his son, Gordon. "Come, Neale. Coming Ivor?"

"After I've had a spot of whiskey and soda and a cigarette."

As Peter stood by the gold piano with its tall crystal vase of deep red roses, he felt a sudden unbearable hatred for the Fragonard wall panels with their simpering ladies and adoring courtiers, all soft pinks and blues, mellow greens and sunny yellows, for the lacquer and gilt and pale-tinted brocades of the furnishings, for the gorgeous bejeweled women and bemedaled men against that background, representatives of the caste system, of families whose names were part of Britain's history and of whose curiosity about the rank outsider, Peter Corey, he was aware. But the scarlet and ermine they represented were a part of Con's inheritance, he reminded himself.

"What will you sing, Peter?"

He saw Ivor Hardwick enter, noted his expression of insolent assurance. That steadied him. He smiled down into the girl's dark eyes raised to his.

"Your favorite, *Ich Liebe Dich*,' darling," he said in a low voice and saw the startled color mount to her hair. She struck a few unsteady chords before she began the accompaniment.

With the sense that he was battling for the girl he loved he sang as he never had sung before. His voice was impassioned, infinitely tender at the close:

" 'I love thee, dear,
I love thee, dear, now and forever more.' "

His singing was fresh and dramatic and disturbing. There was silence for an instant after the last exquisite note of the accompaniment. Then the applause broke.

Peter laughed, caught Con's hand and drew her to her feet.

"Take your bow, darling," he said huskily. "How's that chocolate peppermint heart of yours, now?"

"Peter!" she said breathlessly. *"Peter!"*

"Encore! Encore! Encore!"

"We'll give them 'Deep River,' Con."

" 'Oh deep river, Lord, I want to cross over into camp ground.' "

There was an instant's hush after the last profoundly stirring words of the spiritual. Then the thunder of applause.

He shook his head.

"Peter, you were marvelous! You —"

Someone interrupted Con and he made his escape. His mother was waiting near the door of the salon.

"It's time we were leaving, Peter. I've said good night to Connie and Lord Van. She is to stay here and Tim has left with a party of young people. I'm so glad for him to be with girls of his own age. I — I — wish he wouldn't go to Fordham Manor so —" she

156

broke off the sentence. "Peter, when you sang, 'I love thee, dear,' it was the cry of your heart liberated through your beautiful voice. Con never again can be unaware of your love."

"Sorry, it got me. I've kept my feeling for her under so long that tonight it boiled up and over. Perhaps it's a good thing. Someone has said that if we let our emotions evaporate without doing anything about them they get into the way of evaporating."

"You did something about them tonight, Peter." Angela Corey's laugh was unsteady. "You should have seen Lord Van's expression when you were singing. A thunderhead would be sunny in comparison."

"My mistake. It was unfair to her and to her grandfather, as I have assured him that the Coreys will do nothing to influence her to return to the United States. But she is constantly praising Ivor Hardwick and when I saw him looking at her across the room with that smirk of assurance I went cockeyed."

"I have a feeling that because she knows you don't like the Captain she is championing him, but not honoring him. There's a difference."

"That helps. Perhaps you and I are exaggerating, perhaps Con didn't notice anything unusual in my voice tonight. Whether she did or not, I must assume the big brother role again. It won't be easy. Fortunately I've had a cable from the office which will keep me occupied to a certain extent."

"Oh, Peter! I thought this visit was to be all vacation."

"Most of it will be. Get your wrap, Mother. I will order the car."

Two hours later in rose-color pajamas Con sat before the mirror in the Spanish Bride's room and watched black-frocked Mrs. Bunthorne gently brushing her dark hair. Peter's husky "darling" kept echoing in her memory. It tightened her throat. It tripped up her heart beat. He had said the word twice. Never before had he spoken to her in that tone. Lydia had been alluring in the green frock. Much as she detested her she would have to acknowledge her beauty. Perhaps he had fallen in love with her all over again and emotion had overflowed when he sang. Where did that poisonous suggestion come from? She must have imagined that his voice had been huskily caressing. There could be no other explanation.

"Did I pull, my lady?" Mrs. Bunthorne asked tenderly. "You drew such a deep sigh."

158

Constance shook her head. As she looked at her own reflected face she remembered that there were people in different parts of the world who believed that they saw their soul, not their reflection, in a mirror, or in a shining pool. Was that her soul looking at her through her turbulent dark eyes?

"It was a beautiful ball," Mrs. Bunthorne commented in hushed rapture. "The Towers hasn't seen anything like it in years. Next, we'll have a wedding, I hope and pray."

Not mine, Con thought. Aloud she evaded:

"Don't brush any more, Bunny. My hair shines like black satin. You must be tired. I'll feel lost in that huge four-poster with the Trent-Gowan crest carved on the headboard. How many times does that coat of arms appear in this house?"

"I couldn't tell you, my lady! Get into bed and I will raise the shade so you can see it enameled on the window by which the Spanish Bride enters. Sometimes when the moon is going down its light shines through and shows all the lovely jewel-like colors."

She drew the bed clothes to the girl's chin.

"Now go to sleep. You have had a hard day."

Con sat up and clasped her hands about her knees.

"It has been a gorgeous day and night, Bunny. I am too excited to sleep. I can't believe that I'm really in the room I have heard my father describe so often. If only he could have been here tonight. If only the ball had been to welcome him, not me."

"Don't think of that, dearie." Impulsively the old woman pressed her lips to the girl's hair. "Think of how happy we all are that the heir has returned to the Towers. Good night."

At the door she snapped out the light, that electric current which seemed such an anachronism in the old house. A soft gloom settled into the room. There was glow enough in the sky to show up faintly the design on the long window.

Con sat with her arms embracing her knees and lived over the events of the evening. It had been incredibly gorgeous. She had been so proud of the three Coreys as they came up the stairs. Peter had said "darling," had sung "I love thee, dear, now and forever more," as he never had sung it before. She mustn't think of that. It did things to her heart. She hadn't liked Ivor so much tonight — it was last night now. When she had thought it over she hadn't liked the secrecy he had insisted on about her mother's photograph. She had been so thrilled by the ball that she had forgotten she had planned to meet him until she opened the door of the Tower room to tell Peter that the Duchess wanted to hear him sing.

She had hated Ivor's jeers at her country, his satiric "Miss America." She pressed her hands to her hot cheeks and buried her face in the pillow as she remembered her declamation of the Pledge to the Flag. Ooooch! How could she have done it? How could she have been so schoolgirlish? While she was speaking he had been laughing at her inside his mind, of course.

Probably he would tell Lady Hanford, and perhaps she would tell Tim. Why did Tim like the woman — Peter had said he couldn't make out what the boy was up to — Peter — "darling" — how hazy the coat of arms on the window — "now and forever more." What had Bunny said about the moon — funny — she couldn't remember — she couldn't keep her eyes open — either.

XI

Four days later as Peter Corey strolled toward the Chettle farm he thought of his assurance to his mother that his stay in England would be largely vacation. His mistake. A portion of each day since he had spent in London. Clive Neale had been of infinite help as an ally. He had acted as liaison man between him and New Scotland Yard. It would not do for him to be obviously in touch with that, and yet he must be prepared for an emergency. Were he lucky enough to locate Dafter he might need help. The letter of explanation from the home office had arrived this morning.

He looked up and down the tree-bordered road, before he dropped to the ground beneath the wide-spreading branches of a mighty oak and pulled a sheet of paper from his pocket. Two deep lines cut between his brows as he reread it.

"Dafter's given the FBI the ha-ha again," his partner had written. "The day I cabled you, one of our grade-A scouts had brought in the information that he slipped out of the country tourist class on the very boat on which your family sailed. He must have got away under one of his many aliases on fraudulent papers issued by that fake passport mill which has just been uncovered. It has been grinding for sometime, I understand. Some of the others wanted by us gang and racket-busters have fled the country in like manner, doubtless.

The moment I got the report I beat it down to the ship which was back in port. Was given access to the sailing list. Only three men traveling alone tourist class. Thomson — without the p, take notice. Barclay. Sacks. None of the officers could remember the faces that went with those names. The purser had a 'faint recollection' that one had white hair and matching goatee, 'Southern Col'nel' type, I reckon.

So, there we are. Sorry to intrude on your vacation, but with Dafter on your side of the pond what could I do but sic you onto the wily fox? You expressed yourself fluently and colorfully when we learned that he had slipped through the FBI net, insisted that there could be no excuse for losing him. Now you have the chance of your life to show what a sure-fire detective the world lost when you became a trial lawyer. Go to it!

The wires are laid with New Scotland Yard. I've forwarded Dafter's fingerprints which were obtained eight years ago when he resided, reluctantly, in the State Penitentiary. You may remember, that he said the place 'hampered him' and made his getaway. FBI is sending over two G Men to help you if you need them.

I don't know just why, but I'm betting on you, Pete. This time we'll score an' no foolin'.

Bill."

Peter slipped the letter into his pocket and took to the road again. "This time we score an' no foolin'," he repeated aloud. Bill was an optimist. Behind Dafter lay years of practice in dodging the law, in shrewd trickery, in swift getaways, in doubling back, in brazen defiance of pursuers. Was it probable that the man would let himself be picked up now by a person who had had no experience in following up criminals? Bill was crazy to expect it, but, suppose he were right and it could be pulled off?

Weeks had passed since Dafter had left the United States. He might be in the Belgian Congo, might be anywhere outside the forty thousand square miles of Great Britain by this time. There was just a thread of clue. The name of one of the men who had sailed on that ship had been Sacks. Sacks was also the name of the butler at Trentmere Towers and that same butler had been lividly concerned at the presence of his brother-in-law, Chettle, in the Tower room the night of the ball. Had his concern been because of the intrusion upon Lord Gowan, or because his sister's husband had been caught there? Was it possible that he was in any way connected with Dafter's presence on this side of the Atlantic? A crazy notion, perhaps, but not so crazy that it had kept him from making a try for a look-see at the Chettle farm this afternoon.

Pulling Chettle from behind the hangings and exposing the presence of Hardwick behind the screen had knocked everything else from his mind. He had forgotten that he was to see the papers *in re* Mrs. Gordon Trent which Neale was to show him. What difference did it make? If the record of the woman's death had been found, that chapter of Gordon Trent's life was closed.

He jumped aside and pressed against the black spikes of a thorn hedge as a bicycle grazed his shoulder. It was loaded with brushes and rods. A pail dangled from the handlebar. A man with a sooty face in which eyes shone like white-rimmed marbles grinned at him and dismounted.

"Did h'I 'it ye, sir? Ye stopped suddenlike h'as h'if ye saw somethin'. Mind them thorns. They 'urt ef they 'ardly touch ye."

"You're telling me." Peter pulled a tweed coat sleeve away from his arm. "All right now. You didn't hit me. You surprised me, that's all. I'd like to walk along with you if you're not in a hurry."

"Me in h'a 'urry? Not by no means. Farmer Chettle's missus is in a dreadful way 'bout the chimney. H'it's gettin' on fer five years since it was cleaned afore. 'E's a cheeseparer, 'e is, 'angs on to every penny, an' 'e's a bit in the drinkin' wye too, the bloke."

"Do you have much of this work?" Peter inquired. As they walked on to the accompaniment of the click and clack of rods, brushes and pail, he formulated questions which would lead up to the introduction of Farmer Chettle and his relations.

"Ay, that I do. From mornin' to night I goes. From one village to t'other within forty mile. Not many sweeps left, there ain't. I puts h'out many a chimney blaze. Wouldn't a been surprised any mornin' to 'ear this 'ouse I'm goin' to, ketched fire in the night."

"It's surprising that Farmer Chettle would take the chance of losing his property. That stone house ahead with the lattice windows which looks as if it had been dropped in the midst of an acre of flowers, is his, isn't it?"

"Cripes, sir, h'it isn't 'is, not really. 'Is missus' brother, 'e's the butler at the big 'ouse, leased h'it from 'is lordship, for 'er."

"You mean Sacks?"

"Mr. Sacks, h'it is, sir. 'E's got quite a share in the farm, too, I dessay."

"He must be a generous brother. Perhaps, though, he has no family of his own upon which to spend his wages?"

"Wot's that? No family of 'is h'own? Nobody you might call special, like a missus, but law, 'e's got a mother an' another sister wot live 'bout thirty miles from 'ere, Mr. Sacks, 'as. The 'ole family used to live in this village, oncet. 'E 'ad a brother Tod but I did 'ear as 'ow 'e died somewhere in the States, not that 'e be worth much mournin'. 'E pinched sommick from the castle w'en 'e was second man to the butler, nine years past. Mr. Sacks was fair put h'out h'about h'it, 'e was. 'E got 'im out of England, 'e did. Lookee, sir, the chimneys! Right they is, just right in width and 'eight." He spoke with the enthusiasm of a collector of *objets d'art*.

"Law, Joe, you've been takin' your time, I'll say," a woman called from an open lattice window. She saw Peter and closed it with a bang.

The sweep's red lips resembled nothing so much as a ring of fire in a smoke smudge. He chuckled.

" 'Er's fair put h'out now. 'Ow 'er tongue can run on. 'As to know everything that 'appens in the village. You watch, sir. 'Er'll come h'out. Like as not, ask ye to step h'in, sir. 'Er's brazen, 'er is, 'er'd h'invite 'is lordship to 'ave tea, 'er would. H'it's amazin' to me, who 'as a missus as never talks, who's quiet and decentlike. But 'er do have a gift of makin' posies grow. I'll admit."

Mrs. Chettle was at the gate when they reached it. Her sharp restless eyes reminded Peter of those of a weasel he had caught dragging off his string of trout. Her black-dotted white print dress crackled with starch as she dropped a curtsy.

"Good h'afternoon, sir. You're the gentleman from Cherrytree Farm, isn't you, sir? We're just 'avin' tea. Won't you come in h'after your walk an' sit down an' 'ave a cup, h'if I'm not too bold?"

"Thank you, Mrs. Chettle, but they'll be

waiting for me at home. Some other time when I'm passing, if you'll ask me, I will be glad to join you. Stop at the Farm when you're near and take me along chimney-sweeping, will you, Joe? I'd like to see how it's done."

"Ay, that I will, sir. You got a bike, sir?"

"I'll get one. Good afternoon, Mrs. Chettle. I'll be seeing you, Joe."

No need to linger, he told himself, now that he had learned that "Mr. Sacks" had a brother who had died "somewhere in the States." That information would give him food for thought for some time. As he turned from the gate he bumped into a man — the man with the spatulate nose, whom he had pulled into the Tower room the night of the ball — who now twitched at his forelock by way of salutation. His suspicious eyes roamed from face to face before they came back to Peter's.

"You're the gent from the States wot h'offered to see me h'off the Towers' grounds the h'other evenin', isn't you, sir? I hope I sees you well, sir?" A hint of vinegar sharpened his oily voice. "H'anything I can do for ye, sir? Allus ready to oblige."

Peter lighted a cigarette.

"Nothing, thanks. Sometime I'd like to know what you do to your flowers to make them grow. I've never seen such a mass of color and green."

"H'it's the pigs, sir," Chettle replied with a glance of affection at the masses of bloom. Peter wondered if he had ever given the weasel-eyed woman watching him, so loving a glance. Perhaps if he hadn't, it was treatment she deserved. Seldom had he met a woman he distrusted so thoroughly at first sight.

"An' wot were you a doin' in the Towers grounds of an evenin' I'd like to know, Cam Chettle?" she shrilled. Peter took advantage of the man's growled reply to turn away.

As he walked toward Cherrytree Farm, the light changed from gold to rose. The May sun had been so warm that mist, fragile as the malines Con sometimes wore, hovered above a small pond which reflected the green and lavender and sapphire of the sky till it glowed like a fire-opal set in a fringe of willows. Blue dragonflies shimmered above it. Sheep and cows dotted the surrounding fields. Birds were at vespers, their songs sweet and low. The air was flower-scented. Far ahead rank upon rank of firs mounted a hill like a marching regiment of men of war.

Hands thrust deep into the pockets of his tweed coat, Peter reviewed the information he had gathered in the last hour.

Farmer Chettle's wife was a sister of Sacks, the butler at Trentmere Towers. They had had a younger brother who, because he had "pinched sommick" while he was assistant to the butler at the "castle" had left the country or been banished and had "passed away in the States." Suppose he hadn't died there? Suppose he had been known as Dafter and a few weeks ago had slipped out of the country under the name of Sacks? Was that his real name or one of his many aliases? The supposition that the man he was after was in any way connected with the butler at the Towers was a wild guess, but he would look up that mother and sister who lived thirty miles away. He must do it cautiously. How could an American visit them without rousing suspicion? He might pretend that he had known the long-lost brother.

He thought back over the last hour, of his conversation with the sweep. He stopped short. He had it! Joe had said that from morning till night he went from one village to another. "Not many sweeps left, there ain't," he had added. What a break if he could put his plan across.

He was aware of his broad grin of anticipation as be reached the entrance of Cherrytree Farm. He'd better straighten out

171

his face or he would be mistaken for the Cheshire Cat. How lovely were the velvet lawns and how mighty the oaks that laid purple shadows on them. The rosebuds on the brick wall that enclosed the garden were showing a faint trace of color. They were earlier here than at Red Maples.

Red Maples. Did Con ever think of it? long for it? His eyes flashed in the direction of voices. She wasn't thinking of it this minute. She, in white, with Ivor Hardwick in gray flannel bags and crimson pull-over had stopped where the river path opened into the garden. He was holding something high above his head and she was standing tiptoe trying to reach it.

"Going! Going! Going! for one kiss," the Captain sing-songed.

Con's hands dropped.

"I don't trade in kisses. Keep it. I'll find another somewhere."

"Not one like this," he replied quickly, almost as if he were afraid she would find that other, whatever it was. He saw Peter. "Oh, there you are, Corey. Miss America and I have been investigating that bally broken-down mill by the river. She thinks it's awfully picturesque. I think it's a frightfully dank, dark menace."

"It is picturesque, Peter," Con spiritedly

defended her opinion. "It set my imagination on the rampage. All sorts of romantic things might have happened there. Sometime you and I will take the tea basket and investigate its mysteries — the mill's, not the tea basket's. I know those by heart. Here comes a car! It's Lydia. She hasn't come to see *me*. Ivor, let's you and I have tea with grandfather, then you can give me —"

"Con!" Peter's protest came too late. Hand in hand she and Hardwick were racing back along the path.

XII

Peter abandoned a furious urge to follow the fleeing figures and watched them till they disappeared among the trees. Con had said, "Keep it. I'll find another somewhere." What had Ivor Hardwick been offering? Why had he looked alarmed when he had replied, "Not one like this"?

"What luck to find you, Peter." Lydia Austen laid her hand on his shoulder. "Do you realize that I haven't seen you since the ball? Four whole days? Where have you kept yourself?"

In the instant before he turned he said something more emphatic than elegant between his teeth.

" 'Doing' London among other things. Four years since I've been there."

"I came to talk over the ball with your mother and Con. Wasn't it gorgeous? Hollywood could produce nothing more glamorous. You'll admit that is the ultimate in praise. I saw the Honorable Miss Trent dashing out of sight as the car stopped just

174

now. Avoiding me, I presume. Well, you know how I feel about her."

"Won't you come in and have a talk-fest with Mother?" The courteous habit of a lifetime prevailed over Peter's mounting anger.

"Thanks, I will. I'm fainting for my tea. To return to Con. Is it true, the county is fairly ringing with the gossip, that a marriage has been arranged between Major General Lord Vandemere Trent-Gowan's granddaughter and Captain Hardwick, the heir to the title? I can't imagine a more appropriate match, can you?"

"I can."

"Don't snap, Peter. Think what it will mean to you. Relief from care of her business affairs and the renewal of our engagement. It was your quixotic sense of responsibility for her which separated us."

She was still talking when they entered the lounge. The lady with the yellow rose simpered above the mantel, the massive silver kettle on the tea table bubbled a welcome. The only sign of human occupation was a pair of white slacks draped over the arm of a deep chair, with tennis shoes dangling below them.

"Where's Mother, Tim?"

Peter's crisp question stopped the flow of Lydia Austen's voice with the quick efficacy of a patch on a leaking tire and brought his brother out of the chair with a groan. He patted lean fingers over a prodigious yawn.

"Guess I was asleep. Five straight sets of lawn tennis put the kibosh on me. This champ must be getting old. Where have you kept yourself, Pete? Slim was looking for you a couple of hours ago. Wanted you to take her canoeing. Captain Hardwick appeared and off she went with him. Hi, Lyd! Where did you come from? Were you hiding behind Peter? I thought for a minute a pale green ghost had materialized from the everywhere into the here."

"Not hiding, hesitating." Miss Austen shivered daintily. "These stone houses are so cold, even in May, that I was wondering if I would better stay, my throat is so delicate. Go find a maid to light the fire, Tim," and, "Don't come back," her tone implied.

"*Just* a minute!" The eyes of the brothers met before Peter added, "We Corey men may be living the life of Riley, but we are not so soft yet that we have to call a maid to light a fire. Besides, we could ring for her. It is still being done in this country. Touch a match to the kindling, kid. Take out some of it first. The servants here pile on enough to make an able-bodied smoke screen."

Tim's lips tightened. He regarded Miss

176

Austen with intense aversion. Suddenly his expression changed to an impish grin.

"Okay, Pete. In the language of Farmer Chettle, 'I'm allus willin' to oblige.' " He dropped to his knees before the hearth.

"Where's Mother?" Peter asked again.

"Gone to see a garden," Tim flung over his shoulder as with one hand he groped in the chimney.

"I'll pour tea for you boys. It will make me feel quite like one of the family again." Miss Austen stripped off her gloves and smiled engagingly at Peter.

"We couldn't put you to all that trouble, Lydia."

It was Con's somewhat breathless voice. Con, who slipped behind the tea table so quickly that Miss Austen was left with her alluring smile suspended in air, as it were.

"I was halfway down the river path," she continued, "when I remembered that Angel had gone with the General to see a garden and being a perfect lady I raced all the way back that our guest might be hospitably received."

"How sweet of you, Con dear. And what did you do with your — achew!"

Miss Austen's violent sneeze was followed by another.

"Tim!" Con was on her feet. "What have

you done to that fire! The smoke's pouring — achew! The room's — achew!"

Tim who was standing with one arm on the mantel looked down calmly.

"Heavenly day! It is smoking, isn't it? Guess I must have closed the dam— achew —per instead of — achew!"

"Open it — quick! Why didn't you take out some of that kind—ling?" choked Peter who was throwing wide the mullioned windows. He looked over his shoulder. The smoke coiled like a great serpent from the fireplace and broke in waves and billows. Tears were streaming down Con's cheeks as she fumbled blindly in the chimney with tongs.

"*Courage, mes camarades,* the worst will soon be o—over," Tim sneezed the last word as he worked beside her with poker and shovel.

Came the clatter of iron and a spurt of golden sparks. Con sank back on her heels.

"We've pulled the dam— achew —"

"Woman, cease thy profanity —" chuckled Tim, who squatted tailor-fashion opposite her. He brushed back a lock of light hair thereby adding another streak of soot to his already sufficiently begrimed face.

"How can you joke, Tim Corey," Con demanded hoarsely. "There, I stopped that sneeze, but goodness, how my nose tickles and my eyes smart. I thought for one awful moment we had set this adorable house on fire. That would be the perfect return for the loan of it, wouldn't it? The smoke's clearing. I can see across the room. Where's Peter? Where is Lydia?"

Tim's grin was a cross between that of satyr and gargoyle.

"She must have removed her delicate throat from this polluted atmosphere."

Con's red-rimmed eyes glowed like black diamonds in her grimy face which was streaked by the river beds of her tears.

"Tim Corey! You closed that damper on purpose!"

His chuckle was one third laughter and two thirds sneeze.

"If you'd seen Pete's face when he came into the room you would have known that his fascinating ex-fiancée was getting under his skin. When I saw the muscle in his cheek twitch, it's the only sign of inner excitement I've ever seen him show, I rushed to his rescue and smoked her out. You know me, 'allus ready to oblige.'"

"Lydia is an expert at getting under skins. Doubtless in some circles that gift would be called 'fulfillment of personality.' Has the mail come?"

"Not yet. Why the tone of tense anxiety?"

"I'm not tense, foolish. The *Times* comes in the afternoon, doesn't it? I adore the Personal Column. It is packed with story plots. We'd both better dash up and remove the soot. I will be down in a minute and pour the tea."

One minute had stretched to ten before she returned to the lounge. The air of the room was reasonably clear. Peter and Tim, with all traces of the smoking party removed, were standing by the mantel.

"Sorry I kept you waiting," she apologized, "but my white knit was as grimy and smoky as if it had been chief mourner at a chimney sweep's obsequies. Where's Lydia, Peter?"

"She departed, smoky but unbowed. I like that soft yellow you've changed to, Con. It does things to your gorgeous eyes. The psychologists list the emotional state invoked by yellow as comfort, happiness, warmth and joy.

"Curious that you should have spoken of sweeps," he went on as he lavishly sugared his tea. "I met the genuine article this afternoon, rods, brushes and all the paraphernalia. He was on his way to clean Farmer Chettle's chimneys."

"A real sweep! How thrilling. I thought

they were as extinct as the *Dinosauria*. We'd better engage him to clean out this chimney — apparently it needs it. It's huge. Twin Santas could slip down without rousing the family."

" 'Slip down! Without rousing the family.' Now, that's an idea!" Peter agreed with an earnestness so out of proportion to the importance of the suggestion that Con and Tim glanced at him in surprise. "Joe, he's the sweep, was so interesting I would like to talk with him again, would like to ask if he ever drops down a chimney, by mistake or otherwise."

"Joe must be a knockout, Pete. I thought you were about to burst into tears of enthusiasm. Chettle is the guy who looks as if he had fallen on his face while still in the wet clay, who's 'allus willin' to oblige,' isn't he?"

"Perfect description. Where have you seen him, Tim? He doesn't move in the circle which you now so decoratively adorn," Con teased.

"Oh, I manage to get around. I've dropped in on most of the tenants. I like 'em. I'm not the only person in what you facetiously call 'my circle' who knows Farmer Chettle. I've seen Captain Hardwick slinking from the side door of his cottage several times."

"Tim! How unfair to speak of Ivor as if he were doing something dishonorable," Con protested indignantly. "He was probably there on an errand for the General."

"Mebbe he was and again mebbe he wasn't." Tim helped himself generously to cake.

Chettle and Ivor Hardwick! Peter repeated to himself. Chettle had carried notes "for young master Ernest to some of 'is lydies." Was he acting as go-between for the present heir to the title? Between Hardwick and whom else?

"We're still here, Peter," Con reminded. "You appear to be a thousand miles away. We were talking of Ivor when you put on your thinking cap. It is apparent that Tim doesn't like him and I know you don't. But, I do. More and more," she declared truculently. "You'd better watch your step, Timothy, my lad, or some day you'll fall by the wayside from too much fruit cake, then what?"

"What a blissful end! Speaking of bliss, how come that the usual assorted half dozen sprigs of English aristocracy aren't in evidence this afternoon, Slim? Didn't you broadcast the fact that you were to be at home? Why not let one of them swallow the golden bait and shake the others off the hook?"

Constance wrinkled her nose disdainfully in response to his gamin grin.

"You are not too delicately intimating that the estate I may some day inherit is my major attraction, are you? Thanks for the orchid. Why pick on me? Why not jeer at your brother for his popularity? This is the first time he has been at home for tea since the day he arrived at Cherrytree Farm."

"That's old stuff, my girl. Hasn't the female of the species been after Pete like a chorine pursuing a movie scout since he first put on long pants?"

"We'll call it a day on that sort of repartee," Peter observed dryly. "Why didn't Hardwick come back with you, Con?"

"He flatly refused to meet Lydia. He said her voice made him think of a hard-shell dor bug beating against a window and that he has a frightful aversion to green, either in eyes or clothes. By the way, how do the psychologists rate the effect of that color, Peter?" Con inquired with a laugh in her eyes.

"Curiously enough, in their chart the emotional state evoked by green is a sense of well-being. Health. Abundance."

"Well, what do you know about that?" Tim drawled. "Miss Austen and a 'sense of well-being.' Somewhere the signals got mixed. I have more respect than I had for the Captain if he dislikes Lydia."

"I suspect that it isn't all Lydia. He and that hard-riding sister of hers, Lady Coswell, — I like her tremendously, she's so genuine, such a grand person, had a duel of words the other day and to my amazement he limped from the field leaving her waving the banner of victory." She glanced at Tim whose legs were draped over the arm of a deep chair while he stared at the oak-raftered ceiling. "It — it was about Lady Hanford." She saw his eyes narrow and his lips tighten.

"Why should those two go into a clinch over that poor little woman?" he demanded. "Must have been a champ fight. I'd say either is capable of drawing blood." The thought apparently gave him inner satisfaction.

"Lady Coswell claimed that Celie, Lady Hanford, had not only had her face lifted but her past as well."

Con felt like a cat digging with sharp claws, but Tim was at Fordham Manor a lot and if he fell in love with the woman who was doing her darnedest to make him, it could mean nothing but unhappiness. She couldn't bear it to have him unhappy. Better scratch now than have him hurt.

"Her past," Peter repeated thoughtfully. He watched a smoke ring mount till it became as misty as a circle round the moon. "I wonder if I met her before that bit of plastic surgery was accomplished? I'm referring to the face lifting, not the past. Each time I have seen her something deep in my memory bobs up then ducks before I can grab it. I think, 'Where have I met you before?'" He turned quickly to his brother. "Ever get that impression, kid?"

"Who — who — m-me?" Tim stammered as if suddenly recalled from a distance. "No. No, can't say I do. She's *sui generis*. Individual, not a type, if you get what I mean."

Peter looked at him sharply. Just what did he mean? He couldn't believe that the boy was in love with the woman and yet, why not? She had beauty, brains and physical appeal, if not heart appeal. Young as he seemed to him, Tim wasn't a boy — he was a man, but not a very experienced man. What chance had he against a woman who knew her power and used it to the nth degree?

XIII

"You're putting on flesh, Tim!" Con observed as he rose to renew his attack on the fruit cake. Her pleased comment changed the current of Peter's thoughts. In love or not, the boy certainly looked one hundred per cent. better than when he left home.

"Sure I'm putting on flesh," Tim answered and perched on a corner of the flat desk. "How can I help it? Jam yesterday, jam tomorrow and always jam today, with a bow to *Alice in Wonderland*. I'm getting to be more English than the English in the matter of eats. And that isn't all, I'm fairly itching to get home to make up work for my degree. Here's the mail."

"And the *Times*!" Con took the bulky post bag from the gray-frocked, blue-eyed maid whose round cheeks glowed with the lovely color of a Delicious apple. "Thanks, Maggie. You may have the letters, boys, and I'll take the newspaper."

On the broad window seat she eagerly scanned the front pages. Tim dropped down beside her.

"What do you find so interesting?" He laid his arm across her shoulders.

"N-nothing."

"Just busting with information, aren't you?" he demanded sarcastically.

As he saw the dark head and the light head close together Peter's heart contracted. Suppose his mother and Con were wrong about Tim's infatuation for Lady Hanford? Suppose he loved the girl who had grown up in his home and she loved him?

"I never realize through what strictly American eyes I am observing England until I read the Court news," Con remarked. "Sir So-and-so and Lady So-and-so have arrived at Castle So-and-so. The first page of our papers at home is a mass of headlines. This is made up of columns headed, Personal, Births, Marriages, Deaths, Kennel, Farm & Aviary, Connoisseurs' Guide, 4 lines 10s. (minimum) and so on ad lib. It pays to advertise. Ever read it, Petey?"

"Never have time, I turn to the news." He noticed that Tim's eyes were on the girl's face, not on the paper, as he asked:

"What are you looking for, Slim? Not advertising for a job or a flat or a husband, any trifle like that, are you?"

Her color deepened. Peter caught the furtive glance she cast at him before she protested:

"Silly! What would I be doing with either one of those things at present? The Personal Column is a veritable mine of mysteries. I'm all excited about one that appeared day before yesterday. 'Antony: Barge puts off on time. Answer, Cleopatra.' What do you suppose that meant, Peter?"

"A cipher probably. 'Antony' may answer today."

Tim's attention had returned to the paper. "Perhaps this is it. 'Box XXZ. Yes.' "

Con shook her head.

"N-no. Too short." She rose. "Time I was dressing for dinner. I'll be seeing you."

Tim watched her as she left the room with a portion of the *Times* tucked under her arm.

"Did you notice how kind of excited Con was over the paper, Pete?" he asked. "I've had my eyes on her for two days. She appears to have an absorbing interest in that Personal Column."

Peter's heart lightened. He had noticed her slight breathlessness and had attributed it to Tim's arm across her shoulders.

"She's the heir to a great estate and —"

"What do you mean, kid? What have you heard?"

"I haven't heard anything so don't go wild-eyed. I had a sort of hunch when she was reading the paper — my batting average on hunches is fairly good — that she was looking for something. Ever since the ball your mind has been miles away and —"

"It's Dafter, Tim," Peter confided in a low voice. "Bill cabled he had sailed for this country."

"Heavenly day! What d'ye know about that! Let me in on the hunt will you?"

"You can help me more by keeping an eye on Con while I'm going over England with a fine-tooth comb. Detecting isn't in my line, but I'll make a stab at it. If she were to get into a mix-up —"

"All right, fella, all right, you needn't finish. I know I'll keep on her trail. Don't you worry about your girl."

"*My* girl!"

" '*My* girl!' Just like that. Think I'm so juvenile that I don't know love when I see it? That the electricity in the air when you and she are together doesn't give me the merry pranks? Her heart must be encased in asbestos not to catch fire."

"Con is not to suspect that I love her, Tim. We Coreys are not to influence her decision by so much as a word as to which country she will choose as hers. Get me?"

"I get you, but I think you're darned quixotic. Why don't you let yourself go?"

"You'd be surprised how many times I've asked myself that question. But no matter from what angle I approach it I always get the same answer. It will not be fair to Con to tell her I love her until she has made up her mind either to become a British subject or remain a citizen of the United States. Lord Gowan won't permit a compromise."

"I still think you've got a cockeyed slant. Suppose she up and marries Hardwick? I can't stand that guy."

"I have a feeling that he has no intention of marrying Con, that he is fooling Lord Gowan for a purpose. Can't account for it, perhaps it's just one of your hunches." He hated to appear to advise Tim, but, the boy ought to know. "I am sure that he and Lady Hanford are — have some kind of an understanding." That was an example of understatement if ever there was one.

"Is *that* so? She's pretty darn fascinating. Get busy on your man hunt, Pete, and I'll keep my glittering eye on the Honorable Miss Trent. You might whisper to her that I don't need her not too thinly veiled warnings about Celie, Lady Hanford; that I'm free, white and twenty-four. Neither do I need yours. With which subtle suggestion we'll bring this confab to a close. Get busy on your man hunt."

Tim's words recurred to Peter as a few days later from the upper deck of a bus he looked down at the group bustling around a newspaper kiosk in the London street. Men and women, boys and girls were pouring from shops and doorways of old and of modernistic buildings in a stream patched with bright colors and blotted with black and drab. They plunged, dodged, charged with militant shoulders through homeward-bound crowds or stood in queues waiting for a red bus much as they did at home, but at home the buses wouldn't wear a huge white plaster proclaiming the merits of merchandise, nor would he be looking at the towers of the Houses of Parliament looming against a sky blushing faintly under the ardor of a slanting sun which also tipped with rubies the silver wings of a soaring plane.

Since the arrival of the letter containing the news of Dafter's escape from the United States, he had spent hours on this same man hunt, in trams, buses, the underground, following clues supplied by officials, sometimes only in the wild hope of meeting up with the man he was after. Hunting for a needle in a haystack was a child's game in comparison to looking for a man he had never seen, whose face he knew only from photographs, whose aliases were legion, but since he had learned that there had been a Sacks who had died in the States whose brother was butler at Trentmere Towers, had met the two unprepossessing members of the family, he had been obsessed with the idea that Dafter had made his getaway under the name of Sacks and that he was in London. No foundation for it, it wasn't a particularly reasonable deduction, it was just a hunch but he was playing it for all it was worth.

He counted the strokes of thirteen-and-a-half-ton Big Ben. Listened to the London bells, heavy bells, merry bells, faint bells, that clanged and pealed the hour until they rolled away in the distance like beads dropping from the string of Time. He was too early. He would walk from the next bus stop. Time enough to reach Hardwick's diggings when the party was about to break up. If he consulted his own wishes he wouldn't go there at all, but this morning Con had told him that she and his mother were to have tea at Ivor's town house after attending a concert sponsored by Royalty.

"Won't you please forget your aversion to my *cousin* just this once, Peter, and call for us?" she had pleaded. "We are going to town by train. Bring the sedan and we'll all drive home together. The country is heavenly in the late afternoon."

Of course he had said "Yes" though he had received no invitation from her host. Equally of course, he would do anything in the world Con wanted.

Would he? Words of his mother's streaked through his memory like lightning. "Unless you decide to make her interests yours and become a British subject," and his reply. "Not even for Con could I do that."

If he had meant it then, he meant it doubly now after weeks of absence from home, weeks when the conflict between his love for Con and deep inner loyalty to the country of his ancestors and his professional commitments, ran like an underground river of doubt and heartache beneath the color and gaiety of his daily life.

Perhaps the strength of his convictions never would be tested, perhaps she would love and marry one of the "sprigs of aristocracy" hanging round her, perhaps loyalty to her forebears would result in her marriage to Ivor Hardwick that title and estates might once more be united.

Why crucify himself with that last possibility? He had promised Tim that he would run away with her himself before he would allow her to marry the heir to the Trent-Gowan title, and he would.

The harsh clang of a bell jolted him to awareness of his surroundings. This was the bus stop from which he had decided to walk. He bolted down the stairs. Leaped as the bus started. The conductor's voice followed him:

"It tykes one of you 'Mericans to do that crazy thing, sir." A grin massaged the worried lines from the man's long face as his late passenger waved a friendly hand from the safety of the curb.

Peter entered a park, stopped to buy a red carnation of a shawled flower seller whose skin had all the crackles of old crockery and none of its smoothness, refused her offer to place it in the buttonhole of his blue coat with her shaky, heavily veined hands, and strolled on. He had left the sedan outside the city thinking that his mother and Con would enjoy the novelty of the bus ride to the garage. From somewhere behind him drifted the music of a drum-and-fife corps, and from a distant highway came the muted roar of traffic with a saxophonic obligato of automobile horns.

He drew a deep breath of the fragrant air. Spring in London. It made one tingle with the sheer joy of living. He passed bronze statues entirely surrounded by stiff flower beds gory with geraniums; benches occupied by men and women, some just sitting, others scanning newspapers with lines of worry graven deep between their eyes.

The papers reminded him of Tim's suspicion that Con had an absorbing interest in the Personal Column of the *Times*. He had diplomatically attempted to get at the reason of it, if there were a reason, but she had laughed at him and replied that even on vacation his Sherlock Holmes complex worked. Why single her out as a case?

Little she realized, that that same complex was occupying his mind almost to the exclusion of thought of her. Between his jaunts to London he had been cultivating Joe. When alone he had rehearsed the sweep's jargon until he was sure he was letter perfect. He hadn't figured out just how he would use it, but, as one of his professors in college had been wont to remark, "It doesn't cost anything to carry round the know how."

He had made several trips as Joe's assistant and was becoming expert in thrusting a brush up a choked chimney, screwing on a rod, adding joint after joint until it reached the height desired and after the job successfully de-sooting his face and hands. He hadn't mastered the art of reversing the brush action and thrusting downward from the top. That required ladders and a catlike agility on the roof. Familiarity with the country chimneys had convinced him that it would be neither difficult nor dangerous to drop down one if emergency required.

He retraced his steps on a street of quaint Georgian houses gay with window boxes blossoming with pink and blue and purple, and dripping with ivy and striped vines. He had been so absorbed in his plans that he had passed the number. Here it was.

He glanced at the man in correct green livery who answered his ring and caught an instant's dilation of the pupils of his eyes. It was gone as quickly as a face at a peek window shut off by a slide.

Queer, he thought. I've seen that look in the eyes of criminals taken by surprise. Apparently it is uncontrollable. A flash and it's gone, but it is unmistakable. I wonder if Captain Hardwick is employing a gangster, unaware? Why think of it? Except for one man gangsters are not my business on this side of the Atlantic.

"This way, sir," the man invited urbanely.

Peter followed him across the octagon-shaped foyer. Between the gold-brocade hangings at the entrance to a dining room, he saw the rich dull colors of a rare tapestry, caught the gleam of massive pieces of silver.

These English bachelors do themselves well, he thought, and remembered that Clive Neale had told him the heir to the Trent-Gowan title was in a chronic state of debt. The perfection of this establishment with its atmosphere of inherited wealth and treasures didn't look like financial embarrassment. Not as he had seen it. At the entrance to a living room the servant announced ceremoniously:

"Mr. Peter Corey."

Ivor Hardwick looked up. He was unmistakably startled and curiously colorless. He had been bending over Con who, in a Big Townish costume of sunny brown crepe rippling with waves of white, smiled a radiant welcome to Peter from under the brim of a rakish white hat.

"Frightfully jolly of you to drop in, Corey," Hardwick welcomed even as his eyes demanded, "Why are you here?"

"I was invited to call for members of my family and drive them home." Peter answered the unspoken rather than the spoken words. He smiled at his mother who in a silvery gray costume was presiding at the tea table. Why didn't all white-haired women wear large pinkish-red hats, he wondered, as he noticed that the color of hers was rosily reflected on her hair and skin. She had the charm of a Marquise escaped from a French fan. Near her, looking for all the world as if a ramrod had been substituted for his spine, stood Lord Gowan.

A butler in correct black at Peter's elbow presented a cocktail on a silver tray. He shook his head.

"You don't drink?" his host inquired with superciliously arched eyebrows.

"Not when I'm driving." Peter smilingly ignored the hint of malice in the question. "It's a trend at home. Ever follow trends, Captain? It's a fascinating study. I chart them so that I'll know what the general public will be thinking and wanting six months or a year from now. With accidents on the highways from automobiles mounting to forty thousand-plus deaths, and no one knows how many cripples, in one year, we've adopted a slogan: 'If you must drive, don't drink. If you must drink, don't drive.' I'm to drive my family back to Cherrytree Farm. Get the connection?" He waved away the silver box the butler offered and took his gold case from his pocket.

"Oh, you're one of those bally reformers."

Above the yellow flame of the light the servant held to his cigarette his amused eyes met the contemptuous eyes of Ivor Hardwick who was perched on the arm of the sofa beside Con.

"A reformer! Heaven forbid. Where'd you get the idea I had come to England as a missionary? I'm merely a lawyer taking a much needed vacation and boy, oh, boy, it's proving a smash hit. Yours is certainly an hospitable country, Captain."

He waved away the cup of tea the butler offered. He would neither eat nor drink in this man's house. He glanced about the room with its choice furniture which he recognized as collector's items; at the Goya above the fireplace; at the boxes of pink geraniums, blue lobelia and trailing vines which topped the ornate iron railings of the balcony outside the long windows; at the elaborately equipped bar in a corner of the room and the massive silver bowl of crimson roses which set the air vibrating with their color and fragrance. His glance met his mother's intent dark eyes, touched the stern face of stiff-necked Lord Gowan, and returned to the girl on the sofa.

"Here I am, Con," he said lightly. "Whenever you are ready —"

"Out of my way. Of course I'll go in!" stormed a woman's voice in the hall.

XIV

The angry protest was followed by the appearance of Lady Hanford on the threshold. Her chic black costume accentuated the metallic redness of her hair, the matching color of her lips and the sheen of her triple string of pearls.

"Ivor, I wish you would employ servants who know that I am welcome here at any time. That new man at the door —" She stemmed the torrent of words in pretended confusion as if aware for the first time of others in the room. The diamonds in her sumptuous bracelets twinkled with a million iridescent sparks as she clasped her black-gloved hands in theatrical apology.

"Really, my dear, I hadn't a suspicion that you were entertaining, Ivor. I am *de trop*. Neither had I an idea that you would be here, Peter, because I saw your friend Lydia Austen in the foyer at the Ritz. And was she impatient? Evidently waiting for someone who had forgotten her. *Dear* Lord Van, don't glare at me. I wouldn't have come had

I known that I was intruding on a family party. Ivor usually tells me all his plans, but he forgot this one."

Lord Gowan vigorously cleared his voice for action. Before he could speak Angela Corey rose.

"But, you are not intruding, Lady Hanford," she assured graciously. "Captain Hardwick has been so entertaining that we have stayed an unconscionable time. Come Connie, we have a dinner engagement remember, and a forty-five-mile drive before we reach home in time to dress."

It would be apparent to the most unobservant that Lord Gowan was rigid with disapproval at the presence of Lady Hanford who had seated herself at the silver-laden table with the air of a woman in her own home, and that the heir to his title was white with anger, Peter reflected, as they made their adieus.

The butler led the way across the octagon foyer and opened the door. In the street waited the gleaming black limousine from Trentmere Towers. A man in maroon livery was at the wheel, another at the curb touched his cap.

Peter looked back at the house. Why had the butler opened the door for the departing guests? What had become of the servant who had admitted him? When the pupils of his eyes had dilated, he had thought for an instant that the man had recognized him. That was absurd —

"Chettle and Hardwick!"

The name shot up from his subconscious and rang through his mind as if broadcast by a microphone. Tim had seen Captain Ivor "slinking" from the Chettle cottage and the name of Chettle's wife had been Sacks!

A man named Sacks had sailed on the ship on which Dafter had fled the U.S.A. Lord, he had been dumb. Lady Hanford had complained that the man at the door was new at his job. Add that to the uncontrollable widening of the pupils of his eyes when he had opened it for him and the result might be Dafter, Dafter who had recognized him. There was only one chance in a thousand that it was, but he couldn't go back to Cherrytree Farm until —

"Mrs. Corey is returning with me." Lord Gowan's domineering announcement derailed Peter's train of thought. Then, as if realizing that he was not giving army orders, he qualified, "If you will do me the honor, Madam?"

"Thank you, Lord Van." Angela Corey included both the girl and her son in her smile. "Connie, Peter has been away so

202

much lately that the drive home will give you a grand chance to bring him up to date on our recent hectic round of gaiety. Remember that we have a dinner engagement and don't be late."

Late! The word catapulted Peter's mind back to his surroundings. He was about an hour late on his job of following up the man who had opened the door. He said quickly:

"Take Con with you, Mother. I can't go back yet. I've just remembered an important appointment that I must keep. You won't mind, will you, Con?"

"Certainly *not*, Mr. Corey."

The girl's face was flushed with lovely color. She avoided his eyes and held her head high as she passed him and followed his mother into the limousine. She leaned forward in the seat to add, "You'd better hurry. Lovely ladies do not care to be kept waiting at the Ritz."

Lord Gowan stepped into the car. The footman closed the door, touched his cap and mounted beside the chauffeur.

"Confound that Hanford woman! Con thinks I have a date with Lydia," Peter muttered under his breath as he walked on. In the seconds since the possibility of Dafter's proximity had burgeoned in his mind he had decided that it would be a mistake for him to inquire at the house as to the servant. Some-one else should do it. He would get in touch with Clive Neale at once.

He telephoned his office. He had gone. Tried his club. It seemed but an instant before Neale answered.

"I must see you," Peter told him.

"Meet me at my flat in ten minutes."

This was quite a different atmosphere from that of the Georgian house he had left recently, Peter reflected as a dour Scot took his hat at the door of Neale's apartment. Furnishings rich and heavy, but few of them. The walls of the library were lined with books.

"What's happened," Neale demanded as the servant closed the door.

Peter told him of his suspicions. Seated on the arm of an enormous chair upholstered in tan leather Clive Neale tenderly mas-saged the lapel of his blue serge coat as he listened.

"Of course it may be merely a brain wave," Peter concluded.

"I think you've got something, Corey. Keep out of this. I'll send a man to Hard-wick's house. He'll pretend that he is a butler, that he has heard that the second man there is looking for another situation, that he would like to interview him for his employer. Stay here and dine with me. Make yourself comfortable while I get in touch with the man I want."

"Comfortable," Peter muttered, as Neale left the room. As if he could be when he was facing the possibility that once more Dafter had slipped through his fingers like a wriggling eel.

He paced the floor, thinking, planning, smoking, while the clock ticked off the seconds. Suppose his hunch was but a bubble of suspicion which would dissolve into nothing when pricked by the report of the investigator? Because of it he had lost the chance for a talk with Con to which he had been looking forward all day. He had intended to lead up to the subject of Hardwick and to learn, if he could, what he had offered to sell for her kiss. Tim's suspicion that she had a special interest in the Personal Column of the *Times*, had scratched in his mind like a burr. He had planned diplomatically to lead up to that also and now the opportunity had passed and she had left him thinking he had a date with Lydia.

He would straighten out that misunderstanding tonight if he waited hours for her return from the dinner. Why not tell her he loved her? Tim was right. Holding back was quixotic, and yet, he wanted her to be free to choose her homeland without being influenced by his love for her. There was so much to be considered, not only her future but the future of her children. He wouldn't tell her. He wouldn't welsh. He would wait, no matter what the result.

"That's started!" Neale exclaimed as he entered the room. "Now we'll dine."

The Scot served a simple but delicious dinner. Peter watched the clock. Clive Neale followed his eyes.

"We ought to hear soon, Corey. That servant may be the man you are looking for but I can't see where Ivor Hardwick fits into the picture, why he should be harboring a criminal from the United States."

"Neither can I, nor why the Captain should be slinking from the house of Farmer Chettle. A piece of the puzzle is missing."

"A man to see you, sir," the Scot announced.

Peter paced the floor waiting for Neale's return. The seconds seemed to drag into hours, though it was only a few moments by the clock when he came into the room.

"Well, what's the report, Neale?"

"Our man could get no information about the servant who opened Hardwick's door for you. The butler was indifferent. Said he knew nothing about the 'bloke' — that he was a person hired by the master for the afternoon. That he had collected his pay and gone."

"It's darned improbable that an unknown man would be given a job in an establishment so rich in portable treasures as that one."

"I agree, Corey. It's a lot of flapdoodle. We'll have the place watched."

"On the chance that the doorman at Hardwick's was the younger Sacks whose visit to his mother and sister may be imminent, be sure to have those four Scotland Yard men on the job in that village tomorrow as we planned, Neale. I won't rely on the local constable. Joe, the sweep, will pick me up at a certain tumble-down tower about a mile from there at noon, after which I am to assist him on the Sacks' chimney job. My hunch may be nothing but a hectic brain wave, but if it should prove right and the long-absent son and brother should visit his family I want to be able to grab my man if Tod Sacks proves to be the much-wanted Dafter. Get me?"

"I get you. Good luck, Corey."

The end of a perfect day, Peter thought grimly as under a cobalt sky sequined with stars, through air steeped in coolness and scents from dewy gardens and damp box hedges, he drove between the square ball-topped gate posts at Cherrytree Farm. The mullioned windows of the lounge showed a faint light. He had gained mighty little information and had lost Con for the evening at least.

The glare of the headlights revealed a face which shone white against a hedge. Some-one waiting for him? Had Dafter realized that he had been recognized and come here to silence him? Cheerful thought.

"Hsst! H'it's me, Joe!"

Peter swallowed a lump in his throat. Not strange that he had not recognized the sweep. He never before had seen him with a clean face. He stopped the car.

"What's up," he inquired in a whisper. Joe grinned as he leaned against the door of the sedan to speak through the window.

"I dessay, I come a little h'unexpected, didn't I? Been takin' me 'arf bitters h'at the pub till I thought ye'd be along. I puts that little plan through, proper, sir." His low voice was of the very essence of conspiracy.

"When do you start work?"

"I've started h'already, dye afore yesterdye, sir. Hit's gettin' on fer seven years since I did see them Sacks women afore, but they remembered me, sir. They think Tod passed away in the States, I wasn't long gettin' h'at that. They said h'as 'ow 'e become an h'American citizen, did ye know that, sir? I give 'em a little scare about fire ketchin' in the chimney an' p'haps settin' the 'ole village a-goin', an' they 'ired me, quick. They're goin' to talk to their neighbors to 'ave theirs done too. Looks like h'I'd 'ave two weeks' work, sir. Now then, ye'll be along at noon t'morrer as we planned, sir?"

"Sure, Joe. Better do a little chimney cleaning at one of the other houses in the morning, before you meet me. I've made a note of the route. I am to leave my car at a certain farm and walk to the old tower where I'll find clothes, bike, rods and brushes and wait till you join me. Straight?"

"Straight it be, sir. Prompt h'at noon. H'Ive told the women h'as 'ow I'd found so much work to do, h'I'd 'ave to 'ave h'a 'elper, sir. You've certain got the talk down proper, h'I could almost think h'it is meself speakin' when I 'ears ye, sir."

"Thanks to the coaching you've given me, Joe. It wouldn't get me far in my pretense that I'm your helper if I couldn't speak your language, would it? Remember, this is strictly between you and me. I've trusted you to the limit. I have told you what I am trying to do. Our success depends on secrecy."

"Law, sir. H'I never was much h'of a talker an' h'I'm too proud you trust me, an' you such a big gent in a legal wye, to clack, sir. Besides, with twenty pounds jest waitin' for me to h'earn h'it, h'I never see so much money h'at one time in me life afore, ye don't think h'I'll lose h'it, do ye, sir, an' me countin' on gettin' meself an' the missus a wireless set with h'it? Not likely, sir."

"All right, Joe. Carry on." As the man replaced his cap, Peter said hurriedly, "Just a minute. Was Captain Hardwick friendly with the younger Sacks who passed away in the States?"

"Wot's that? Tod Sacks an' the present heir to the title friendly, sir? Blimey, thick as two thieves they wus, w'en they wus lads an' master h'Ivor used to visit 'is lordship h'an' the Sacks fam'ly lived 'ere in this village. They'd go rabbit snarin' together. They did worse 'an that, later. They used the h'old tower, up the coast a wye, the very one w'ere ye're to stay till h'I comes fer ye, to try their 'ands at robbin' fishermen. False lights they used, to snag 'em on the cliffs. Nothin' was proved, not h'against his lordship's relative, but the 'ole village wus in a dreadful way 'bout them an' their tricks. Did ye say somethin', sir?"

"Nothing that would improve your mind

or your vocabulary, Joe. Good night."

"Ye're a bit h'in the wye of bein' a scholard, with your long words, isn't you, sir? Good night."

Peter watched him out of sight. Now he knew why the younger Sacks whom he suspected was Dafter, had been employed as second man by Hardwick. As boys they had been partners in deviltry. Hadn't Tim said that he had seen Captain Hardwick slinking from the side door of the Chettle cottage and wasn't Mrs. Chettle a Sacks? Another piece to fit into the puzzle. What were the two planning now?

He glanced at the dark windows of Con's room, said under his breath, "Good night. Good night, my darling." She had not come home. He couldn't wait for her.

He drove into the garage. He must get the information to Clive Neale that Ivor and the younger Sacks had been "rabbit-snarin' pals." More than ever now he must be sure that there was no hitch in the arrangements for tomorrow. No need to mention their one-time piratic escapades at the old tower. He didn't dare telephone with the possibility that the man he was after was the returned Tod Sacks. He would change to his roadster and go back to London.

He shut off the headlights of the sedan.

Started toward his own car. Stopped. Had he imagined a sinister sound?

In the instant after, he thought, "They've got me! Joe will carry on. Lucky I told him —" he sank down and down into soft, smothering darkness.

XV

The midday sun streamed down on Trentmere Towers which loomed frowning and dark in the golden light. It picked out the vivid new green on the ends of tendrils of ivy climbing the turrets, played like a floodlight on diamond windowpanes, crept to the very edge of the covered terrace where its brilliance diffused and stole forward a pale golden glow, until it faded at the feet of a man and girl seated at a low table at which they had been having luncheon.

A servant in maroon livery removed the table. Another drew forward white wicker chairs with turquoise-blue cushions and placed smoking paraphernalia on a low stand.

"That will be all."

"Very good, your lordship."

Lord Gowan settled into a deep chair and filled his pipe.

"Sit down, Constance. Don't stand there as if you were waiting to take off."

She wondered as she obeyed if she had

shown so plainly her eagerness to be on her way.

"I'm not rarin' to go. I was considering you. You like your forty winks at this time, don't you, General?"

"Usually, but today I want to talk to you." He cleared his voice in his characteristic manner. "It is four weeks since last I mentioned the subject of making this country your home. I have been very patient. There are some aspects of the situation you cannot have considered or you would not hesitate."

He regarded her over the top of his pipe and frowned at her rosy-nailed fingers outlining the white pattern on her dusty-pink frock.

"You are not listening to me," he reminded sternly.

The truthfulness of the accusation sent soft color to her hair. She had not been listening. She had been wondering if Peter had given up driving her home yesterday that he might meet Lydia? If he had the two must have had a grand celebration for last night Angel had found a message written by Maggie that toward midnight he had phoned the house that business would prevent his return to Cherrytree Farm until late today.

The afternoon at Ivor's had begun to go blooey when Lady Hanford appeared. Before Peter's arrival and hers, under pretext of showing her a rare silver tankard, Ivor had taken her to the dining room and had hurriedly given her a card photograph. She hadn't paid for it with a kiss, either.

"Quick! Hide it! It may have frightfully unpleasant consequences for me, if anyone knows you have it and the fact gets to Lord Van. You'll recognize your father's writing on the back."

What would Peter think if he knew she had the photograph? Since the night of the ball when he had called her "darling," when he had sung "I love thee, dear, now and forever more" as if he were singing to her, the mere thought of him set not only her heart but her mind and body a-quiver. Yesterday when he had entered Ivor's living room her voice had left her, she had sat like a dumb Dora and just smiled at him. There was no one like him for distinction and charm and strength of mind and character. Ivor had been abominable with his hateful question about drinking. Peter had replied in a light, friendly tone which had ignored his host's rudeness. There had been no holier-than-thou hint in his explanation.

Never before had he spoken to her as he had that evening in the gold salon with its Fragonard panels, and never since, she reminded herself dryly. The afternoon in the lounge when Tim had smoked out Lydia he had been the same big-brother companion she had known for the past ten years. She must have imagined that night that his voice was huskily caressing; there could be no other explanation.

"Constance! I insist upon your attention!" Lord Gowan commanded in his best Major General manner.

"I'm sorry. You will forgive me, won't you? You always do forgive me, don't you, your lordship?"

Laughter faded from her eyes as she admitted wistfully:

"If you knew how much I think about the matter you want to discuss — it is always in my subconscious waiting to pop up like an undersea boat — you would forgive a few moments' mental detour. To stay or not to stay in this country is the first thing I think of in the morning and the last at night. Can I bear to renounce my American citizenship? I would have to do that, wouldn't I? Now I'm beginning to dream about it. Also the matter is presented for my prayerful consideration several times weekly."

"Quite so! Quite so! It is those young cubs who hang round you who are asking you to marry them, I presume?"

"Modesty forbids me to go so far as to say *all*, my lord," Con replied with exaggerated humility, "but you've got the right idea. A sufficient number of them propose to keep the subject uppermost in my mind were I inclined to forget it."

Lord Gowan's grim mouth twitched in sympathy with the mischief in her eyes.

"Heartless hussy —" he accused between puffs at his pipe.

"I'm not heartless, really, I'm not. If I thought that one of those boys — somehow they don't seem grown up to me because I'm used to men, even quite young ones, who have serious objectives, who give their lives direction, who feel they owe something to the country in which they live — was deeply, honestly in love with me, I wouldn't jest about it. Love is too sacred, too soul-stirring an emotion to treat lightly."

"What do you know about love? Ever been in love?"

"Oh, I have! I have," she exclaimed with mock ardor. "Listen, your lordship, while I tell the story of my love life."

She clasped her hands behind her head. Eyes on the infinite blue of the sky she spoke dreamily as if she were evoking a picture from the depths of memory to flash on the screen of his mind.

"I was in love, desperately in love when I was fifteen. The object of my passion was the dictator pupil at dancing school. They called him 'Sniper' Blake, because he always brought down his girl. His real first name was Dexter. I was his teeth-banded slave. I was not his only conquest. There were other girls who, figuratively speaking, sat at his feet. He was the biggest boy in the class and showed his scorn of our adoration by stepping on our feet and twisting our wrists excruciatingly when the instructor wasn't looking. The masterful, red-blooded, he-mannish type, if you get what I mean. But, believe it or not, the more he stepped and twisted, the more infatuated we became. Perhaps you can explain that?"

"It's a problem for a psychologist, not an officer in His Majesty's service. What became of the brute? By Jove, you don't love him still, do you? It isn't *he* who is luring you back to America?"

His consternation was funny. Con visualized the irresistible Sniper's present waistline and chuckled. Before she could speak Lord Gowan flared:

"I believe that man is the reason you won't stay here. You are in love with him!"

His accusation was too amazing. Before she could deny the charge he went on:

218

"It's this Sniper person and Corey who are influencing you against England."

"Sniper, luring me back! That's the funniest thing I ever heard," the words were sunlit with laughter. "As for Peter influencing me! If he only would tell me I'd better go back to Red Maples I would know what to do. He won't even talk about it. Neither will Angel. They say that I am the only one who can decide upon the way to take at the crossroads I've reached, and remind me that I am choosing not only for myself but for my unborn children."

"Quite so! Quite so! Mrs. Corey is a remarkable woman. She's right. If you remain in England and marry a British subject all this will go to your son." Her eyes followed the comprehensive gesture of his fine hand with the ring with its Trent-Gowan crest.

"I know. And why can't I say at once, 'I'll stay'?"

"If it is because you will feel separated from the Coreys, that's nonsense, when from the Tower room you can talk across the ocean to them at any hour of the day or night."

"Of course that isn't the reason. I'm not quite such a child. I could see Peter or Tim depart to settle in darkest Africa for life without shedding a tear, were I convinced that it was for their best interests. It isn't the Coreys, much as I love them, it is something here," she laid her hand over her heart, "a sort of 'now and forever' reminder whenever I consider remaining in this country."

"Hmp! It is that 'now and forever' song of Corey's. I thought it would make mischief."

"You mean *'Ich Liebe Dich'*? Of course it isn't. Maybe the ghost of an American patriot who died for his country lays a restraining hand on my shoulder when I think of staying. I know nothing of my mother's people. Maybe she had a long line of ancestors who have bred the same sense of loyalty in me that kept my Trent-Gowan forebears fighting for their kings through the centuries. When I left Red Maples I would have been furious had it been suggested that I would consider making this country mine. And now — well, it just shows how insidious your arguments and the pull of what you call 'all this' has been."

Her hand duplicated his comprehensive gesture. Sunlight lay evenly on acres and acres of fertile land patched with fields, green, gray-green, yellow-green; honeycombed with lacy streams and hedged paths; shaded by century-old trees; dotted with villages, some of color-washed houses, some of age-worn stone, others rosy and warm-looking of red brick, each with its white church steeple pricking the sky; rimmed with faraway hills, emerald at the base, purple as amethysts at their peaks and in between spotted with the isolated agate-gray houses of shepherds. Near at hand a cloud cast a shadow on the lichen-covered stones of the gray chapel. In the gardens, pink, lavender, white, yellow and blue blossoms drooped delicate heads in the hot, scented air. Over them shimmered iridescent gossamer wings. The sun was so warm that a mist fragile as malines hovered above the blue pool of the fountain.

Her heritage. There it lay with the thin patina of sunlight gilding it. Mute. Appealing. Offering her its richness, its beauty and its centuries of tradition. Everything she could see except the blue dome of the sky was hers for the taking. What should she do? The world was as still as if it were holding its breath. She wondered if her grandfather could hear the milling of her thoughts.

"And if I don't remain in England?"

She didn't realize that she had spoken the words until he rose impatiently. His face was a choleric red, his blue eyes sparked.

"If you don't remain the estate goes to Ivor. Not one shilling to you."

His domineering assertion roused a little demon of opposition. Did he think he could ignore her for twenty-three years and then dictate to her? She'd show him! On her feet she faced him defiantly.

"Do you think I care for your money, that I would give up about everything I love in the world for that? My country? The Coreys? My friends? Why should any one person want thirty thousand acres and this great ark of a house? I don't. If I remain it will be because of what this house and its traditions meant to my father, because it stands for my family."

"Quite so! Quite so! It is the only family you have. All you know of your mother is the date of her marriage and the fact of her tragic death, the record of which I showed you this morning when you insisted upon seeing it. She's a blank. You have imagined that American patriot ancestry. Neale could find out nothing about her before she married your father."

A blank. One part of her mind picked up the word. Perhaps not such a blank after this afternoon. If the person who had advertised really could tell her —

"This is your background." Lord Gowan's loud voice brought her attention back to the present. Why did he have to

222

roar? "What background have you in America?"

"Quite as fine a one as this. The Coreys are —"

"But, you're not a Corey. You have been merely a child brought up in their home, thrust upon their charity."

"Charity! *Charity!*"

Con's eyes blazed beneath pools of angry tears. She clasped her hands tight behind her. She wanted terribly to grab the lapels of her grandfather's coat and shake him till his teeth rattled.

"Charity!" she repeated furiously. "Where did you get that crazy idea? My father paid my way. Not only that but he left money which has been enough for my living ever since. Besides, I am trained for a business position. That nasty fling of yours settles it, I won't stay now. I'm not yet an ancestor worshiper."

He caught her shoulder.

"You will stay here! You'll forget the 'Sniper' person. You'll marry Ivor and in time be Lady Trent-Gowan of Trentmere Towers. From now on you'll do as I tell you!"

His voice was so commanding, his eyes so fierce that for a frightened instant she wondered if he could force her to his will. Self-

223

confidence surged back. She twisted free and met his fiery glare squarely.

"Try to make me! From now on I'll go under my own power," she defied. "Do you think I will attempt to rival the 'chawming' Lady Hanford in Ivor's affections? Not for a minute. You saw her, heard her yesterday. She behaved as if she had a right in his house, didn't she? She'll adore being mistress of Trentmere Towers. *You* make much of this estate as an inheritance for my unborn children, *I* think it much more important to give them a father whom I and they can respect. It may be a bourgeois point of view but it's mine. Ivor is out of the picture. *Definitely* out. Now that the matter under discussion has been so amicably settled, I'm going. I have a date."

She watched for even a slight sign of weakening in his face, but it was hard as stone. She ran across the terrace and jumped into the roadster she had left in the broad drive. Whiskers, who had been dozing, sat up and barked a welcome. Her grandfather followed her to the top of the steps. She looked up:

"You handed down to me a beastly temper, didn't you, your lordship? It's almost as hot as yours. Goodby!"

XVI

The beauty of the early afternoon, the smooth action of the dark-green roadster quieted Con's pulses and nerves which the battle with Lord Gowan had set jangling.

"I shouldn't have flung that last taunt about his temper, should I, Whiskers?" She rubbed her cheek against the dog's black ear as he whined understanding. "Even if I did inherit it, it was up to me to discipline it, wasn't it? I thought I had, but he makes me so furious. I set fuse to dynamite when I told that yarn about Sniper Dexter in my best dramatic style. I was merely trying to give a light touch to the conversation, instead of which I blew it to smithereens. Moral of that is, don't strike joke sparks in a powder magazine. You're a lot of company even if you can't talk. I'm glad I brought you, young fella."

No use regretting the blowup now, with the present expedition ahead of her, she reflected, and resolutely gave her attention to her surroundings.

She entered a covered bridge which spanned the river, the gay little river she had followed through a lovely valley, hill-bordered on one side. She looked at the azure sky across which a cloud like a ghostly galleon was majestically sailing. Did her father know that his father was trying to force on her a husband she didn't want? Where was he? Sometimes she felt he was very near. Did he know that since she left Trentmere Towers her teeth had developed a curious tendency to chatter? Even in this sunny, moist air icy chills rilled through her veins whenever she thought of the date she had made with an unknown person. This morning she had seen the certificate of her mother's death, a tragic death, and yet she intended to keep the appointment. Often mistakes had been made in identification.

She had sent her answer to the first note to the *Times*. Later had come written directions for her to reach a meeting place. Perhaps this expedition was crazy, but not so reckless as it appeared on the face of it. It was broad daylight. Kidnaping wasn't an industry in England. She had left a sealed note addressed to Angel propped up on the desk in her own room, telling where she had gone, just in case she did not return. Cheerful thought. Tucked in her bag was

226

the photograph of her mother with "My wife, Viola" in her father's schoolboy writing on the back. Ivor's anxiety for fear she would get one elsewhere had puzzled her. Did he know where there was another?

What would Peter think if he knew that without consulting him she was faring forth to a strange town to meet a person who claimed to have information about her mother? She eased her prickling conscience with the reminder that she couldn't have told him about it had she wanted to. He had been away from Cherrytree Farm almost constantly during the week and last night business had kept him in London. The few times she had seen him his thoughts had been miles away. Had his absorption to do with the cable he had received or was it Lydia? No matter if he wouldn't approve, she wanted to find out what the mysterious writer had to tell her.

She slowed down to consult a sign post. Directions sent with the day and hour for the interview had been: "Turn left at end of bridge and run ten miles to next town. At market place, park car and walk to Stag Lane. Knock three times at stone cottage with blue door."

She glanced at the speedometer, looked at the distant hills upon the tops of which rested wisps of cloud like the white caps on haystacks.

"Gorgeous day, but like an old kill joy I sniff rain, Whiskers," she predicted to the dozing terrier beside her.

She sent the green roadster smoothly ahead and picked up the train of thought interrupted by the necessity of checking the route. If Peter were again in love with Lydia Austen he was being given every chance to test the state of his affections. When he and Tim were not at Fordham Manor, they were at some county estate for lawn tennis, riding, boating, luncheon, tea or dinner and the intriguing Lydia invariably was among those present.

So was she, herself, and where she was, there also was Ivor. She had begun to take his devotion as a matter of course. At first she had disliked it; it had bordered on the saccharine and she detested men with sugary manners. But lately he had seemed straightforward and likable and she had enjoyed being with him, had even wondered what sort of husband he would make. But yesterday, when Lady Hanford had staged that theatric appearance at the door of his living room, she had known by his eyes that he was afraid of her, that in some way, she held the whip hand. A man like that, if he were heir to a dozen titles, was not good enough for her. She hoped she had made that plain to Major General Lord Vandemere Trent-Gowan. The fury in his eyes had left no doubt but that she had.

She knew by the taste of salt on her lips and the gulls spiraling above the sandstone and marble cliffs scarred and slashed by time and the sea, that she had almost reached her destination. Had the roadster startled the birds? They were screaming as if broadcasting a warning.

Sun-gilded waves broke into lacy white frills as they gently embraced the base of rock and crag. At the end of a scraggly, overgrown lane, sagged a stone tower. Ivy covered it. As if to brace the crumbling ruin a great trunk had climbed to the tumbled-in dome. Limbs encircled it like the arms of an octopus about to squeeze out its life. Green tendrils swayed in the misty breath of the sea, clung and clutched at crevices and window openings, as if their very life depended upon holding on.

Even in this glorious sunshine the ivy-strangled tower dispensed gloom. It was the perfect answer to a mystery writer's prayer. Just the place for a headless body or two. That was a cheering thought.

She caught the terrier's collar and

dragged him back as he started to jump from the roadster. He yelped and twisted, whined and tugged.

"What's the matter with you, Whiskers? Scent a headless body or do you think you can catch those birds wheeling above the old tower? Have you never seen gulls before? Quiet down!"

Instead the dog wrenched free, jumped to the ground and dashed toward the ruin. Standing in the roadster, Con called and whistled. She followed him with her eyes till he vanished into the tower. Instantly it appeared to go up on wings. Screaming, screeching gulls flew out and took to the air.

"Now that helps," she said aloud and frowned at her wrist watch. She must keep her appointment. If she went on perhaps Whiskers would follow. If he didn't she would pass this place on her way back and pick him up. Serve him right if he thought she had deserted him. It was a mean break for the gulls to leave him here. He would make life a nightmare for them.

He is too intelligent to get lost, she comforted herself as she drove on. I'll drive slowly and he will come tearing after me. She looked back before the road took a sharp turn inland. No sign of Whiskers. The

gulls were still soaring, diving and screaming madly.

She tried to forget him, tried to think only
of the beautiful country she was entering.
The air was clear, she had known that clarity
to precede rain. Sunny fields were patterned
by cloud shadows, enameled with Queen
Anne's lace or spangled with the gold of
buttercups. An occasional half-timbered,
gable-roofed house with lattice windows
nestled beneath the overhanging branches
of a huge oak like a chicken poking its head
from under the feathers of its mother's
breast.

A man in blue jeans and a dirty red cardigan pedaled rapidly toward her. As he
passed she noticed that a broad hat was
pulled low over a sooty face. Long rods,
brushes and a pail dangled from the handle
bar of his bicycle.

She turned to watch him and wondered if
he were Joe, the sweep, who had so interested Peter. If he were, she wished he were
going her way. It would have been reassuring to have someone whom Peter knew
within hailing distance.

Don't get jittery at this stage of the game,
she prodded herself and sent the roadster
forward.

She passed a wayside church with its war

memorial. Birds planed swiftly from tree to tree. Fragrance drifted from flower beds which were gay with pansies, candytuft, purple and yellow iris and roses just showing color in their buds. There were kitchen gardens patched with corn, pens from which drifted the grunts and effluvia of pigs. Far away a cathedral spire tapered to a vanishing silver point in the blue.

Beautiful country, she thought again, and my grandfather expects me to make it mine. Could she do it? The question kept tugging at her mind like a dog on leash determined to go his way instead of his master's. She was so tired of indecision. It was so unlike her to wobble. Indecision? Hadn't she decided after that row with the General this noon that she wouldn't stay, that she wouldn't give up the flavor and sparkle, the warmth and zest of life as lived with the Coreys?

With them she had had the best in companionship. Nothing less could satisfy her. She loved Trentmere Towers and all it stood for, but, if she were to remain in England permanently, she could see her heart leading a separate life, secret, aching, turned forever to that land across the sea, while her mind was concerned with a thousand details of daily living, with the social responsibilities and problems of the caste system, and became moss-grown with tradition.

Don't get that on your mind now, she warned herself. One thing at a time, gal. Something tells me that you'll need all your gray matter to deal with the hour immediately ahead.

She passed a grove of birches, whose slim silver bodies swayed like dancers under lacy veils of tender green leaves; next a large rambling house where a peacock on an ivy-covered wall spread iridescent plumage that glittered like jewels. A cuckoo called and from the distance another answered. It seemed but a moment later that she entered a town. Graceful ash trees stood like sentinels beside small thatch-roofed houses clustered around a market place, houses with shining windows and scrubbed doorsteps. Beyond them the stone tower of a church loomed against the turquoise, cloud-clotted sky. Rooks circling above looked like flies crawling on a blue ceiling.

As she parked the roadster an icy shiver of excitement splintered through her veins. She was faring forth to meet she knew not what. If only she had Whiskers for company. If only she could stop feeling guilty about deserting him. Why torment herself? He had deserted her, hadn't he? Perhaps even now he was pegging along in the roadster's wake.

Comforted by the thought of that possibility she glanced at her wrist watch. She was ten minutes ahead of her appointment. Slowly she walked toward the teeming square. The breeze which came to her now was not flower-scented; it was strong with the smell of animals and not-too-well-cared-for human flesh.

Directly ahead stood a stone-pillared market arcade; beside it squatted a quaint inn with a swinging sign. Beyond that glowed a picture house. Garishly decorated with crimson and gold scrolls in the baroque manner, it stood out against the quaint charm of its surroundings like an ugly blotch on a lovely woman's skin. The market place was bordered by trestle tables and carts, half-filled with green vegetables, or butter, eggs and poultry. One was gay with flowers. Another displayed a depleted stock of gingerbread and something which looked like coffee cakes. Cheap jacks shouted their wares.

The square was crowded with men in high gaiters and smocks who were gesticulating, waving sticks, arguing; with pink-cheeked girls in crisp ginghams and women in clumsy farm clothes; with children, racing, shouting, playing; with animals tugging; rearing, bellowing. The air vibrated with yells of "Gee!" "Woa!" "Rope it!", the clatter of hoofs on cobblestones, the lowing of cattle, the barking of dogs, large and small, of excellent breeds and of no breed at all.

For an instant she hesitated, then charged into the crowd. She steered between men and women, dodged children and animals. No one moved out of her way. She might have been a ghost slipping by, so little attention was paid to her.

She darted in and out of a drove of bleating black-faced sheep; did a running high jump over a squealing pig; ducked under the nose of a pawing colt; skirted a dog fight and shooed away a flock of cackling geese who showed a hectic interest in her dusty-pink skirt by nipping at it.

She stopped to inquire the way of a farmer in a blue smock whose long, coarse, yellow hair was like nothing so much as frayed rope. Her question might have come from a disembodied spirit for all the notice he took of the girl asking it.

"Stag Lyne? Tyke the furst left turnin'," he answered and whacked the back of the green smock of his companion who had shot a gimlet-eyed glance at her when she had asked the question.

"Stranger, it's this wye!" he shouted and

picked up the vociferous argument her voice had interrupted at the exact word where he had dropped it.

There were two stone cottages in the lane into which Con turned. The first had a blue door and an enormous chimney. There was a ladder on the roof. Another stood upright by the side of the house. The deep solemn stroke of a distant bell set the air vibrating. Three o'clock. She was on time to the minute.

She followed the stepping-stone path between flower beds gay with a profusion of yellow, pink and purple blossoms. The air was sweet with their fragrance. For an instant she stood rigid with excitement like a watch spring wound too tight. With a supreme effort of will she raised her hand and knocked three times at the blue door.

She looked up at the man who opened it. A tough-fibered man, if she were any judge. Tall. Dark. Forty. Perhaps forty plus. A neat mustache. The flash of his white teeth made her think of the wolf in Little Red Riding Hood, "The better to eat you, my dear." His eyes were opaque. A reddish scar cut across one cheek from ear to chin. But it was his mouth, his brutalized mouth, that betrayed him. She knew at once that it was he who had plotted and organized this scheme, if it were a scheme. She controlled a frightened urge to turn and run. She would see this thing through. Could this man be kin of her mother? A relation of her own? The possibility chilled her heart but her voice showed no sign of nervousness as she announced:

"I'm Constance Trent."

"Anyone with you?"

"I came alone."

"What's that ladder for, Pansy?" he called over his shoulder.

"H'it belongs to my lodger, Brother," a woman answered from the hall behind him. " 'E took a room one week ago. 'E's h'a sweep come to do the village chimneys. They mostly need it. You wouldn't 'ave me give up four bob a dye, cause you come back from the dead an' dropped in on us with h'out warnin' at midnight, would you?"

The sturdy honesty of the voice gave Con a feeling of security.

"Quit your cackling! Keep him out of the setting room. He's been fiddling round the roof all morning," the man scolded over his shoulder before he swung the door wide with a gruff, "Come in!"

Sunlight through leaded windows spotted the scrubbed pine floor of the room into which Con followed him. Heavy timbers raftered it. A huge stone fireplace with kindling and logs neatly laid for lighting occupied one end. A moon-faced clock ticked loudly on the shelf. There were a few ladder-back, rush-bottom chairs and a sofa in one corner of which huddled a woman bundled in shawls. Dark glasses concealed her eyes.

Con looked from the swathed figure to the man. She never had seen a hypnotist, but his eyes fastened on hers were precisely like what she had thought the eyes of a hypnotist would be, opaque and motionless with a flicker in their depths. Instead of terrifying her, the thought steadied her. Nervousness departed. She had the curious feeling that a tide had swept through her and washed it away.

"The *Honorable* Miss Trent." The man might have been announcing her at the door of a drawing room.

"Here I am. So what?" Con asked and marveled at the crispness of her voice.

"Won't you sit down?" he invited suavely.

"No."

She drew a ladder-back chair in front of her and gripped the top till her knuckles showed white. If worse came to worst she could swing it. It would deliver a nasty crack.

"Go on," she prodded. "You claimed that

you could tell me of my mother. What about her?"

The woman on the couch threw back the shawl and pulled off the dark glasses.

"I am your mother."

XVII

"I am your mother," the woman repeated.

The theatric whisper echoed through the raftered room. Con stared at the face rouged and powdered to the pinkness and whiteness of a wax doll, at the deeply undulated hair which glistened like cheap gilt, at the crow's-feet at the corners of eyes which were now black with intensity and triumph, at the painted scarlet lips parted over cigarette-yellowed teeth. A terrible travesty, this woman who claimed to be her mother. Passé. Showy. Dowdy. And yet, she was the person grown older and harder of the photograph Ivor had given her. She had pored over that picture until she knew it by heart.

It couldn't be true. It was too horrible. Even with "My wife, Viola" in her father's handwriting on the back of the photograph in her bag, that photograph which was undoubtedly that of the triumphantly leering person on the sofa, she couldn't, she wouldn't believe it.

She disciplined a shudder and brought up

240

reserves of coolness and control she hadn't known she possessed. She even managed a contemptuous smile.

"So, that's the way it is. You are standing me up for money, I presume?"

The woman dabbed at her eyes with a scrap of blue and rose kerchief which was the legitimate offspring of her garish silk dress and caught the sleeve of the man brooding like an evil spirit behind her.

"George! Ge—orge! My girlie talks of money when all I wanted was to see me — che—ild!"

Melodrama. Cheap melodrama. *Girlie!* For one devastating instant Con feared she would scream with hysterical laughter. Fright at the tumult of her senses steadied her. She scurried through her memory like a mouse in an attic. Had she ever heard that her mother had been an actress before she married Gordon Trent? That wail smacked of stage or screen.

"Good film stuff!" she approved and laughed.

Was this the psychical moment to announce that Clive Neale had found the authenticated record of her mother's tragic death or would she better wait until this crafty couple had disclosed more of their scheme?

"Wait. Don't give them information," advised that inexplicable inner voice, the wisdom of whose counsel she always recognized the moment she violated it.

"Taking it that way! As a joke, are you?" The strident question with no hint of English inflection whipped Con's mind to attention. "You, the granddaughter of a lord, you *think*, won't be so toppy when I tell you a few things, will she, George?"

"Keep your shirt on, Viola!" The woman cringed at his harsh reproof.

That's pure Americanese, Con thought. The man may be English but he has been in the United States recently. He called her "Viola," my mother's name. What had been meant by that sly "granddaughter of a lord, you *think*"?

The realization that she had walked into a trap tightened her throat. Only for the space of a heart beat, and then some subtle fusion of reason and humor relieved the tension. This was nothing to be afraid of and was as amusing as a comic strip. What about the resemblance to the photograph? The reminder was like the twist of a thumbscrew.

"Before you tell those 'few things' why not produce the proof that you were my father's wife, if you can?" she inquired.

"George, show my snooty daughter the

marriage certificate." The woman wasn't so calm as she was trying to appear. The knuckles of the hand with which she gripped the arm of the sofa showed white as if the bones were coming through the skin.

As the man drew a folded paper from a breast pocket of his tweed coat, Con asked:

"If I'm not too inquisitive, just who is 'George'? Where does he fit into this thrilling scenario?"

"I'm Viola's present husband," the man answered and regarded her with a fixed stare.

"Oh, I see. Then you're my present step-father?" Con rigidly crushed back an hysterical giggle. "My goodness, but I'm lucky, acquiring two parents in one day."

She shouldn't have said that. She was crazy to anger them. His eyes glowed like the red coals of a smoldering fire. These people were out for money. They might do anything to her. She had been stupid when she had made this appointment without consulting Peter. Tim had accused: "You're a terribly reckless person. You dash into a situation without stopping to think where it's coming out. Millions of the living are already dead." He was right. She hadn't thought this situation through, hadn't thought of the dangers and difficulties into which it might lead. Her common sense had been quite, quite dead when she had answered that note. If only Peter would *feel* that she needed him and come!

He won't. God's in His Heaven and Peter is far away, she paraphrased. Alone she had gotten into this mess. Alone she would get out of it. She'd better stop being panicky and do some constructive thinking and be quick about it. The patches of sunlight on the floor had vanished. Time was marching on.

"Let me see that certificate," she commanded sharply.

"She hasn't gone to sleep," the woman drawled. "She has all the airs of a ladyship, hasn't she? Show it to her, George. She seems anxious to leave us."

"She won't leave till I say the word." The man's smile was smug. "Here's the paper, take your time examining it. You see how we trust you. Why not? If you destroy that we can always get a copy from the registry."

The noise of a ladder being dragged across the roof drowned the last word. He flung open the door.

"Pansy! What's going on overhead?" he shouted into the hall.

"Wot a row you do make, Brother." The woman's voice Con had heard before answered fretfully. "I've telled ye that h'it's h'a sweep wot's come to clean the village chimneys. 'E's a doin' mine free on 'is off time an' 'e can make all the rumpus 'e likes. Ef ye don't care fer h'it ye go back w'ere you come from, you an' thet —"

The bang of the door, a click, did things to Con's nerve centers. She was locked in. He hadn't put the key in his pocket. That was a break. She forced her hands to steadiness, her attention to the words printed and written on the certificate they held. The names, dates and places were correct. Before she left her room this morning, she had refreshed her memory in regard to them from her Bible in which her father had recorded the data of his marriage as well as her own birth. She folded the paper and returned it.

"This is correct. But, can you prove that you are the person named in it?"

"Easy." Con's confirmation had poured the elixir of assurance into the woman's voice. The triumphant toss of her head precluded any chance of failure. "Get the album and the letters, George."

"Not so fast, Viola. Let's hear what the Honorable Miss Trent thinks finding her long-lost mother is worth or else —" His low laugh dripped innuendo.

Con drew a sharp breath. It had come. At last she knew what she was up against. A scheme to extract money. Evidently they knew she had not seen her mother since she was a very little girl. Hadn't her grandfather warned her that it was common knowledge? Knew that they could foist anyone on her as her missing parent, and this shoddy, gloating female was their attempt.

But, shoddy, dowdy, gloating as she was, the woman facing her now was the woman of the photograph Ivor had given her, which had "My wife, Viola" inscribed on its back in Gordon Trent's writing, and Gordon Trent had sent it to Ivor's father. Why be so sure that she wasn't the person she claimed to be? What did she herself remember about her mother's appearance except that her hair had been golden and wasn't this woman's touched-up yellow?

She shook off the spell of memory. She was in danger, no doubt of that. If only she had Aladdin's lamp with which to summon a friendly genie. She hadn't. The only magic lamp she had was within her brain, and rub that as she would no dazzling idea for escape from this room came across.

No use to make a dash for the door. It was locked. The key was there, but if she tried to turn it the saturnine George would stop her.

In spite of photograph and inscription she never would believe that this cheap woman had been her father's wife. There was a trick somewhere.

"Get going. What's the job worth to you?" the man prodded.

Con flexed stiff lips.

"If you ask me, hunting up a parent like her isn't worth anything — to me."

Her heart stopped as they approached with menacing scowls. Samson and the temple. She had shaken the pillars of protection and conservatism under which she had grown up and had brought an amazing and terrifying adventure tumbling down upon herself. Could she crawl out from under? She must.

"This is a hold-up and you know it," she accused. "If you had looked up the record of my mother's death it would have saved you a lot of trouble and possibly a jail sentence."

The woman burst into coarse laughter and squeezed the man's arm.

"Didn't I tell you she'd say that, George? Well, my snooty daughter, it was my twin who died. After I left your father, I wanted to do a complete fade-away. When my sister and I were caught in a fire what was easier than for me to swear that it was me, not her, who jumped from the burning building and was killed? I gave my name when the death certificate was made out and took hers and I was free."

Con's heart froze. Only this morning she had learned that that had been the way her mother had died. The woman's statement was devastatingly convincing; even so, she wouldn't believe her. If she had been through such a terrible experience could she speak of it so lightly?

"If that is true why didn't you go to Lord Gowan's lawyer?" she demanded. "Why contact me? I haven't any money."

"Is that so? Well, you can get it out of your grandfather. Write a note like we tell you. We think our information worth about twenty thousand pounds."

"You'll break your neck to write it, girlie, when —"

"You're told that while you are Viola's daughter —" the man snatched the sentence from the woman's lips, "the late Gordon Trent was not your father."

"What do you *mean?* Not my father!" Con's shocked whisper was barely audible.

The woman registered embarrassment by a smirk and wriggle. She looked down at her broken-nailed, not too clean fingers heavy with cheap rings.

"You see, girlie, your real father died on

me just after we married, and soon I met Gordon and he never knew —"

"That's a lie! You've overacted your parts. You're a couple of blackmailers! You —"

The man clapped his hand over Con's lips. "That'll do for that!" he warned. "Keep your voice down or you'll get what's coming to you. Understand?"

She nodded. He freed her mouth. She had to make two attempts to produce a voice before she said:

"Yes. I understand. If I agree to write that note —"

"Asking for twenty thousand pounds," he interrupted. "You'd better get busy because your *mother* and I intend to keep you safe with us until we get the money. *See?*"

Con saw. She was neatly caught in a trap into which she had walked with her eyes open, wide open.

XVIII

"Joe will carry on — lucky I told — him —"

Who was repeating those words over and over, Peter Corey wondered dully. If only the voice would stop. It went on and on like a merry-go-round in his brain, the voice and that monotonous swish, swish, swish. Where was the person? It was too dark to see him.

He tried to lift his head. Was it his head? That thing on his shoulders felt as heavy as a Civil War cannon ball. It dropped back against something hard with a force which jarred him to fuller consciousness. He peered into the dark. Where was he? He could see no one. Could that have been his own voice sing-songing, "Joe will carry on"?

He stared up at the deep indigo dome, polka-dotted with faint specks of light. Turned his head with experimental caution. His neck wasn't broken. He had thought from its stiffness that it might be. Early morning. He knew by the faint pink stain in the east. Water, oceans of water spread ahead of him until it fused into the rosy horizon. It was a whirling universe.

He looked in the opposite direction, this time with less discomfort. He frowned at the crags and cliffs, ghostly in the faint light, which broke into pinnacles and serrated edges at the top. Above them something dark loomed toward a darker sky which seemed to bend down to meet it.

Where was he? What did all this mean? Nightmare? He closed his eyes. Perhaps he could hang onto his thoughts better if he shut out this strange world of dark sky and water and ghostly gray cliffs. No sooner would he get one well started than it slipped away into blankness like a launched ship sliding down greased ways to the sea.

How had he come here and where was "here"? What was the last thing he could remember? Joe! Joe, meeting him outside the garage at Cherrytree Farm, Joe telling him —

He caught at memory which had begun to fade like a radio broadcast and dragged it back. What had he been thinking? It was about — he had it! Joe had told him that the younger Sacks had been pals with Ivor Hardwick. Hardwick. He held onto the name as it tried to do a fade-away. Hardwick. What was it about Hardwick? He remembered. When Joe had told him that they had been — pals — he had caught that word before it eluded him — something in his mind had clicked. He had been sure then that the man who had opened the door of the Captain's Georgian house was the younger Sacks, alias Dafter, who was wanted by Federal and State law-enforcement officers. Dafter, was the supposed-to-be-deceased Sacks, hadn't a man sailed from New York under that name?

Memory swept back on the job like a river breaking through a dam. It cleared away the debris of scraps and fragments of unrelated thought which had been clogging his mind. Dafter had recognized him. The uncontrollable dilation of the pupils of his eyes was proof of that. Hadn't he immediately decamped from the house of his old pal, Ivor Hardwick? He had beat it from London to Cherrytree Farm. Of course he had known where to find him, the man whom he suspected might be on his trail. Hadn't the newspapers publicized to saturation point the Corey family's connection with the long-lost heiress of Trentmere Towers and her return to the home of her ancestors? Sacks, alias Dafter, had lain in wait in the garage. The chance had come to crack his unsuspecting victim on the head. He had cracked — and how. Had brought him here. Where the dickens was "here"? Wherever it was it was darn cold. He was frozen.

He opened his eyes. The sky was a shade lighter and steady. He looked down at his legs or where his legs were supposed to be. They were invisible. He was hip-deep in water. No wonder he was cold. The jagged rock against which his coat had caught had saved him from entire immersion. Apparently he had been flung or slid down the cliff to the sea.

It had been a good try and one quite in character with the gangster who had attempted to settle his score against the man whom he knew had been as relentlessly on his trail as a bloodhound on the scent. A chill not induced entirely by the icy water shivered through Peter as he thought how nearly successful the scheme had proved.

The realization brought up his shoulders with a jerk. He pressed his hands hard against his temples. His head was no longer a cannon ball but a squirrel cage whirling on high. Dafter must have put all he had behind that blow.

He moved his legs carefully. Numb but not broken. He looked up at the broad path worn smooth as a toboggan slide by centuries of water drainage from the top of the cliff to the sea. Had he been sent down that roller-coaster fashion? The rest of it was jagged, sharp. His body would have caught, never would have reached the water had he been flung over that. As it was, it was a miracle his bones had not been splintered. His unconsciousness had saved them, his body must have been as relaxed as a bundle of old clothes. He felt dead from the waist down. Better that than dead from the shoulders up, he told himself, and knew by his chuckle that he was fast returning to normalcy.

The world was taking on opalescent tints. Light spread evenly. Dawn was mounting to the sky, brushing from her way the trembling stars as she trailed rosy skirts behind her. He must pull himself out of this trap and be quick about it.

He struggled to his feet. His knees doubled under him. His numb legs wouldn't hold him up. He couldn't wait for them to come alive. He must get on.

He crawled between rocks, through slimy seaweeds and creamy foam to a pocket of marble pebbles, stopped there to get his breath and to beat the circulation into the useless legs which had dragged behind him like sticks.

It was light enough now to see the crags and crannies of the cliff he must scale. It was not so stern and forbidding as some he had noticed along this coast. That was a break for which to give thanks. No use to try the smooth marble slide down which he had been coasted. It would be impossible to get a toe hold.

Slowly he climbed. Clutching at tussocks of gray-green grass and plants of sedum in the clefts between jagged crags which tore at his hands. Stopping to get his breath, to beat at the legs which were like so much dead cargo. On and up. Slipping back. Hanging in air while he reached frantically for a hold with feet coming to prickling, excruciatingly aching life. Forcing himself onward and upward. Startling sea gulls from their nests, great birds and small birds, white birds and gray birds which flung themselves on the air mewing and screaming an alarm through their yellow bills while dawn spread and the sky turned to orchid and turquoise and the marble beach and limestone cliffs to rosy silver.

With a final supreme clutch and lurch he went over the top. He lay on the grass-covered plateau where he had fallen and brushed his hands across his eyes. Was that looming thing the ivy-covered tower where Joe was to pick him up? It answered the description, even to the tumbled-in dome. It couldn't be. It was too easy. He must be seeing things.

He dropped his face to his arms while he pounded circulation into his toes. He would rest a moment, then when he opened his eyes if the tower were still there he would know it was real and not a mirage.

He cheated himself and peeked. It was there. If he found within it the paraphernalia Joe was to leave for him he would be sure that it was the rendezvous. If it were, what a coincidence. One that might be used on the screen but wouldn't occur once in an hundred years in real life.

He sat up. His breath was coming easily now. If it weren't for the smart and burn of his legs and the lump big as an egg, a super-ostrich egg he'd bet, on the back of his head he would be fit as a fiddle. What did the lump matter outside if the machinery inside was working again? And it was, boy, it was!

He choked back a whoop of exultation. His being here wasn't coincidence. It was one more missing piece in the puzzle. Joe had said that Hardwick and Tod Sacks had used the old tower up the coast a way, the very one where he was to stay till called for, to try their hands at robbing fishermen. What more natural than that Sacks, alias Dafter, would think of the cliff on which the tower loomed as the number-one place over which to chuck his enemy? That wasn't all.

It meant that Sacks, now that he was near, undoubtedly would visit his mother and sister in the village in which he, himself, had planned to do a bit of investigation under cover of Joe's chimney activities.

"At noon tomorrer," Joe had said. Was this mother-of-pearl morning, "tomorrer," or had he been lying at the foot of the cliff for a day or more? What had the family thought when he did not return? He always phoned his mother if he were not coming home at night. Would Con be anxious? Better not think of her, he must keep his mind focused on what he had to do in the next few hours.

For the first time since the return of consciousness he looked at the watch on his wrist. It was light enough to see the hands. Four o'clock. Was the thin going? He held it to his ear. Its steady tick was like a friendly voice in the midst of chaos.

Four o'clock. It must be early morning of the day on which Joe had planned to pick him up at the old tower. It wasn't reasonable to suppose that he had been lying at the foot of the cliff longer than one night. Had he been, sooner or later he would have been swished free of the rock by the tide, his coat wouldn't have held. Also, there were nine chances out of ten that his assailant would have returned to the scene of his crime to make sure he had finished the job and finding him jacked up against the rock would have dumped him into the water.

As it was, Dafter was likely to appear for a check-up at any moment. He'd better beat it for the tower which, besides providing a hiding place, presumably held the clothing Joe was to leave there, dry clothing. His own wet garments were getting colder and clammier every minute. The slightest current of air set him a-shiver. He measured the distance to the yawning hole which indicated a doorway. It seemed miles away. If he stood up to cross to it the gulls who had quieted down and were floating with folded wings on the water would begin their infernal wheeling and mewing and screaming, would betray his presence. He would creep.

Dropping flat to the coarse green grass and nubbly ground at every sound, poking up his head cautiously to make sure of direction, he crawled on hands and knees while the light spread, rocks and stunted trees and bushes which had been shadows stood out in bold relief and the world was washed with silver in the purity of the shimmering morning air.

It seemed hours to his strained nerves, it was five minutes by his watch, before he reached the millstone which served as a doorstep and tumbled into the cavernous dampness and darkness of the tower. In that instant the air was rent by deafening screams as gull after gull flew over his head grazing it with wildly flapping wings to crowd through the opening which once had been a doorway.

"Walk, do not run to the nearest exit," he quoted aloud. His words echoed eerily. That exodus hadn't helped. If Dafter were within hearing distance he would suspect at once that the tower had a strange human occupant.

He stood up, tried not to breathe in the nauseating stench of dead fish. Listened. No sound but the swish of the tide and the diminishing screams of the gulls. He was safe for the present. Feeling had returned to his legs. Okay so far. Now to find Joe's cache. Aside from dry clothing he needed nothing so much as an electric torch. The place was dark as pitch.

A hurried dip into the pockets of his waistcoat produced his cigarette lighter. Had dampness put it out of commission? He snapped it. A tiny yellow flame licked at the darkness. He could see nests made of dead grass, brown twigs and feathers tucked into interstices of the stone walls.

With one hand shielding the precious light, he crossed the floor carpeted with ivy which laid snares for his feet. He passed under a tipsy arch into a room from which sagging iron stairs twisted upward. A bicycle leaned against one crumbling wall and near it on the ground lay a heap of clothes and iron rods and brushes tied together. Dirty as those garments undoubtedly were they looked as good to him as an outfit from a Bond Street tailor.

Better save the light. He snapped it off and fumbled for the dry clothing. As he changed, splinters of pink sifted in between cracks and crevices in the walls. The sun was up. "Tomorrer" was here. What had it up its sleeve for him?

Whatever it was, he would have to wait for it. Joe wasn't due until noon. In spite of the dry, if sooty clothing, he was chilled to the bone. There was light enough now to see the twisted iron stairway and the broad flooring at the top. He would stretch out on that and let the hot sun bake the stiffness out of him. Better take his wet clothing along in case Dafter returned to check up on the thoroughness of his late villainous attack.

The rods and bike must be hidden. Where could he put them? He couldn't get the stuff up those sagging steps. He would hide it on the ground under the ivy. That was an idea.

He covered wheel, rods and brushes smoothly with vines. Regarded the result and found it good. There was no sign of human occupation in the tower.

As he mounted cautiously the iron stairway swayed and groaned like a tree in the grip of a tornado. When he reached the top he pulled himself to the broad remnants of floor and filled his lungs with the fresh salt air. Would he ever get that sickening fishy smell out of his system?

He stood up to stretch the stiffness from his muscles. What a world. A realization of its beauty surged through him Was it because he had so nearly left it that he was so sensitive to its appeal? On the far horizon a faint mist was being crowded back to show the green slopes of distant hills. The water, blue as the sky above, glimmered where the light touched it, turned to amber near the rocks, russet above the seaweeds and to milky whiteness where it laved the pebbly beach. The clefts and crannies of the cliffs were patterned with pale green, pink and rose. On the peak of a marble pinnacle poised a white gull, wings outspread. In a crevice between two big rocks was a nest with mottled brown eggs. From somewhere rose a lark singing an impassioned greeting to the morn.

Sunlight which had warmed the air was creeping toward the tower. He spread his own clothes to dry, made a pillow of his coat and lay down on the platform. Except that he was cold and that his head throbbed he was okay and darn lucky to be alive to feel the cold and pain, he reminded himself, as he visualized the spot in which he had regained consciousness.

He turned over. The flooring was not any too broad, but it would serve. Elbows on the coat pillow, chin in his hands he watched a creamy fluff scoot across the azure sky after a great white cloud-bark for all the world like a fussy little tugboat hurrying to escort an ocean liner into her berth.

That ocean-liner stuff reminded him that his vacation was more than half over and that from now on the days would put on ten-league boots and stride and soon the Coreys would be on their way home.

Would Con return with them or would she remain and take on the honors and responsibilities of Trentmere Towers? Wanting her, loving her as he did, could he stick to his resolution not to tell her, not to show her that he loved her until after she had decided to which country she would belong? Even then, would it be just to ask her to marry him when his work made him fair game for an attack like that of last night?

He thought of Lord Gowan's determination to keep his granddaughter with him, of what life in England offered her, and he thought of his mother's suggestion that he might compromise and live here himself. If he were given the choice between England with Con or home and the work to which he was pledged without her, which would he choose? He dropped his head on his crossed arms. Once he wouldn't have asked himself the question. Was his loyalty to his own country, to his sense of right, weakening?

"Pledged" was the word, his thoughts trooped on. He had established a law office and before he realized it he had been drawn by a privately financed crime commission into law enforcement. He had determined to do his part toward smashing the alliance between the corrupt politician and the criminal; to expose perjuring witnesses; to show up the law's delays which aided the guilty; and to checkmate crooked lawyers who bribed and lied to protect their underworld clients from conviction and, if they were sentenced, by chicanery, pressure and the intimidation of their jailers to help them escape. He was pledged to enforce the law and secure conviction where guilt was proved. That was the most important of all. To secure conviction.

He had been eighty per cent. successful in the cases he had handled. Justice had been geared to speed. If he caught Dafter he would secure a potent weapon against the underworld. Step by step he reviewed the bits of information he had secured as to the man's habits, the way he swooped on a job and vanished, the type of his pals, the women with whom he traveled, his mannerisms, his physical appearance — apparently he changed that with every alias. He had been dark, light, white-haired, bald, smooth-faced and pink-cheeked, hawk-nosed and swarthy, mustached, bearded. Would any of these descriptions fit a person by the name of Sacks?

How warm the sun was getting. He'd better dry his knees. He turned over stiffly. He flinched as the back of his bruised head burrowed into the coat pillow. He covered his eyes with his hand to shut out the glare from the luminous blue sky and yawned. The heat and his throbbing head were making him confoundedly sleepy. He must keep awake or he might miss Joe. What had he been thinking of when he turned over?

Con? No, he had tried with all his strength to keep her out of his mind. Dafter! If Dafter were Sacks, Tod Sacks — that wasn't right. If Sacks were — were what? The words kept slipping away. He had caught them again. If — Dafter were —

What a racket those gulls were making. Was the world going up on wings? The sky was alive with them. What was lap, lap, lapping at his face? The tide? Was he back in the water? Had he only dreamed that he climbed the cliff?

The horror of the possibility brought his shoulders up. He stared at something white on his knees. Closed his eyes. Opened them.

"Whiskers!" he exclaimed. "Are you real? Where did you come from? Did you trail me from home, you scamp?"

The terrier whined and licked his cheek. Clutching a stone of the parapet Peter struggled to his feet. Good Lord, but he was stiff. Sleeping on a board — *sleeping!* How long had he been asleep? He glanced at the sky. At his watch. It couldn't be so late. It was. It was midafternoon!

Someone was moving below! Peter caught the terrier's nose in a grip of steel. The slightest sound would betray his presence. He stood motionless! Was it Dafter? Had the man traced him?

"Blimey, sir! Blimey!" The shout from below was followed by Joe's sooty face at the head of the iron stairs. "I thought h'I'd lost ye, sir, w'en h'I didn't find ye 'ere h'at noon. Come back to try h'again. Wus goin' h'away w'en h'I 'eard ye talkin' to the dog. 'E's come! Tod Sacks 'as come! 'E's got h'a woman with 'im. H'if we don't 'urry, we'll be h'a losin' 'im. H'I 'eard 'im tell 'is sister as 'ow h'a boat was to pick 'im h'up h'off this point."

Peter was on the ground disinterring the bicycle before the sweep had finished speaking.

"Help me load these brushes, quick. He mustn't get out of that house. Everything ready there?"

Joe shook his head doubtfully. "Blimey, sir, h'I wouldn't wonder ef we'd h'a lost 'im by this time, sir. 'E allus was h'as slippery h'as h'an h'eel, wus Tod Sacks."

XIX

"Caught in a nice, neat little trap."

The words whirled round and round in Con's mind like a repeating record in a phonograph as she faced the man and woman who were regarding her with triumphant malice. This was an attempt at kidnaping, kidnaping in England where it was almost unknown. They intended to keep her prisoner until her grandfather paid a ransom. Where? Not here. They wouldn't dare.

She must not appear frightened, they must not suspect that her heart was a lump of ice. She could get out of this trap if she would stop being jittery and nail her mind down to constructive thinking. If she appeared to bargain with these people she would gain time. Time was what she needed. There was a scream gathering chokily in her throat but she mustn't let it out yet. The realization that the two facing her were gloating, like hovering buzzards, brought her mind out of a tail spin. She tried desperately to steady her voice.

"Twenty thousand pounds!" she repeated. "I am to write a note asking for it." She paused as if to examine the suggestion. "I get the idea. If my grandfather pays that money — I forgot, you said that he is not my grandfather — well then, if Lord Gowan pays the ransom thinking I am the child of his son, you will keep the secret and I will inherit his big estate, subject to lifetime hush money paid to you, I presume. If he doesn't pay — something tells me he is allergic to ransoms — you will tell all and I won't get it. Nice work. Nice work. It must have taken months and a master mind to think it up."

She felt as if every drop of color had been driven from her face and looked quickly away from the narrowed eyes which she had been defying. She hadn't deceived the man with her bravado, not for a minute, but she knew by the woman's smug expression that she had fallen for it.

"She's caught on, George," she exulted. "I told you a daughter of *his* and mine would know the side her bread's buttered on."

"Now what?" Con was fencing for time. She had a sense of physical sickness as if she had been breathing poison gas. These two persons exuded malice, intrigue, slyness, evil. If she could get a sense of her peril over the air waves to Peter, he would come to her rescue. She couldn't. Her mind wasn't equipped with broadcasting mechanism. Only a few hours ago, it seemed years, she had boasted to the General that in future she would proceed under her own power. She now had the chance of a lifetime to demonstrate what that boast was worth.

The man and woman, as if tensed to spring, were waiting for her to speak. She must say something. What? As if in answer to that challenge her inventiveness, or whatever it is in the mind that comes to the rescue of bemused humans, leaped into high. Could she outsmart them? Could she produce a light, indifferent voice through lips which were stiff? It was worth a try.

"So that's what this talk boils down to? No money for George and Viola, no father, no grandfather, for me." Her laugh was not too steady. "Low down as you two are, it has been pretty mean of me to lead you on to spill your plan, when your information has no money value, for you see, I know all about my mother. We've just let people believe that she died; we are not very proud of her. I could see her tomorrow if I wanted to." As surprise, stupefied surprise, stiffened the woman's face, Con added for good measure, "She's right here, in England." She had heard of pale-pink and baby-blue lies, this one of hers was a deep dark purple.

"Has that guy double —"

The man silenced his alleged wife's furious outburst with a glare which sent her cowering back to the corner of the sofa. He gripped Con's wrist.

"Think you're smart, don't you? You won't get away from us until we have that —"

The last words were lost in the racket on the roof. Bump! Bump! Bump! The sweep and the ladder! He was taking it away! He mustn't until she could make him hear. If I can shout "Help!" up that chimney, Con thought wildly and tried to free her hands.

"Nothing doing!" The man's grip tightened. "You're going on a boat with us. We'll —"

His voice died in a choked stammer, his hand on her wrist loosened as an avalanche of soot streamed down the chimney and billowed into the room in gun-metal clouds. From the midst of it like a genie shot from a trap door emerged a figure. Fiend or devil, Con wondered in the instant before she saw something glint in the hand of "George."

"Sorry, folks," apologized the apparition. "H'I've come h'a little h'unexpected like, h'I 'ave. H'I didn't ought to have let h'all this sut down chimney, but it got h'away. H'I slipped, an' 'ere h'I am."

His eyes shone like bits of coal in the surrounding blackness of his face as he stared through the milling cloud of soot.

"B-blimey, blimey," he stammered, "h'if h'it ain't Tod Sacks, come back from the dead, h'I'm seein'! Remember me, don't ye? H'I'm Joe —"

"Shut up, you —"

"George! Ge—orge! I can't breathe." The woman's choking wail broke into the man's curse. "The soot will spoil my dress. My best dress."

"Blimey! H'is thet yer missus, Tod?"

Con watched the sweep breathlessly through smarting eyes. Would he help her? He must. A muscle twitched in his cheek. The room whirled. Peter! Could it be Peter? It was unbelievable. Her mind steadied. That cable. His absorption in business. His inexplicable interest in a chimney sweep. He hadn't come on her account. He didn't know she was here. Had he been hunting the very man who had planned to kidnap her? She must not make a sound which would attract his attention to herself. Had he seen the revolver "George" had slipped back into his pocket? Could she warn him? No. He must not see her. It might distract him and

271

every cell of his brain geared to high would be needed to checkmate this villainous couple. She crouched behind the chair she had been gripping.

"If you won't let this soot out, I will, George," the woman scolded and groped toward the door.

"Don't open it!" he roared and pulled out his gun. Too late. Already she had unlocked it, flung it wide.

Two powerfully built men in green smocks stepped into the room. Con recognized one as the man with the gimlet eyes who had been arguing with the farmer in the market place. Two more moved up and stood like sentinels on the threshold. With them was the sweep in a dirty red cardigan whom she had seen pedaling away from the square. Their leveled automatics covered the man backed against the chimney piece. His eyes glimmered through thinning clouds of soot like points of polished agate.

"Drop that gun, Dafter!" the sweep beside him ordered. As the metal clattered to the floor, he commanded, "Pick it up, Joe."

Dafter! Dafter! The man whom the law-enforcement officers had been after for years! Con's mind did a merry-go-round and steadied. She hadn't been mistaken. The sweep who had dropped down the chimney was Peter! He had caught his man!

In her excitement she stood up. Without an instant's warning her knees doubled under her. She clutched the chair back and clung desperately, heard Peter shout:

"Quick! Don't let that woman get away! We may want to question her."

She must have made a stifled sound. He turned. His eyes were flames in his sooty face.

"My God! What are you doing here, Con?"

In the instant his attention was diverted Dafter sprang on the open-mouthed, staring Joe, wrenched the revolver from his slack grasp and leveled it.

"You go to —"

Horror restored Con's circulation.

"Look out, Peter! *Peter!*"

He pulled her arms from his neck and flung her aside as two shots echoed. Dafter's gun dropped from a limp hand at the end of a useless arm. He grimaced with pain as his wrists were manacled.

"What's it all about?" he demanded hoarsely. "What dy'e mean calling me 'Dafter'? I'm Sacks, Tod Sacks. Ask the women in the back of the house if I ain't. Dafter! You're crazy, you there who came down the chimney. Not a real sweep are you

273

— but —" His eyes in his livid face bulged as if starting from their sockets.

" 'Peter,' the girl called you! Well, if I don't believe it's man-eating Corey! and I thought you were a-floatin' out to —"

"Better not talk," Peter advised coolly. "You've hung yourself recognizing me. Tod Sacks wouldn't know me."

"Well, if I did, you ain't got nothing on me in England. Who squealed on me? Who told you I was Sacks? When I saw you yesterday you didn't know me, did you?"

"You've grown a black mustache and acquired a villainous scar since yesterday, Dafter, but they haven't saved you this time."

"I've been framed! I —"

"Wot's goin' on here, Tod Sacks?" A stout, worn-faced woman brushed by the smocked guards on the threshold. Her harsh breathing denoted a tired heart, the wisps of gray hair, rampant, a distracted mind. "Mischief, I'll be bound. You've been up to your ears in it since you was a little tyke playin' with his lordship's cousin. You didn't ought to be 'ere anywye. Why did you come back with that cheap woman 'angin' on, w'en yer mother an' me wus thinkin' you wus dead an' glad of it so's we could 'old up our 'eads once more an' ye not be a shamin' us again." She drew her breath in a racking sob.

"Shut up your cackling, Pansy," the man gritted between clenched teeth.

"Take Miss Sacks out."

"Yes, Mr. Corey." One of the guards linked his arm through hers. "Come along with me, Marm, you can't do any good here and it's making you kind of sick, isn't it?" he sympathized kindly.

The sardonic eyes of her brother followed her, came back to Peter Corey.

"She sure gave me a character. Looks like you won't get that grand you were promised for putting on the act, Viola, unless you go after it. That's an idea! These guys can't hold you. They haven't got anything on you. *Go after it!* Find him!"

"What act?" Peter demanded sharply. "Viola! Your mother's name." He looked at Con. "Is that why you are here?"

"She says she is my mother," Con answered faintly.

"And so I am." The shivering woman huddled in a corner of the sofa, whined, "Ain't I, George?" She began to whimper.

"Can't take it, can you?" he sneered.

"That's enough from you, Dafter. Take them both out to the car," Peter Corey commanded.

The man put up a fierce fight as the guards closed in on him. Surprisingly the woman came to life, clawed and scratched in his defense.

"Go, Con! Quick!" Peter flung over his shoulder.

"Can't I help?"

"*No!* How did you come?"

"In my roadster."

"Go home. Wait outside till one of these Scotland Yard men joins you. I will follow as soon as possible."

She was only too glad to escape from the horrible place now that Peter was out of danger. She didn't want an escort. She wanted to go alone. She would get away before the Scotland Yard man could find her.

She slipped through the crowd of whispering, jabbering, round-eyed townsfolk gathered outside the door. Evidently news of the presence of officers of the law had spread. The market place was deserted as she ran across it.

The sun had disappeared. Ragged, rain-filled clouds were racing overhead as if trying to catch up with the tail end of a plane. Trees swayed and creaked. A broken branch blew across the road. Rooks cawed harshly and flapped angry wings.

Excitement, plus speed, was pumping her

breath in hard gasps when she reached the roadster. She stopped and stared. The wire-haired terrier, curled in a white and black heap on the seat, regarded her with one reproachful eye.

"Where did you come from, you bad dog? You ought to be scolded for running away, but to tell you the truth, Whiskers, I had forgotten you were in the world." She stepped into the car, unlocked the engine and kicked at the starter.

"Where have you been? My goodness, but you're dirty and smelly. It's a break you found me. Suppose on my way home I had had to stop at that old tower and hunt for you on top of everything else, I ask you?"

The terrier put his paws on her shoulder and tried to lick her cheek as an expression of apology.

"Hold it, Whiskers. You are too dirty to come so near. I know you are sorry. Settle down. I have a lot that needs thinking about, and I'll have a lot more before we get back to Cherrytree Farm if that sky means what I think it means. Feel those drops?" The dog whined and snuggled closer.

"It's more of a drizzle than rain, one of those soaking drizzles and it's getting darker every second. No use to stop and put up the top. The canvas is snugged down so tight I would get drenched trying it. I'd better shoot for home as Peter ordered. He's furious with me for being in that Stag Lane house, I could tell by his eyes. By the time he gets home he will have calmed down. Man-eating Corey can be rather terrible when he's angry, can't he, Whiskers? Why don't you answer? Don't you realize that I'm talking aloud in the hope of keeping the picture of that revolver leveled at Peter out of my mind?"

She bit her lips hard to steady them and with startled eyes regarded the world about her. The wind had died. The cawing, flapping rooks were still. In eerie silence a thick fog was creeping forward like a smoke screen preceding an advancing army. It transformed everything moving and motionless into grotesque shapes and shadows. She switched on the lights. The dog yelped and squatted on his haunches.

Con peered into the wet gray mist. Where was she? The lights hadn't helped. She couldn't see. How the wheels bumped. She must be off the road. She could hear and smell the sea. Better not keep going. She might pitch over a cliff if she kept on.

She stopped the car. Listened. There was no sound save the oily rhythmic lap of the tide, the dog's low frightened whimper and the muffled chime of a distant bell.

"You ought to know that dark thing looming black against the mist, Whiskers? It must be the old tower which so intrigued you that you ran away," she said to the dog in an effort to shake off a chilly sense of impending peril. "We might take refuge in that until the fog lifts. It would save us from getting wetter than we are."

She felt of her drenched shoulder. She couldn't be wetter than she was. Besides she didn't care for the tower — hadn't she thought it the perfect hiding place for a headless body? She patted the shivering terrier snuggled against her.

"Not so keen to investigate the place as you were, are you, Mr. Whiskers? Satisfied the hanker the first time, didn't you?" It bucked up her courage to talk to the dog though her voice, which sounded weird and hollow, gave her the jitters.

"There goes the tower. It faded away in the thickening mist like the grin of the Cheshire Cat. The glow from the roadster lamps hardly shows. I hope the tail light will shine enough to keep anyone from crashing into us. Can't see an inch ahead so we'll park right here until the fog lifts; it always does lift, doesn't it, young fella? Cold, aren't you? I can feel you shake. Hear my teeth chatter? If only we had something. The rug! Under the canvas top! How dumb of me not to have thought of it before!"

With some difficulty she drew out the rug. It was dry and woolly. She threw it over her head and shoulders, tucked her feet up on the seat and pulled the shivering dog into her lap.

"Ooch! You're dirty! You'll add the last ruinous touch to this dusty-pink frock, but I can't let you freeze. Heavenly warm, isn't it? Does the fog seem full of groping fingers and threatening whispers, to you, Whiskers? It does to me." The terrier whined agreement.

She tried by the exercise of imagination to conjure pictures of Angel and Tim in the lounge at Cherrytree Farm. On this kind of a day tall scarlet and orange flames would be leaping and licking up the great chimney. Perhaps guests would be there, Lady Hanford for instance. Tim was apt to bring her home for tea. How could he like her?

She resolutely shut out that picture and substituted the silver-laden tea table. The massive kettle would be steaming merrily in the midst of piles of hot scones, golden toast and crystal pots of orange marmalade. There would be plum cake too, rich, dark fruity slices of it. The room would be scented by the aroma of tea, burning wood and the fragrance of roses.

But the pictures wouldn't stay. They were crowded into the background by the sordid vision of the man and woman in the room of the stone cottage in Stag Lane, by the memory of their threats and innuendoes, by the horrible conviction that cheap, sordid, repulsive as she was, the woman who claimed to be her mother was the woman of the photograph in her bag.

"You won't get the grand you were promised for putting on the act, Viola."

The rough taunt of the man seemed to cut through the thick fog.

"Putting on the act," she repeated to herself. That meant that someone had hired the woman to pretend that she had been Gordon Trent's wife, didn't it? Pretend! That was the word. Of course. Her father's writing had been forged on the back of an old photograph!

How had it come into Ivor's possession? He had found it among his father's papers. Had the person who had conceived this blackmailing scheme placed it there? If there had been any truth in that horrible woman's claim that she was not Gordon Trent's daughter wouldn't the two blackmailers have gone straight to Lord Gowan?

When Ivor learned that it had been the trump card in the scheme to kidnap her, he would be furious at the deception which had been practiced on him. Her elation cooled. If the woman was an impostor how could she have known so well the circumstances of Viola Trent's death?

She had argued in a circle. She was back where she had started. If only Peter were here that she might pour out the story to him. He wasn't and she might not see him for hours. If only he would feel that she needed him and hurry home. Why weren't there thoroughfares in the air to carry thoughts as well as voices and harmonies? Perhaps there were if one were psychic and knew how to use them.

She held her wrist near the light on the instrument panel. Almost five o'clock. It seemed hours since she had knocked on that blue door. The melodrama in Stag Lane hadn't consumed so much time as she thought. Would Angel be anxious about her? She peeked from under the rug. The fog rolled and drifted. Was it breaking up? What was that sound? A motorboat? The ghost of one perhaps; its put-put was no louder than a specter's sigh.

Were her strained eyes playing tricks or was that a faint glow where the sea should be? It was. It was rising. A flare! Another. Merely pale-yellow streaks in the fog, but they were flares. Signals? To whom?

To "George"? She felt again the tightening of the man's grip on her wrist, heard his voice. "You're going on a boat with us." Was this the boat? Were the flares signals to him?

She held her breath to listen. A splash. That was a dropped anchor. A weird sound but unmistakable. Muffled dip of oars. Coming ashore? The boat was being beached. Would whoever it was climb the cliff? Suppose he did? Suppose he found her? Would he carry her off without waiting for "George"?

The terrier sniffed and whined. She muzzled his nose in a grip of steel.

"Halloo! Halloo!"

It might have been the wail of a phantom on the shore so faint and hollow it sounded.

"Halloo! Halloo!" Came the call again.

XX

Lord Gowan stood back to the fire in the lounge at Cherrytree Farm and scowled from beneath ragged gray brows at Angela Corey seated in a low chair with a mass of camelia-pink wool in the lap of her orchid-color frock.

A smile twitched at the corners of her lips as if begging them to widen in a laugh. He was behaving like a great boy who knew he had done wrong and wanted to be assured that he had been right. Many a time she had seen her young sons with that half-shamed, half-defiant expression shift from one foot to another as they prepared for confession.

He had been gloomy when he arrived. It was as if he had brought into the room with him some of the thick fog which hung like heavy curtains outside the windows. She had tried to lighten his mood with gay bits of county gossip. She liked and admired him, thoroughly understood and sympathized with his point of view in regard to keeping his granddaughter in England, even though the mere thought of Connie's staying on this side of the ocean, of Peter's loss of the girl he loved, twisted her heart unbearably.

"I say, I've muffed it!" His harsh voice broke into her reflections. "You warned me not to push Constance, not to ask her questions, to let her alone, but I did push today after luncheon, Angel."

The last word sent a flush as rosy as the wool in her lap to Angela Corey's forehead. He had never used Connie's name for her before and he was quite unaware that he had now, she realized.

"What happened?"

"I told her I was tired of her indecision, that I would decide for her, that she *would* stay in England, *would* marry Ivor and in future do as I ordered."

"Is *that* all? And you call that pushing? I'd call it using a rope and tackle. Of course, she replied sweetly that her life was yours to *order* as you saw fit?"

"By Jove, don't go sarcastic on me. Can't you see that I'm frightfully torn up about this?"

"You deserve to be shredded to rags, and I hope you are. You forget when you attempt to dictate to her that the child saw her father live and die with his heart bruised and bleeding because of your harshness. Why

285

should she respect your judgment now?"

"I know. I know. Life has evened the score since I turned Gordon out of my house. I have been lashed to the quick with shame and humiliation by the weakness of my elder son. There is no need to remind me of my treatment of the younger."

"I'm sorry. I had to defend Connie. There has been no limit to her sweetness and tenderness to those she loves. What answer did she make to you this morning?"

"When I referred to the estate which sometime would be hers she asked why one person should want thirty thousand acres and a great ark of a house. Ark! Trentmere Towers which her family has owned for centuries!"

"Hers is the point of view of many of the modern young people, Lord Van. Unless they belong in the upper millionaire brackets, and often when they do, they do not want great estates, do not want the care and expense of them. They do want a charming house and garden, not too large, superb educational advantages for their children and if they can afford it, two saddle horses in the stable, two automobiles in the garage and as few servants as possible."

"How do you feel about the care of a large estate?"

"I? I'm not modern. I like the formalities of life, the pomp and circumstances. What else did Connie say that ruffled you?"

"Ruffled! By Jove, it was more than a 'ruffle.' When I spoke of her marriage to Ivor she declared that it was out of the question, 'definitely out,' said something about Lady Hanford's presence at his house yesterday. She intimated that she is in love with a man at home."

"Connie in love with a man at home!" Angela Corey's heartbeat quickened. Could she have meant Peter? Was it possible?

"Also she said I had handed down to her a beastly temper. Have I a beastly temper, Angel?"

Troubled as she was at this news of Connie, why hadn't the child come home to her after the battle with her grandfather? Angela Corey had difficulty in controlling a smile at the wistful question.

"I would hardly call you a sunny person. You see, you belong to the vast, vanishing race of domestic overlords. The modern girl and woman isn't overlord-minded."

" 'Vanishing race'! By Jove, you make me out a fossil. Do I seem so old to you? I'm only sixty-eight."

She met his eyes, so like those of a hurt boy, squarely.

"And look not more than fifty-eight, Lord Van," she replied in an honest attempt to comfort him. Being sorry for what one has done, even if one richly deserves to be drenched in remorse, hurt terrifically, as she knew from experience.

"You have come to the wrong person if you expect me to change Connie's mind about Captain Hardwick," she declared. "He is not a fit husband for my lovely girl and I warn you I shall do everything I can to prevent her from even considering marrying him."

"Ivor will settle down once he's married. He has lived the life of a single man —"

"But, all single men have *not* lived the life of Ivor," Angela Corey cut in crisply.

"Quite so. Quite so. 'Overlord,' fossil, that you think me, no woman has touched my life in any way since my wife died. You may put that down on the credit side of my character, if there is a credit side for me in your book."

Something in his voice warned her of deep water ahead. She scrambled for land.

"Where did Connie go after she left Trentmere Towers?" she asked with a hint of breathlessness.

The twinkle in his blue eyes as they met hers increased her sense of danger.

"In the language of your son, Timothy, something tells me I got that confidence across. I am asking you to marry me. Don't forget that you have assured me that you like the formalities of life, the pomp and circumstance." He held up his hand as her lips opened impulsively. "Don't answer now. Think it over. I don't know where Constance went," he went on as calmly as if he had not taken her breath away. "She said she had a date and shot off in the roadster with that fighting dog of hers squatting beside her like a bodyguard."

"A date. That's curious. I didn't know it. She usually talks over the day's engagements with me at breakfast. I wish she wasn't out in this fog. Perhaps she has gone off alone to work out her problem. I have been thinking lately that it might be easier for her to make up her mind if we Coreys were not here."

"Not here! By Jove, Angel, what bally nonsense you —"

"Not so loud, Lord Van. Here come Lady Hanford and Tim in her roadster."

"Why do you allow that adventuress to come here? You know I don't like her? What does the boy mean by hanging round an older woman like her?"

"I don't know. I can't understand him,

but I am trying hard, desperately hard, to practice the advice I gave you about Connie, not to ask questions. Here they come. Please be nice."

He made a courtly bow and smiled.

"I won't eat her, if that's what you're afraid of. She'd be tough, that woman, frightfully tough. Remember, I am yours to command, Madam."

His tone sent a faint flush to her face. She rose to welcome her son and his guest. Lady Hanford held out both hands in greeting while Tim, with an air of devotion which made his mother wince, removed the short cape of her white sports suit.

"How charming to find you here, Lord Van," she exclaimed gaily. "Really, my dear Mrs. Corey, we were almost lost. If Tim hadn't an uncommonly keen sense of direction, we would have been in London at this moment instead of nice and warm in front of the fire here. I can't remember ever before having been caught in such a quick, dense, short fog. This year has broken all records for freak weather. The sun is coming through now. Perfection, I'm perishing for my tea."

Perfection! Was that what she called Tim? Angela Corey's heart was heavy as she seated herself at the table. Lady Hanford's voice had caressed and flattered. Could he resist the lure of a woman who knew the world from A to Z? If she fascinated a sophisticate like Ivor Hardwick, what chance had a boy like Tim?

"Where's Con, Mother?"

"I don't know. I wish I did. Perhaps she is waiting somewhere for the fog to lift."

"Where's the fire, Maggie?" Tim asked as the little maid flew into the room. Her usually pink cheeks were white.

"Oh, Marm! Your lordship! Mr. Tim. There isn't a fire. One of you please come to the telephone. Someone's a sayin' Miss Connie's in a 'orspital an' — an' —" she choked on a sob.

"Tim! The phone! Quick!" Angela Corey's voice was harsh with apprehension. Water overran the cup she was filling as her son dashed from the room followed by Lady Hanford and the sobbing maid.

Lord Gowan took the kettle from her hand. "Sit down, Angel, you are shaking."

"I'm quite all right now, really I am. Just for an instant the room whirled. I can't sit down. I must get to my lovely girl. Tim, what did he say? Where is she?"

Her son put his arm about her. Back to the fire, Lord Gowan made a sound like the growl of a wounded grizzly and glared as if about to charge an enemy. At the window Lady Hanford looked out upon a shining world.

"Steady, Mother," Tim comforted. "A man phoned for us to come to the hospital at Folkestone, that Miss Constance Trent had met with a serious accident and was asking for you."

"I'll go at once. Connie hurt and alone. She, who is always so tender with anyone in trouble, always the first to help. I can't bear the thought. Bring round a car, Tim."

"Not so fast," Lord Gowan interposed. "We must know where we're going? Which hospital, Timothy?"

"Before I could ask he had rung off. Is there more than one in Folkestone?"

"There are six. Put through a call to Police Headquarters there. Quick. Use this desk phone. I'll talk when you get the connection."

"Why waste time, Lord Van? Why not start at once?" Angela Corey protested feverishly.

"We'll gain time if we know where to go. Change into something warmer. It won't take long to get the report. We can start at once if you are ready."

"I'll go up with you, Mrs. Corey, perhaps I can help," Lady Hanford offered. Even

292

Tim's lips were colorless as he held the receiver to one ear. "What could Con have been doing in Folkestone, of all places, Lord Van?" he asked. "If only we knew where to page Peter. I've been so taken up with — with business of my own that I haven't kept an eye on her as I promised. He'll go berserk if anything happens to — Yes — Yes — Here you are, sir."

Lord Gowan seized the phone.

"Folkestone? Head Inspector? This is Trent-Gowan of Trentmere Towers speaking. Have just received word that my grand-daughter, Constance Trent, has been seriously injured and is in hospital at Folkestone. The party didn't say which one. Locate her. Work fast. I'll wait here. Report to Cherrytree Farm. Yes. Quite so. That's the call."

Tim who had been pacing the floor stopped beside the desk.

"Doesn't it strike you as strange that a person summoning a seriously injured girl's family didn't mention the name of the hospital where she was to be found?"

"It's so strange, my boy, that I won't permit myself to *think* of what it may mean, of what may have happened to my son's daughter, until I get that report. If only your brother Peter were here. Dealing with criminals is not in my line."

The clock ticked away the seconds. Lord Gowan paced the floor. Stopped at the table and prepared a cup of tea. Once he went to the foot of the stairs and listened. Outside the mullioned windows the flowers in the garden were turned blood-red by the slanting sun. He seized the telephone in answer to an imperious ring. With military carriage he walked back and forth as he listened and talked.

"Quite so. Quite so. Contacted every hospital? All relief stations? No one by that name reported? Set your best man to tracing the call to Cherrytree Farm about an accident. What time?" He glanced at the old clock. "Under five minutes before I first called you. Report here."

He cradled the telephone. His face was chalky.

"I was sure of it. That hospital call was a hoax. Where is she? Where can she be?"

"Soft pedal, Lord Van. Here comes Mother," Tim warned.

Angela Corey was breathless as she ran into the room with an envelope in her hand. Her black frock and turban accentuated her pallor. Lady Hanford flitted after her like a white wraith.

"After I changed I went into Connie's room to see if I could find a clue to her pres-

294

ence in Folkestone on her engagement pad and I found this addressed to me," she explained breathlessly. "I flew down here with it. Read it. Quick. I couldn't. She hasn't — But, why should she? I —" her voice broke.

Tim pushed her gently into a chair and took the note from her hand.

"Steady, Mother, steady. Con is too level-headed to do anything crazy. If she is in a jam she has plenty of what it takes. Sit there, please, while I read it. Lady Hanford, you'd better sit down too." He pulled the folded sheet of paper from the envelope and read:

"Dear Angel,

This is to let you know where to look for me if I'm not back by dark. (Sounds like an old-time mellerdramer, doesn't it?) I was informed, no matter how, that in a stone cottage with a blue door on Stag Lane in the village of Parsley which is thirty miles beyond the bounds of the Trent-Gowan estate, I would learn something about my mother. Don't want to bother Peter. He seems to have a lot on his mind, so after luncheon with the General I'm off by my lonesome. Not quite, I'm taking Whiskers for company.

Perhaps I'm crazy, but I'm going.

Connie."

"Crazy!" Tim exploded. "I'll say she's crazy. If she had only told me!"

"Parsley! Thirty miles away. Why are we standing here? She has been kidnaped. That phone call was a blind. If only Peter were here!"

"He is, Mother." Peter Carey reassured from the threshold. Except for his wet hair he looked in his blue serge as if he were dressed for town.

"Peter! Peter! It's Connie. Something has happened to her."

"She's safe." He put his arm about his mother. "I saw her not more than an hour ago. She probably waited for the fog to lift. The sun makes short work of it this time of year, I'm told. I pushed through across inland roads."

"Safe! Then what did the man mean who phoned she was terribly injured? Was in hospital at Folkestone?"

"Injured! Folkestone!" Peter Corey's face was livid.

"She started for home in the roadster. She left me to start. I sent a Scotland Yard man after her, but she had disappeared. Who phoned?"

"We don't know, Corey. The call was a hoax. She is not in Folkestone."

"Then you think — ? Kidnaped?" he

296

hardly breathed the word. Lord Gowan nodded. Peter caught Tim by the shoulder.

"Why are we standing here when Con is in danger? Come on, kid, we'll turn this island inside out but we'll bring her back safe and —"

He wheeled at the sound of a slowly opening door.

XXI

No answer to that faint "Halloo!" No sound but the oily lap of the tide. The world was blanketed in silence. Eyes wide, breath suspended, Con peered in the direction in which she had seen the lights. Where could she hide if she saw a man approaching? The fog was denser than before. She strained her ears to listen. Muffled voices. Scrunch of pebbles. Splash of oars. Was the boat leaving?

She sat tense and breathless as the sound dwindled into silence. Came the muffled put-put of a motorboat, fainter and fainter till the dense gray world settled back into its uncanny stillness. Whoever had shouted had gone. He would not wait for "George." She was safe.

The stiffness went out of her. A rag doll had nothing on her for limpness, she told herself. That boat had come to meet the man and woman who had planned to hold her for ransom. If Peter hadn't dropped down the chimney doubtless she would be put-put-ing away in it this minute. To counteract her shivery chill at the possibility she confided:

"They'll have to go some to meet up with 'George' and his girl friend, Viola. Doubtless they are being personally conducted toward London. Is that her real name, Whiskers? Is she my mother? Peter will find out the truth of her claim when I tell him what she told me. If only I had gone straight to him with that first note. I didn't. But, the next time, young fella, I won't be such an idiot. Believe me or not I've had a warning to Stop! Look! Listen! which will last the rest of my life. See that faint red light? Has the boat come back?"

She leaned forward. Held her breath. Suppose the boatmen had learned by radio that she was on this road? What would she do? Where would she go? The light was growing! Too big for a flare. Could it be the sun?

"It is the sun, Whiskers! It is! The wind has changed! It's blowing my hair! Dirty as you are I must hug you." The terrier yelped a protest. "Sorry old dear, I'm fairly jittery with relief, I've just got to hug someone. I have felt like Robinson Crusoe on a desert isle with you for my man Friday. You're soaking wet, I would think you'd like to be hugged. The fog is lifting! Understand?"

The dog threw back his head and answered with a prolonged howl.

One moment she had been imprisoned by an impenetrable gray wall and then, almost in the drawing of a breath, the heavy mist crept back slowly, almost apologetically, as if sorry it had to go out to sea and leave behind it blue sky and the green slopes of hills and gleaming cliffs. The sun and shadow of late afternoon swept victoriously over the country changing color values as it passed.

As the fog drew back its vaporous curtains something happened in Con's mind. It was as if in their slow retreat they drew away veils of mist which had hung between her and Peter and she knew all at once why he had been the dearest person in the world to her, knew why his caressing "darling" kept echoing in her memory no matter how hard she tried to silence it. She loved him.

Why hadn't she known before? She was grown up, wasn't she? Hadn't a number of men proposed to her? Peter and Tim had been really like brothers, she had never thought of them otherwise. That was why. A girl didn't fall in love with her brother, did she? Curious, this sudden change from warm, sisterly affection to something which throbbed and clamored as if her pulses had broken loose and were running wild through her body. What had brought it about? That revolver leveled at him? Terror for his safety? She loved Peter. Her pulses stilled. That realization brought a problem to be reckoned with, perhaps to fear. He didn't love her.

Why was she waiting? She shook off the rug and started the engine. The car bumped back over the rough ground to the road. The terrier crawled out of her lap, sat up, sniffed the air and yawned.

"If he doesn't love me, Whiskers, I'll stay in England," she confided. "Now that I know how much I care for him I couldn't bear it to go back to Red Maples and see him married to someone else. Fate steps in sometimes and settles problems for one, doesn't it?"

She turned her heart-shaking discovery over and over in her mind as she drove on. What would she do when she saw Peter? He must not suspect that she loved him.

Angel must not know. Tim mustn't know. She had lived long enough to be able to disguise her feelings, hadn't she?

Had she? The question recurred as she slowly opened the hall door at Cherrytree Farm and saw Peter standing as if turned to stone staring at her. Why was his face white, why were the others behind him in the

301

lounge looking as if they couldn't believe their eyes? He caught her hands and drew her forward.

"Here she is! Con! Con! Where have you been?" he demanded hoarsely.

They surged toward her. She smiled at her grandfather. She had forgotten that his face was so deeply lined, pressed her lips to Angela Corey's white cheek, made a saucy face at Tim, nodded to Lady Hanford and laughed.

"Why all the excitement? I waited for the fog to lift. How did you get here so soon and so clean, Peter? Why are you all looking at me as if I had returned from another world?"

"Heavenly day! Why shouldn't we stare at you when we thought —"

Peter's lifted hand checked Tim's unsteady outburst. He said quickly:

"I was motored across country at a speed which took my breath, the fog meant nothing in the life of that driver, sneaked in the back way, removed the chimney soot and beat you to it."

"Connie, dear! You and Peter have been together? What does it all mean?" Angela Corey demanded and laid her hand on the girl's arm.

"Don't touch me, Angel, I'm wet to the

302

skin. Look at Whiskers. He insisted upon digging for a mole on our way from the garage. As if his previous excursion hadn't made him dirty enough. His nose and paws are black with mud. Was that a gasp or a sniff, Tim? I could do with a cup of hot tea before I change."

She shook her head as Peter pushed forward a chair. Better not look at him yet, she decided. His voice had set her pulses racing. She felt gay, riotously happy. Just to be near him set her heart singing. What did that woman in Stag Lane matter? What did anything matter? She loved Peter.

"Constance!" Lord Gowan said gruffly. "Constance. Someone —"

His voice broke. Tim stopped feeding the wet terrier with tantalizing bits of cake.

"Shall I tell her now, Pete?" As his brother nodded he went on. "Someone phoned that you were hurt, that you were in —"

Con lost the rest of the sentence. The light in her heart went out like a candle flame in a cold wind. She was back at the stone cottage defying the villainous man and the woman who claimed to be her mother. Evidently a confederate had telephoned that she was injured to cover up her disappearance at first. They had planned to keep her prisoner on the boat which had come to the cliff. The realization made her so faint that she swayed.

"Give Con her tea, Tim," Peter commanded. "Be quick about it. All right and safe now, darling. We all need tea, Mother," he suggested to divert attention from her, Con knew. She wasn't faint any longer, the tenderness of his voice had rallied her slipping senses. She laughed shakily.

"I'm steady as a rock now, Peter. While I was curled up on the seat of the roadster, chilled to the bone, waiting for the fog to lift, I pictured this room, Angel behind the tea table, the nice warm fire. I could smell the tea and toast and roses. I pretended I was nibbling plum cake rich and dark and fruity. You weren't in the picture, General, but Tim was and so was Lady Hanford sitting in the low chair she likes, only her hair didn't look so golden as it does now in the fire light and I didn't picture her in white, she so often wears black."

"That foolish boy, Timothy, insists that I wear white, don't you, Perfection?"

Tim's face reddened to the color of well-baked brick as all eyes in the room turned toward him. As if to cover his embarrassment he broke off a large piece of cake and held it up.

"Want it, Whiskers?" Whiskers yelped

with eagerness. "Then get it!" He threw the cake directly into Lady Hanford's lap. The terrier jumped after it. She rose with a shriek of anger, slapped the dog's head, shrilled:

"Don't touch me, you dirty thing!"

Something snapped in Con's brain.

"Mother!" she breathed. *Mother!*

The shocked whisper cast a spell over the room, stripped a veil from Peter Corey's memory. Incredulously he regarded the woman and girl who stood as motionless and white as marble statues. Now that the blood and expression had drained from the two faces he could see that the bone formation was the same, there was the same thin modeling of the nose, there were the same planes of chin and forehead. He remembered the inexplicable sense of familiarity which had teased him the first time he spoke to Lady Hanford. It had been her likeness to the photograph of Gordon Trent's wife, of course.

He glanced at his brother whose eyes were burning coals of excitement in his flushed face. Had he thrown cake into the woman's lap and sent the dirty dog after it in the hope of bringing forth the exclamation which was the only memory Con had of her mother? It was a long chance but, boy, it had worked.

Had Tim's devotion to Lady Hanford been based on the suspicion that she was the missing wife whom they had been trying to trace for years?

Con's eyes were the eyes of a somnambulist suddenly wakened to terror of her surroundings. Peter took a quick step toward her and the petrifying spell was shattered. Angela Corey released her breath with a shocked, "Impossible!" Lord Gowan cleared his throat with a force which brought a sympathetic yelp from the terrier. Tim choked down a sob of excitement. The girl brushed her hand across her eyes as if to clear them.

"You are my mother, aren't you?" she demanded.

The pallor of Lady Hanford's face changed to stone gray. She flexed stiff lips into the semblance of a contemptuous smile and stared at Con with cold eyes.

"Really, my dear Miss Trent, are you rehearsing for a play or trying to be funny? If you are, drop it. This situation is neither dramatic nor amusing."

"And to think that almost every week since I came to England I have seen and spoken to my own mother and haven't known her. It is a dramatic situation," Con attested brokenly as if the woman hadn't spoken.

306

"Are you sure you know now, Constance?" Lord Gowan asked gravely. "Remember that Clive Neale has proof of the death of the wife of my son Gordon."

"She isn't dead. She's standing there looking at me as she looked the first time I saw her in this room. She hates me now as she hated me when I was a child. Her voice and words as she slapped me then are seared into my memory and when she struck at the dog and shrilled the very protest she had shrilled at me, it tore my mind wide open. She may deny it till doomsday but I know she is the woman who deserted my father and me."

"It isn't true!" Lady Hanford countered furiously. "My car is outside. Perfection, take me home before the girl goes entirely crazy."

"She isn't crazy." Tim drew a card photograph from his breast pocket and passed it to his brother. "I knew, although she rarely spoke of her mother, that Con had the welfare of the missing parent on her mind. I had a hunch and followed it. I've split the deception wide open. You carry on. I'm through." There was a hint of buoyancy in his voice as if now that his task was accomplished he was inexpressibly relieved to be through with deception.

Peter looked from the tinted photograph to the face of the woman who was staring at Tim as if she doubted her ears. It was the same face if one allowed for the changes time and experiences had wrought in it and thanks to wealth and beauticians, except for red hair in place of blond, they were mighty few. Why didn't she admit the truth? What could she lose by acknowledging that she was the widow of Lord Gowan's son? Widow! Memory challenged with a promptness that chilled his blood. It was a split second before he could summon his voice.

"You are the crazy person, not Con," he asserted, "when you deny that you were Gordon Trent's wife, Lady Hanford. And what's more you were still his wife when he died five years ago."

"I warned you, Angel, that the woman was an adventuress," exploded Lord Gowan.

Angela Corey slipped one hand under his arm and patted his sleeve with the other. His voice moderated perceptibly as he added:

"By Jove, she hasn't the right to the titles or the fortunes of those two men she duped into marrying her, has she, Corey?"

"If you're quite through with your vicious insinuations —"

"I'm not insinuating, I'm stating facts."

"I'm going," Lady Hanford icily announced as if quite unaware of Lord Gowan's growl.

"Just a minute!" Peter caught her arm as she reached the threshold and swung her back into the room.

"Listen to me! No one here cares how many men have been fooled into leaving you their fortunes, that's a matter for the courts and legitimate heirs, but I want to know, and you won't leave this room until you tell me, how you are mixed up with the woman who claims to be Gordon Trent's widow and Con's mother."

"I say! What's that? What's that?" Lord Gowan demanded.

Lady Hanford ignored him.

"I haven't the slightest idea to whom you are referring, Mr. Corey. Is it possible that you *too* are a little mad?"

If the woman was lying she was making a mighty convincing job of it. As if she had read Peter's mind Con answered quickly:

"He is not mad. A woman insisted this afternoon that she had been my father's wife and when I told her we had the certificate of my mother's death, she said she had given her own name when a twin sister perished in a fire. I wondered then how she could speak so lightly of what must have been a tragic experience. She was lying. Perhaps you know something about that? Perhaps you are the twin sister?"

"I never had a sister. The woman probably was your father's wife. Changing names with a dead person has been done before. In fact, it's quite a threadbare trick," Lady Hanford added flippantly.

"Why are you afraid to acknowledge the truth?" Con's contemptuous demand set flames in the woman's eyes. "Afraid that I may expect something from you? Do you think I *want* it known that I am the daughter of a cheat? Before I came to England I tried to find you because I feared you might be in want, that because of that you might be driven to —" she choked on the word. "Now that I know you are rolling in wealth I hope and pray I may never see you again. Peter, I'll leave it to you and my General to get at the truth about that woman in Stag Lane. There is one bit of reality in this hideous nightmare. I can be sure now that I am Gordon Trent's child." Her teeth chattered on the last word.

"I'm freezing. Come with me, Angel. I must get off these wet clothes. We are dining with my *grandfather*, Major General Lord Vandemere Trent-Gowan, this evening, remember. Lady Coswell and her sister are to be guests. We must make ourselves gorgeous not only for them but to celebrate an event in my young life. I've just buried a mother whose fate has been haunting me for years, buried her so deep that she'll never trouble me again."

She laughed, blew a kiss to her grandfather, waved an unsteady hand to Peter and Tim.

"Courage, mes camarades," she rallied gaily, linked her arm in Angela Corey's and left the room.

XXII

Tim brushed a hand across his eyes as one brushes away tears. Peter twitched at the collar about his tight throat. Con's stricken eyes, her broken voice had hurt him intolerably. If only he could have saved her from this grueling experience.

"High of heart," Lord Gowan murmured as his glance rested on the doorway through which his granddaughter had passed. He polished his monocle as if the fate of the Empire depended on its transparency. His fierce eyes flashed to the woman.

"Tell the truth," he thundered. "If you don't, by Jove, I'll drag you before a magistrate and make you prove that you are not Gordon's widow, make you prove that the fortunes of the two men you tricked are legally yours. When I get through, you'll wish that you, not those men, had died. What have you to do with that lying creature in — what the devil's the name, Corey?"

"Stag Lane." Would the woman crack under Lord Gowan's broadside, Peter wondered. She looked small standing there with her short white skirt smooched with dirt from the terrier's paws, with the red of her hair, which accentuated the lined pallor of her face, shining below the brim of her white hat, with the diamonds of the bracelets she always wore glittering in the fire light. No, she wasn't the cracking kind. She tilted a defiant chin and nonchalantly tucked a curl back of her ear.

"Better come clean, Lady — Mrs. Trent," he advised.

As if weighing her chance at brazening out the situation she glanced from face to face of the three men intently regarding her. Common sense tipped the scales.

"Very well, I'll admit that I was Viola Trent if you two men — three, I forgot you, Perfection, you're such a cunning boy — will swear that you won't reveal what I tell you."

"You! Laying down conditions! You'll tell without a promise from either one of us," Lord Gowan declared furiously. "At the same time I'll remind you that I'm not eager to have the criminal dishonesty of my son's widow and my granddaughter's mother blazoned in headlines, broadcast from one side of the Atlantic to the other. Get on with your story. This is your last chance. In ten minutes I leave this room. As you may have heard, I am expecting guests for dinner."

A grand old man if a rather terrible old man, Peter thought, as he noted the glow in his eyes like light blazing through blue glass. The last two hours had deepened the lines responsibilities, sorrow and disillusionment already had etched in his fine face. The woman was regarding him defiantly, then, as if she could no longer endure the shriveling fire of his gaze turned to Peter. She shrugged.

"Lord Gowan is right. Neither he nor the Coreys want publicity. I'll take a chance on that fact. I did marry Gordon Trent. I didn't want a child. Children bore me. I did run away. I'll spare you my experiences with the world's worst liar. After he deserted me I got a chance in a chorus; I had been on the stage when I met Gordon. I was rooming with a girl in the same company when one morning at about three o'clock we were awakened by a scream, 'Oh, Lawdy! Fire!' We jumped from bed. Scrambled into our coats — we had no time to dress. From the window we could see flames and smoke coming from the basement of the six-story frame and brick building. My roommate flung up the sash. 'Jump!' she shrieked. 'Jump! We'll never get to the stairs!'

"I looked down at the crowd, at the engines, at the licking red tongues of fire." She closed her eyes and shuddered. "The girl leaped. I couldn't. I would take my chances on the stairs. Down. Down I went. Stumbling through smoke that stifled. Cringing through heat that scorched.

"I reached the second floor. Flames burst through. I climbed out of a window. Crept on hands and knees along a ledge for what seemed a thousand miles. I was seen. A ladder was run up. I was rescued unhurt, except for a deep burn on my forearm." She pushed up her bracelets and revealed a wrinkled white scar. "My roommate was lying on the sidewalk. Dead. I saw the circlet on her finger, my wedding ring with my name engraved inside. I had sold it to her. I didn't want it. She needed it.

"The gleam of that gold roused me from the stupor of fear and exhaustion. I had my chance to begin again. And this time I wouldn't blunder, I swore to myself. Nothing simpler than to give my name and age to the ambulance driver in place of that of the girl who had jumped, and I was free. Born again."

She shivered violently, pinched her ghastly cheeks till color flooded them.

"For the first time, and the last, I have

told of that flaming horror. It's like opening a tomb and letting out a specter. Will I ever crowd it back again?" By a supreme effort she steadied her voice to flippant lightness. "The manner of my change of name is all that the person who claims to be Gordon's wife and I have in common. It is such an old trick no wonder she, and whoever was scheming with her, thought of it."

"And after you had been born again?" Peter prodded for Lord Gowan who had tried to speak but whose voice had been but a growl of unbearable pain.

"I worked till I had money enough to get to France. I was a show girl in Paris when I met and married a baronet. I know what you are going to ask, Lord Van. I knew I wasn't divorced, but, Gordon Trent's wife had been reported dead, hadn't she? This was my chance for a step up. I stepped. He died and left me a fortune so securely settled on me that no court can upset it. I saw to that. Besides money I had a title and my beauty. I came to England and married a baron." She spread her hands in a gesture of accomplishment. "Now may I go?"

She really knew nothing of the woman in Stag Lane, Peter decided. The fake Mrs. Gordon Trent was a creation of Dafter and

— who else? "May the lady go now, Lord Gowan?" he asked.

"By Jove, the sooner she takes herself out of this room the better. How could my son, who had generations of lords and ladies behind him, and a long line of soldiers who had been decorated by their kings, who had died for them, marry this common person?"

"Common!" she flared. "*You* call me common and your granddaughter called me a cheat. You boast of the ancestors of your son. Now that we are on the subject, what about mine? Did you think I hadn't any? That I materialized out of the air?" Her low voice was harsh with fury. "One of mine was appointed governor of a colony in the new country by his English king; one of his descendants fought, starved, died as a Major at Valley Forge. My grandfather was a captain in the Army of the Potomac. So, you see, my daughter has soldiers who died for their country on her mother's side of the house as well as on her *distinguished* father's, my lord."

"Is this true or is it a lie like the story of your death?" Peter demanded. If it were true it would mean so much to Con, would help her bear the knowledge of her mother's dishonesty. "Can you prove this?"

"I can." Her voice attested her scorn of his

317

doubt. "It was a man of your profession, Peter Corey, who convinced my father that a huge fortune was awaiting him in the Bank of England if he could prove his descent from that Colonial governor. He spent every dollar we had proving that he was the rightful heir to that money, fighting in the courts for it, only to discover that there was no fortune, that all he had was his authenticated family tree and a sheaf of receipted bills paid to a crook lawyer. We were desperately poor. I met Gordon Trent. I married him as a way out of poverty. He was a gentleman. That was all I knew about him. Except for my father gentlemen hadn't been so numerous in my life that I could pass him by."

"Married and deserted him at the first opportunity."

"And who are you, Lord Gowan, to talk about desertion? He spoke of an English home, said he had no family. I know now what that 'no family' meant. You had turned him out. Do you think had I known who he was I would have left him because I was offered more money and easy living? Not I. I would have battered at your door till you took us in, until you had established us at Trentmere Towers. I didn't know who he was until the papers published his death with a discreet reference to his quarrel with his father, and announced that in the event of the death of the remaining son, Ernest, title and estate would pass to Captain Ivor Hardwick. Gordon's child was not mentioned. I presumed she had died."

"By Jove, that was five years ago. Five years ago Hanford bought the Manor and already you had lived with him as his wife two years! You began to scheme then to marry Ivor, didn't you?"

"Dear Lord Van, you must be a mind reader. Having met your elder son I was sure he would not outlive you. Lord Hanford was a sick old man, almost as old as you, my lord, not quite. If I were established in the neighborhood, well, it was a gamble but I am not unattractive, it would be a bit of dramatic justice if the title I had missed should in time come to me. Then a few months ago your granddaughter was discovered. Too late for me to claim my social position as her mother. If a suspicion of the truth leaked out I would lose Lord Hanford's fortune. I had burned my bridges. Viola Trent was dead."

"In all these years have you felt no desire to see Con?" Peter demanded.

"Don't be quaint. Why should I desire to see a child for whom I cared so little that I left her? Did you expect me to clasp her to my heart, cinema style? I swore I would climb. I have. If you men pull me down you know who will go with me. You wouldn't care to have that happen to *her*. *I* can see by your faces that you wouldn't."

"I want a copy of your family tree."

"Really, my dear Peter, for a reputedly brilliant advocate, you are very stupid. Those papers vanished with Viola Trent."

"Give me the names of that Colonial governor and the Valley Forge major or that same Viola Trent will be neatly, speedily and *permanently* exhumed."

The woman's defiant eyes shifted from the steel of his. In a low voice, as if fearful the walls might echo them, she gave the names.

"Now, may I go? I too, have a dinner date," she added flippantly. Halfway to the door she stopped.

"Oh, just a moment. I forgot something." She smiled brazenly at the man scowling at her from under shaggy gray brows.

"Captain Hardwick owes me a large sum of money, a rather colossal sum, Lord Van. If you want him as a husband for your granddaughter, pay it. If you don't, I will take him and his title-apparent off your hands in settlement. *Au revoir*. I *hope* it is not good-by, my lord."

Tim followed her to open the hall door.

"*Toujours la politesse,* Perfection." Her sneering voice was heard clearly by the two men in the lounge. "So, all this time you have been a spy. Operator No. 1. Take that!"

Tim's cheek was a violent red when he returned to the lounge. He admitted:

"I guess I rated that slap. I have parked on Lady Hanford's trail since the afternoon when in this very room she looked up at me and drawled, 'Nice boy.' She made me feel all kinds of a fool, but something in the way she tilted her head, in the shape of her nose, reminded me of Con. In a flash I saw as plainly as I am seeing you, the photograph of Gordon Trent's wife. It was so uncanny it took the starch from my knees for a minute, I had to sit down. Heavenly day! You don't suppose I'm going psychic, do you, Pete?"

His expression was so terrified that in spite of having been mentally and spiritually battered and bruised by Lady Hanford's revelations, Peter laughed.

"No, kid. Though I do believe that when you and I have those hunches some Power speaks to us through our imaginations. What brought about the climax this afternoon?"

"I've been working up to it. Told Lady Hanford I wished she would wear white

321

when she went out with me. I figured that if in some way I could get her to say the only words of her mother's Con remembered, it might crack open the girl's memory. When Con came in with that filthy dog this afternoon I figured my chance had come. It worked."

"I'll say it worked. 'You're a better man than I am, Gunga Din.' "

"I don't feel so good, I feel like a heel, pretending that I liked the woman when all the time I was waiting for a chance to show her up. My only excuse to myself was that I was doing it to ease Con's mind and that Lady Hanford was playing me for a sucker to make Captain Hardwick jealous. Did you notice that her voice lost its English accent and cadence when she told the story of the fire? You're satisfied that she is your son's widow, aren't you, Lord Van?"

"Yes," Lord Gowan answered gruffly.

Peter glanced at Tim. He replied with an understanding nod before he spoke to the terrier who in a sprawl of exhaustion had been twitching and snoring in front of the fire.

"Come along, Whiskers. You're not fit for polite society. I'll hand you over to the groom for a bath. How could he get so filthy motoring with Slim, Pete?"

"He must have deserted her when her car passed an old tower and he sensed that I was there. I'd been asleep hours. If he hadn't awakened me, I don't know what terrible thing would have happened to Con."

"Nothing happened, she's safe, Pete, don't look so ghastly. You were asleep in a tower? Weren't you in London last night? Someone phoned that you would be detained in the Big Town on business and wouldn't be back here until today. Who was it?"

So, that was the way his absence from home was to be accounted for, Peter reflected. He put his hand to the back of his head where a lump still loomed. He answered his brother's startled query.

"Must have been the same super-interested party who phoned that Con had been seriously injured. I'll tell you later. Meanwhile how about removing that much-in-need-of-a-bath Whiskers? There were long-dead fish and thousands of live gulls in that tower."

Lord Gowan roused from deep abstraction. "Sometime, Corey, I want to hear what happened to Constance, to you, this afternoon, but not now. I'm tortured with regret. I am sick with disgust. I have seen all types of bad men but never a woman so cruel and brazen as she who has just left this room. How could my son have married her?"

"Probably she had charm and beauty, then, maybe something like Con's, Lord Van. Perhaps she appealed to his pity. She said she was very poor."

"Perhaps, Corey. He was always championing the weak. I'm going."

"I'll drive you home, Lord Van."

"Thanks, no, Timothy. I will walk. I have much to think of. I can think better walking." He turned on the threshold. Declared furiously:

"I'll be damned if I'll buy Ivor from that woman!"

XXIII

Con leaned against the closed door of her chintz-hung room. The room she loved.

"I — I c-can't s-stop s-shaking, A-Angel." She shivered violently.

Angela Corey put her arm around her shoulders.

"I know, dearest, I know. You have had a tremendous shock. Get those wet clothes off, quickly. After a hot bath and a cup of tea — you didn't have your tea downstairs — you'll be your gallant self again. You are my child, as you have been for the last ten years, remember, my beloved daughter."

She pulled the old bell rope, gave an order to the maid who answered, helped Con remove her drenched clothing, drew a bath. She lighted a fire and pulled a small table and a deep chair before it. It was a relief, to be busy. Her nerves were still twanging from the shock of that telephoned message that Connie had been seriously injured.

Later in a rose-color house coat by the fire Con pretended to drink her tea. She smiled at Angela Corey in a low chair opposite.

"Relax, Angel, relax. I'm steady now. My world has turned right side up again. That last true-story episode coming on top of the nightmare of the afternoon g-got me," she shuddered.

"Better not talk about it now, dearest. Wait until tomorrow."

" 'Never put off until tomorrow what can be done today.' Haven't you drilled that precept into your family, Angel?" The attempt at gaiety drew hot tears to Angela Corey's eyes. "I must talk. Not about what happened downstairs, I never want to think of that again, but of the nightmare. Telling you will help conquer the shivers. If I don't beat them they'll g-get m-me."

"Then tell me, dear. I want to know what happened. I was thinking only of you when I asked you to postpone it."

"The quicker I get the thing out of my mind the quicker I'll bury it deep in the past. I received a note by post which offered news of my mother."

Hurriedly, breathlessly, she told of her decision to follow it up, of her determination not to trouble Peter or let Tim know about it, of her distrust of the man who opened the door of the house in Stag Lane, of the woman who had the data of the marriage of

Gordon Trent and the tragic circumstances of his wife's death at her tongue's end; of her declaration that while Gordon Trent was her husband he was not the father of the girl known as the granddaughter of Lord Gowan.

"But, my dearest, how could you believe that lie?" Angela Corey demanded.

"Deep inside me I didn't and yet she was so like the photograph of my mother grown older I almost had to believe her."

"What photograph? When did you see a picture of your mother?"

Con caught her breath. Almost she had betrayed Ivor's confidence. He had insisted that no one was to know about the photograph he had found among his father's papers. He had been fooled as well as she. She must give him a chance to find out who was behind the deception.

"I saw one, once." She answered Angela Corey's question and hurriedly began to tell of the man's demand for ransom, of his threat to keep her on a boat and of the arrival of Peter in a cloud of soot.

"Peter! Down a chimney?"

"Yes. He was after Dafter and Dafter was after me. Wouldn't you think that gangster would know better than to touch a member of man-eating Corey's family?"

A knock. Peter's voice.

"Con! Are you all right? May I come in?"

She crossed to the door.

"Of course I'm all right, Peter. Quite recovered from my attack of jitters. I'm dressing. I'll be seeing you."

She turned to Angela Corey.

"I — I just couldn't talk with him now." She steadied her shaken voice. "I've been putting on the rescued-damsel act long enough, Angel. It's getting late. Time you and I were making ourselves gorgeous for the General's dinner and when I say gorgeous, I mean gorgeous."

An hour later Peter Corey knocked at his mother's door. As he entered the room she was seated before a mirror clasping a necklace. There was a luscious pink rose at the point of the delicate white fichu which framed her shoulders above the black bodice of her frock. There were broad bands of the same frosty lace on the black skirt which spread like an old-time crinoline. Her mirrored eyes smiled into his as he stood behind her.

"I like you in a white tie, Peter."

"Pretty grand yourself, aren't you? You look as if you'd stepped from a Winterhalter painting. Why the family jewels?"

She rose and faced him. "Connie said 'be

328

gorgeous,' so I've put on my diamonds. Their sparkle lifts my spirit and they always delight her. The child needs all the help we can give her tonight, Peter. Her heart is burning with shame and humiliation. It would have been better had she never discovered that Lady Hanford is her mother. You are convinced that she was Gordon Trent's wife, aren't you?"

"Yes."

Briefly he retold the story of the fire, of the father's fight for a fortune as the woman had told it.

"Do you believe it, Peter? About her ancestors, I mean?"

"Why not? Plenty of persons who have been dragged down by poverty have come from fine families. However, I shall not tell Con until I have checked up on the story. I am glad she knows that Lady Hanford is her mother. Certainty is better than uncertainty for her. If only I could tell her now that I love her. It wouldn't be fair yet, would it? I'm right, am I not, Mother?"

"I am sure you are, my dear. Connie is too valiant to let what she learned today get her down. She wouldn't have broken as she did if the shock had not come on top of the terrifying experience of the afternoon. Do you know what happened?"

"No. I haven't had a chance to find out. Do you?"

She told him all that Con had told her.

"So that was what she meant when she said in the lounge that she could be sure she was Gordon Trent's child. She said the woman was like a photograph of her mother? I didn't know she ever had seen one. Did she mention Captain Hardwick?" he asked abruptly.

"No. I asked her why she had not taken the note to you or Tim. She said she didn't want to trouble you, that she had decided to follow it up and admitted that she knew neither of you boys would approve. The crazy child. Suppose you hadn't arrived."

"But I did arrive. You can imagine my horror when I saw her in that room with Dafter, the racketeer, blackmailer and gangster who has been hunted for years. Well, we have him. Three days from now I will be personally conducting him back to the U.S.A."

"Going home, Peter? Shortening your vacation? Leaving Con?"

"Yes. It will be better for her if I take myself out of her life for a while. Perhaps she will discover that she loves me. Then again, perhaps she won't."

With long slim fingers his mother adjusted the red carnation in the lapel of his evening coat.

"I think you are right, about going, I mean. I think, also, that it would be wise if the other members of the Corey family left with you."

"Now? When Con's heart is so torn up about the discovery of her mother? What's the idea?"

"Tim came here before he dressed. He was troubled by his deception in regard to Lady Hanford and wanted me to reassure him. I did. I was so relieved to find that he wasn't in love with the woman that I cried. It was a short, sharp cloudburst, the culmination of the excitement of all that had gone before. He said he was feeling fit and was keen to get home and back to work. He wants to study this summer to make up lost time."

"What do you think of that?"

"I approve of it, heartily. Do you remember the day this all began, our English adventure, I mean? There must have been a conjunction of the planets which influence the Coreys. Life was flowing along smoothly, when presto, Lydia broke your engagement, Clive Neale appeared to claim Connie for her grandfather. It was as if a river had been suddenly dammed and forced into new and increasingly turbulent channels.

"These last few days I've been doing some intensive thinking. I have concluded that if we leave Connie it will be much easier for her to decide whether she will become an English subject or return to the United States. We go suddenly and there will be no long-drawn out parting. If Lord Van were opening the townhouse for the London season I would feel that I should remain with her; as he is not, the sooner we leave, the sooner she will settle down."

"There's a lot in what you say. Are you sure you want to go?"

"Very sure. Lord Van has asked me to marry him."

"Don't tell me you were surprised. I've seen it coming. Do you want to marry him?"

"I don't know. I want to go home and think it over, get a perspective that I can't get here. I enjoy his companionship, and the companionship of a fine man means a lot as one grows older, Peter. No one but a woman who has lost a tender, devoted husband can know that feeling of utter desolation when she realizes that her man will not be coming home to her at the end of the day." She steadied her lips.

"I think I could make Lord Van happy, he hasn't had much happiness in his life, largely his own fault probably. I like what he stands for. I think he's a grand person. I like the baronial splendor of Trentmere Towers, the tenantry, the tradition, but, your father is still very real to me."

"He always put your happiness first, Mother. With your intelligence and tact and charm you would be a perfect lady of the manor. Have you told Con?"

"No. I don't intend to. It might influence her decision. Lord Van intimated that Connie had told him she was in love with a man at home."

"A man at home —"

"Come in," Angela Corey called in answer to a knock. Tim pushed open the door. Con whirled into the room. Silver sequins glittered at the hips of her bouffant camelia-pink frock, drifts of tulle floated about her, there was a pink rose in her dark hair. Her glowing eyes smiled above an open silver-sequined fan.

"Like me, Angel? Think I'll top the alluring Lydia? Peter!" she stopped whirling. "I didn't know you were here!"

Her beauty and charm set Peter's heart racing. Was he quite demented to leave her without telling her he loved her? Suppose he told her tonight what she meant to him? Why was he dallying with the temptation?

Hadn't he any strength of purpose? Angel and he had agreed that she must not be influenced by them in her decision; only a moment ago his mother had re-affirmed that opinion. He had practically promised Lord Gowan they would remain neutral.

"Why are we waiting?" Con's voice broke into his troubled thoughts. "His lordship will order 'Heads off!' if we are a minute late for dinner, and believe it or not, I love my head."

"Don't we all?" Peter cleared his husky voice. "Where's your wrap, Con?"

"Maggie took it downstairs."

Later as he held the short white ermine jacket for her he asked:

"Why didn't you come to me with that note? You told me once that you would always trust me, didn't you?"

"I do trust you, Petey. I do, but you were busy, and — and, oh, I went Little Jack Horner. Wanted to put in my thumb, pull out the plum of discovery and crow, 'What a big girl, am I.' "

"You sweet soul!"

"Don't speak to me in that voice, Peter, it will burst my control to smithereens. Tears are simmering behind my eyes ready to boil over if anyone is kind to me and my throat is full of sobs."

"Then I'll turn cave man." He gave her a little shake. "Snap out of it, woman. I could eat raw meat I'm so hungry. I haven't eaten since I dined with Neale last night."

"Then you weren't with Lydia?"

"Lydia! I should say not. I was otherwise engaged. Sometime I'll tell you about it. Come on. Your carriage waits, my lady."

XXIV

Peter Corey glanced around the Tower room. The lighted Rembrandts, the rich faded hangings, the stag's head and racks of guns, the shelves of worn books, the folding screen of Spanish leather, were as he remembered them on that night not so long ago when he had pulled Farmer Chettle and later the imperturbable Captain from hiding. Had that evening set in motion a current of events which had ended in a smashing climax this afternoon?

He hadn't a shadow of proof but he was sure that Hardwick had been behind the scheme to get Con to Stag Lane, had given her the photograph of her alleged mother. Otherwise why had he had Dafter, Tod Sacks, in his house as a servant? Perhaps that scene in the lounge at Cherrytree Farm wasn't the climax, perhaps life was sweeping on to more surprises. With the explanation that he couldn't enjoy his after-dinner smoke anywhere but in the Tower room, Lord Gowan had linked his arm in Peter's as the men left the dinner table.

"Ivor, you and Timothy join the ladies in the hall. Corey and I will return for a game of quintract. I have business to talk over with him."

Peter had noted the furtive expression in Ivor Hardwick's eyes as Lord Gowan spoke. Was he apprehensive of what that "business" might be? Seated between Lydia and Con at dinner he had been unusually silent, his skin had been the color of old wax. Con had talked to him earnestly. Had she given him the details of the happenings in Stag Lane? Why should she? She didn't know of his connection with Dafter. She liked him. Her heart had been hurt enough today with the discovery of her mother's dishonesty. No reason why she need ever know, unless she decided to marry him; in that case, he himself would break the story wide open.

"By Jove, you look as fierce as if you were about to harangue a jury, Corey."

Lord Gowan spoke from his chair in front of the fire. He forcefully cleared his throat. Roustabout, the bulldog, who had been dozing, rose to squat beside his master's chair. Head tipped, fat face wrinkled and furrowed with loose rolls of skin, he looked up at Peter as if asking, "What now?" A question he was asking himself. What was

337

the business he had been brought here to discuss? Was he to be asked to tell the story of Con's near escape from tragedy this afternoon or was he to be questioned about Hardwick? If the last, he had nothing to say — at present.

"Corey, you like this country, don't you? Great Britain, I mean?"

Peter drew a sigh of relief. This was a question he could answer with enthusiasm.

"I do, sir. In between what may have appeared to be a ceaseless round of festivities I have studied British methods. I have a tremendous respect for them and for the commonsense and absence of hysteria which greets any pronouncement of the government. Last week I heard a discussion in the House of Commons on the proposal for financial assistance to utilities in connection with air-raid precautions."

"By Jove, what a comment on our so-called civilization that air-raid precautions are necessary. What else do you like about us, Corey?"

"Your police." Peter laughed. "I would like to take a bunch of them home. I have been impressed by their unfailing courtesy toward the driving public."

"Quite so. Quite so. They are trained at Hendon to acquire advanced technique in driving. They are good. Well, you like us. That's a step in the right direction." He leaned a little forward.

"Corey, you know that I want my grand-daughter to carry on at Trentmere Towers after me. I had hoped that she and Ivor would marry and unite title and estate. That is out of the question after what that terrible woman told us today. You love Constance. Will you marry her?"

Would he marry Con? Exultation shot Peter's heart to his throat. As if he had any other desire! Realization dropped it with a sickening thud. What was behind that question? Lord Gowan didn't intend that his granddaughter should return to the United States, of that he was sure. He waited a second to get his voice in hand before he replied:

"You know I love her, that I want her for my wife, know that I care enough for her happiness to keep my own feeling under control until she has made her decision as to whether she will become an English subject." At least, I've tried to, he qualified to himself.

"I'll credit you with having made a good attempt. But you backslid with that 'Now and forever' song you sang straight to her that night in the gold salon. If the girl hadn't

339

been in love with a man at home —"

"A man at home!" His mother had commenced a statement like that which had been interrupted, Peter remembered. Had his suspicion been correct, was it Tim? But he wasn't at home. Face after face of Con's stag line flashed and faded on the screen of his memory with lightning rapidity. She never had encouraged one of the men more than another. With whom was she in love?

"How do you know, Lord Gowan?"

"She told me after luncheon today. Was it only today? I've lived years in these last hours."

"Did she tell you the man's name?"

"Yes. Queer name. By Jove, what was it? What was it? Something to do with shooting — guns."

"Shooting? Guns? I can't think of — You don't by any chance mean Sniper Blake?"

"Quite so! Quite so! That's the name. She said she had been in love with him since she was a little girl."

Peter drew back his head and laughed as he had not laughed for years, not since he had engaged in racket-smashing, to be exact. The relief, the incredible relief to know that Con had been improvising about bulky Sniper Blake.

"What's so blasted funny in that?"

340

"You — you would think it funny if you could see the man Blake now, Lord Van. He is almost as broad as he is tall, chews gum on all occasions and is the proprietor of a fleet of taxis in our town. Still single, though. Con in love with Sniper!" As Lord Gowan's face darkened with anger he soft-pedaled another laugh.

"What did the girl mean by telling me a story of her fervid first love?"

"It was a yarn about dancing school, wasn't it? She thinks it's a huge joke now. You probably interrupted her before she had a chance to bring it up to date."

Lord Gowan sank back in his chair. Had he been anything lower in the army scale than a Major General Retired one might say he slumped.

"I did. It precipitated a frightful row. Perhaps if I hadn't she wouldn't have kept that appointment in Stag Lane. Trifles so often change lives. I accused her of being in love with him now, and that he and you were influencing her to return to the United States."

"What did she answer?"

"She laughed at first, then said soberly that neither your mother nor you would advise her what to do."

"I told you you could count on us to play

fair. To remove ourselves from temptation the Coreys are departing for home in three days on the *Queen Mary.*"

Lord Gowan was on his feet. He dropped the monocle from his eye and replaced it.

"Home! Do you mean that your mother is leaving?"

"She is. We three are agreed that while we are here it will be almost impossible for Con to make her decision."

"But, by Jove, you can't go. Corey! I have a plan. It has been teasing at my mind to be heard for days but I wouldn't listen. During my walk home this afternoon it took control. You are to become a British subject. Marry Constance. Live at Cherrytree Farm, if you don't want to live at the Towers during my lifetime. I'll settle an independent fortune on you and in time you will represent this constituency in Parliament."

They stood facing each other, burning blue eyes on a level with eyes black with intensity. Peter tried twice to summon his voice before he said:

"I appreciate your trust in me and your faith in my ability, Lord Gowan, but I can't do it."

"Why can't you do it?"

"Because I am pledged to carry on important work at home." He had lowered his voice in the vain hope that his host would reduce the power of his.

"Pledged! Do you mean that you will give up the girl you love, refuse to marry my granddaughter, refuse the fortune, the career I am offering you, for some petty office in the *States*?"

"It isn't a petty office, sir. I shall give up my law practice because I have an opportunity to do constructive work for my city. I will have four years assured me to carry out my plans. I am pledged to the men who believe in me and trust me. For generations my forebears were Americans. They fought and died and worked to make the country what it is. I am proud of their part in its development. I count their heroism and achievements the most valuable legacy I can leave my children. I was born an American. As an American I'll die."

"By Jove, don't you realize that what I am asking of you has been done before? A number of your countrymen have become English subjects."

"Doubtless for excellent reasons. That's their business. Remember what Balzac says? 'Behind every human action lies a labyrinth of determining causes of which God reserves the right of final judgment.' Even to marry Con, the only inducement you offer which for a minute tears at my determination, I can't do it. She believes in me, knows that I am committed to important work at home. I would fail her in the supreme moment of our marriage, I would violate that deep inner sense of loyalty upon which her character is founded, were I to accept your offer."

"You don't love her, Corey, or you wouldn't refuse to marry her! You don't love her." The walls reverberated with the ring and power of his voice. "You are still dangling after that — Come in!"

Ivor Hardwick opened the door. He smirked self-consciously.

"I say, I'm sorry to interrupt this session which sounded frightfully stormy as I waited in the corridor for the psychical moment to enter, but Lady Coswell is beginning to champ at the bit, you know. She's keen to get at the cards."

"Quite so! Quite so!" Lord Gowan growled. "Go along and tell them we're coming."

Ivor Hardwick's narrowed, speculative eyes roved from the younger man's white face to the other, darkly flushed, before he closed the door. How long had he been in the corridor? He would have to be stone deaf not to have heard his host's roar in any part of it, Peter decided.

Lord Gowan held out his hand and straightened his fine shoulders.

"Forgive me, Corey, for blowing up. I get your point of view. It isn't only your refusal of my suggestion that hurts frightfully, it is that your mother — no use talking about it. They are waiting for us."

Con speculatively observed Ivor Hardwick as he returned to the hall. During dinner he had been unattentive, unlike his usually suave self. She had not a chance to tell him that the photograph he had given her was a fake. She would ask him to let her show that forged inscription to Peter. It might prove a clue to the person behind those kidnapers in Stag Lane.

The memory set her heart thumping suffocatingly. She must not allow that villainous couple to get back into her mind or the scene in the lounge would inevitably follow and set her a-shiver again. She forced her attention to Tim. Lydia Austen in a pencil-slim green frock which glittered like a sea serpent was entertaining him with a story, emphasizing the points with a gesture of her right hand on which flashed a three-jointed diamond ring, one joint of which covered the nail. She could be as brilliant, as brittle and unfeeling as her jewels; she could be softly alluring. She had turned that stop on full power at dinner while she talked to Peter. Her absorption in him had been a challenge to Con's own courage, her pride, her smarting heart not to reveal how intolerably it hurt to see him bending toward her, laughing with her.

To switch her train of thought she looked at Ivor Hardwick. He had stopped beside Lady Coswell whose face suggested blood-pressure on high, whose neck and bosom were adorned with an incredible number of strings of pearls and diamond-studded chains and whose frock of blinding black and white stripes suggested nothing so much as a barber's pole. He left her with a curt nod and dropped down beside Con on the broad sofa.

"And where have you kept yourself today, Miss America?" he asked. "I tried twice to get you on the phone but the bally line was busy."

Was it her imagination, Con asked herself, or was he tense? Perhaps he had found out that he had been fooled about the photograph.

"I've been adventuring," she said lightly; then added quickly, "You look worried. Have you found out about the photograph?"

"Found out *what?* What are you talking about?"

"The photograph you thought was a picture of my mother. It isn't."

"How do you know? Where is it?"

She spread her fan of silver sequins and said very low behind it:

"What's the matter? Your voice sounds frightened. I have the photograph but the writing on the back is forged. May I show it to Peter? He will find out —"

"Peter! Peter! I say, always dragging in that chap, aren't you?"

Con's fan clicked shut. She regarded the scowling man beside her incredulously. Could this be Ivor, the suave? Why the outburst?

"Don't you want to —"

"You think Corey is awfully in love with you, don't you?" he interrupted furiously. "He isn't. Not five minutes ago I heard your grandfather offer him you. Heard him decline *you,* even with a fortune and a career tucked on as an inducement if he would marry you. Rather neat, what?"

His words swept over her like a scorching tide. Peter had refused to marry her! Turned her down as easily as he would a business proposition he would not consider. Burning alive must feel like this, the intolerable smart and sting and ache of it. What could she say to show Ivor that his words had missed fire? Something light, inconsequential, something which would show she didn't care.

She had faced those two blackmailers in Stag Lane without — Stag Lane! She caught her breath. Hadn't she met a situation as heart-wrenching as this this afternoon? During her life wouldn't she be called on to face perhaps hundreds more? In the space of a pulse beat she had herself in hand.

She leaned back, opened and closed her glittering fan and smiled at him.

"Naughty! Naughty! You've been listening at keyholes, Ivor. I wish you had been where I was this afternoon, you would have heard something there worth remembering. I was among those present when a man, Tod Sacks, was arrested. His language would have been barred from radio or screen after the first sentence as he started to denounce a certain, we call him the man higher up at home, for double-crossing him after he had schemed and planned a little kidnaping job — I was the job — upon which he and a woman, the very woman whose photograph you gave me, were at the moment engaged. And *you* talk about kidnaping being one of the bally industries in the United States."

"What do you mean? Kidnap *you?*" His eyes burned into hers, his hands clenched. She drew back quickly. Into the surcharged atmosphere broke Lord Gowan's aggrieved voice.

"What's this I hear about you Coreys sailing for home on the *Queen Mary* in three days, Mrs. Corey?"

Home! Three days. Con started to her feet. Ivor's story of Peter's refusal to marry her was true! He was leaving to escape an impossible situation. But Angel? Tim?

"Connie, Connie, dearest, don't look like that!" Angela Corey pleaded.

"You were going? Without telling me?"

"No, no, dearest, of course we would tell you. You don't understand. Peter, you explain."

"He needn't. I understand. I —"

Lydia Austen slipped her hand under Peter's arm.

"How *wonderful!* How did you know I was returning on that very ship, Peter?"

Lady Coswell flung a first-I've-heard-of-it-look at her sister. "Lyd! You're an opportunist," she rasped.

Lord Gowan approached his granddaughter. "By Jove, Constance, I thought you knew it, I wouldn't have blurted out the news like that. I am frightfully sorry."

"Let me explain, Con."

"No, no, Peter. Neither you nor Angel nor Tim need explain. Why should you? Why should you tell me your plans? You are not tied to my apron strings, are you?"

She felt as if her eyes were burning like headlights, that a steel band was closing round her throat. Were they leaving because of her mother, her terrible mother? Peter must never know she loved him. She caught Lord Gowan's arm and smiled at him.

"Only this morning I read that new factors are bound to intrude in complex situations and bring to a sudden end the problem which has seemed permanent and insoluble. In an instant my problem has been solved. General, I am ready absolutely and entirely to renounce my citizenship and allegiance to the land of my birth.

"God save the King!"

XXV

Silence fell on the flower-scented room like one of those instants of complete calm before the bursting of a shell. Against a background rich with dull gold and warm colors two white-faced men, shaken by the passion of the girl's voice, looked back at her. Peter and Tim. They were the only persons whom she really saw. She dimly glimpsed Angela Corey, felt Lady Coswell's cynical enjoyment of the theatric situation, sensed Lydia Austen licking her lips at her chance to recapture her ex-fiancé; while through her mind whirled the words:

"My mother deserted me. Now they are leaving me!"

"You've been speaking in headlines, Con, which should clear everything up." Tim spoke in a tone intended to be teasingly jovial, but which stopped just short of being convincing. "Now that that's nicely settled let's play cards."

His voice had the immediate effect of an electric current applied to mechanical toys.

Each person in the room moved, a hand, a foot, released a sigh of relief. Peter's eyes met Con's with a look which sent down her lashes.

"Now that's a suggestion as is a suggestion, Tim," he approved. "Lord Van, suppose you and I take on Mother and Lady Coswell and let the younger set fight it out among themselves?"

One moment there had been emotion-charged stillness, then almost in the drawing of a breath the great hall was filled with voices and laughter. Ivor Hardwick drew out a chair at one of the card tables.

"Play with me, Cousin? I'll promise we'll set Miss Austen and Tim so frightfully far down they will never rise again." As his eyes met Con's his smile flickered and went out like a burning match flung on wet grass.

He hates me, she thought; why? Peter looked at me as if he had shut me out of his life forever. If I don't pull myself together I'll be crying in a minute and one outburst like that of a few moments ago from me in an evening is about all that should be inflicted on this company.

"To mop up the earth with Tim at cards would be the perfect end of a superperfect day." She accepted Hardwick's challenge as gaily as her aching, smarting heart permitted. "The defeatist in me urges me to warn you, Ivor, that my five-suit bridge is more of a prophecy than a game at present."

"Dear Con is always so frank in acknowledging her limitations," Lydia Austen purred.

"Sez you! You may take it from me, Lyd, that 'dear Con' hasn't any limitations in card playing or anything else. She's an ace in all games. Your deal, Captain."

Con restrained an almost irresistible urge to throw her arms around Tim's neck and kiss him. His defense eased the ache in her heart. Perhaps he didn't want to leave her behind in England, perhaps Angel and Peter had persuaded him. How could they —

"Waiting for you, Cousin," Ivor Hardwick reminded suavely.

"Scoop up your mind on the point of that pencil and fix it on the game, Slim," Tim advised with an impish grin.

She wrinkled her nose at him.

"Thanks for the implied compliment as to the size of my mind. Subtle I calls it. Three hearts."

Sacks, the butler, approached with his catlike tread. Con stopped studying her cards to watch him. Something came with him, something vaguely sinister like a ghostly presence. His face had the hollow-eyed look of a skull over which the yellow skin had been tightly drawn. Had he already discovered that his brother Tod had been taken into custody? Had the sister in Stag Lane telephoned him the facts?

"I beg pardon, Captain Hardwick," he apologized. "A woman is asking for you, sir." His face was expressionless but his voice was heavy with hate and the settling of old scores.

"What the devil do you mean, Sacks, coming here to tell me a woman is asking for me?" Hardwick demanded. "You said three hearts, partner?"

"I beg pardon, sir. She seems to be proper bothered, sir. She says to tell you if you don't come, she'll come in here, an' from the looks of her, I'm sure you wouldn't want that, sir."

From the corner of her eye Con saw her grandfather rise. That brought the other men to their feet. They stood motionless as Ivor declared angrily:

"It's your business to put the woman out, Sacks. She's some bally beggar —"

"She's not a beggar but she's come for money, all right, Captain Hardwick," a shrill voice interrupted.

The woman who had spoken approached swiftly over the thick rugs. Con pressed her hand above her heart to still its pounding. Her throat tightened unbearably. It was the terrible person who, in Stag Lane, had claimed to be her mother. The woman of the photograph whom Ivor had said was her mother. She had come to him for money! She was still wearing the gaudy blue-and-rose print. A blue hat drawn low over one eye only partially covered her hair which glistened like cheap gilt. Her eyes were black with vindictiveness, her painted scarlet lips were twisted in an evil smile.

"Well," she sneered. "Here I am, Captain, do I get that thousand pounds?"

"I don't know what you're talk—" Hardwick's jaw wobbled treacherously and cut off the word. She ground a furious invective between her teeth.

"So, you don't know? You forget quick, don't you? You've forgotten that I was to tell that girl in pink there that she was my child but not Gordon —"

"I'll be darned. If this isn't just one of those days!" Con heard Tim's whisper and his nervous chuckle behind her.

"Just a minute!"

Lady Coswell, roused from a state of paralyzing surprise, interrupted. She caught her sister's arm.

"This is no place for us, Lyd."

"But —" Miss Austen lingered. Her green frock quivered and glistened like a rippling snakeskin.

"Come!" Lady Coswell jerked her toward the door. "Good night everybody. Have had a wonderful evening, Lord Van."

"Order Lady Coswell's car, Sacks," commanded Lord Gowan.

I knew she was a grand person, Con thought, as her eyes followed the two women from the room. They came back to Peter who had stepped forward. Lord Gowan caught his arm. His face was purplish red.

"Keep out of this, Corey, for the present," he ordered in a suffocated tone, quite different from his usual roar. "Ivor, put that woman out of this house."

"I'd like to see him touch me, your lordship, until I get that thousand pounds. There wasn't anything in his bargain with me that I was to make the girl believe what I told her, I was to tell her, that's all. Tod Sacks told me I'd likely find him here, told me to stay till I got that money. I'll stay all right." She dropped to the sofa. "Perhaps your lordship would like to pay your lordship's heir's debt of honor?" she smirked.

Con looked at Ivor Hardwick who had dropped to a chair and covered his face with

356

his hands. He was the personification of guilt. More nightmare! All the time he had been telling her how beautiful she was, how adorable, he had been scheming to prove that she was not Gordon Trent's daughter, so that Lord Gowan's fortune might come to him. His deceit, his treachery, hurt almost as much as the other hideous events of this unbelievable day. What could he say in answer?

"Have you ever seen this person before, Ivor?" demanded Lord Gowan.

"Never." The muffled denial came from behind his hands.

The woman on the sofa sprang to her feet. Her broken-nailed, dirty fingers clenched.

"He says he's never seen me! What if he hasn't? He hired me, didn't he? Sneak," she hissed. "Sneak! Who wrote to Tod Sacks in the States to hunt up information about that guy Trent's marriage? Who planted that old photo of mine on the girl? Who offered me a thousand pounds if I'd swear she was my daughter and not Trent's?"

"Stop shouting!" Lord Gowan's imperious command broke into her coarse laugh. "Go on, finish your story and finish it quick."

"I will, your lordship. Does he think he's going to get away clean while my George,

Tod Sacks to you, he was George Dafter when I married him, goes back to the U.S. to prison? Not a chance! 'Twas him who bribed Chettle to sneak into the Tower room to get the records about the marriage and death of the Trent woman and then stayed behind when you'd all left and got them himself. 'Twas him who put the ad in the *Times*, who gave George the dope about the fire and told him to —"

"Crack me on the head," Peter interrupted the shrill voice, "and roll me over the cliff, I presume."

"I ain't saying Hardwick did that. I'm honest in my way, I am. You recognized George when he opened the Captain's door yesterday, didn't you, Corey? He was planted there so he'd get an eyeful of the girl and know her today. He had to put you out of the way. After he'd rolled you down the cliff he phoned your house you'd be detained in London on business. I told George before we sailed he was crazy to mix into this scheme that had to do with the girl who lived in your family. He laughed. Bragged he'd outsmarted the law for years, easy enough to take care of you. You had to drop down a chimney like a sweep to get him, didn't you? An' now you think you'll send him up for life. Try it, that's all, try it. I'll have a thousand pounds to fight with, that's about five grand in U.S. money. It will go a long way with a lawyer I know. I'll get it if I have to stay in this room a year."

"You won't stay in this room a year." Con's contradiction rang clear as a bell. "You'll be personally conducted along with your Ge—orge, for an attempt to kidnap me. Ivor, were you behind that scheme too?"

The contemptuous question brought Hardwick to his feet.

"No. I swear I wasn't. I knew nothing of it. I'll admit I worked up the story that you were the woman's child, but not Gordon Trent's, in the hope that your grandfather would pay to hush it up. I was desperate. You had refused to pay my debts, Lord Van, I was being pressed for money, frightfully pressed by my chief creditor. After all, you can't prove that the woman standing there didn't marry Gordon. There's that photograph of her with 'My wife, Viola' in his writing on the back." Assurance had returned to his voice and a cocky tilt to his chin.

"Which you forged," Peter asserted. "You're wrong about proof, too. We can prove that she never has been the wife of Gordon Trent." His eyes with a question in them met Con's. "Don't tell him," hers answered.

"Was Captain Hardwick party to the kidnaping scheme? Tell the truth, woman," Lord Gowan commanded.

"If I do, do I get that thousand pounds?" she bargained slyly.

"Answer me. If you don't, by Jove, you'll get clapped into irons and dropped into the Towers' dungeon," Lord Gowan roared and took a menacing step toward her.

She cringed. Her face went livid. Her eyes popped with fright.

"I believe you'd do it. George told me about that dungeon!" Her voice shook. "The Captain had nothing to do with the kidnaping, your lordship. George planned that. I didn't know about it, I swear to God, I didn't, till we were waiting for the girl in that Stag Lane house. Then he told me that a boat would pick the three of us up at the old tower — back in the States he was always talking about that old tower, seemed as if it was drawing him — and that one of his pals was to phone her folks that she'd met with an accident. He said he was going to show England a neat job of kidnaping. I begged him not to do it. If you don't believe me," she rolled up her sleeve to show marks on her arm, already faintly purple. "George has a way of making folks do as he wants."

Lord Gowan held up his hand. The lines in his face from nose to chin had deepened till they looked as if they had been gouged.

"Enough of this sickening story. Bring the woman to the Tower room. Strange that the honorable man in my family was the son I drove from my house. Ernest a rotter and now you, Ivor. Come, Corey. I may need you."

"In a moment, sir." Peter crossed to Con. He took the glittering fan from her hand and closed it. "Look at me. Did you mean it, when you said you would become a British subject?"

She remembered that she had been offered to him in marriage, remembered he had refused her, remembered her dishonorable mother, brought up her shock troops of pride.

"I did. I adore this country. I don't wonder you doubt me after my shilly-shallying," she confirmed as lightly as she could with his eyes boring into hers.

"Remember what you promised? That you would trust me and believe that no matter what I did, it would be because I thought it best for you?"

"Did I promise all that? It must have been back in the Dark Ages. I've forgotten," she replied flippantly.

"Then that's all. There isn't any more," Peter said and followed the woman, Hardwick and Lord Gowan from the hall.

The three left behind watched them go. Angela Corey's quick breathing set the diamonds in her necklace sparkling like rain drops in the sun. The silver sequins on Con's pink frock quivered in response to each hard beat of her heart. Tim's chuckle broke the strained silence.

"Like the Northwest Mountie the gilded blonde got her man. Hi! Look out, Con! Your eyes are like black coals stuck in the face of a snow woman! Don't fade on us now." He flung his arm around her. "It was a grim party but don't you see? It's over. The party's over."

She smiled at him gallantly.

"Of course I see, foolish. The party's over. Quite over."

XXVI

In turquoise-blue pajamas and a diaphanous matching lounge coat Con sat on one foot in a corner of the seat under the open lattice window in the Spanish Bride's room.

"The party's over." She wondered how many times the words had echoed through her memory since that night weeks ago when Tim had spoken them in the hall at Trentmere Towers. Then it had been May, now it was mid-August. The flowers in the gardens were changing from pastel tints to strong yellows, reds and purples. Tomorrow she and the General would start North for grouse shooting on the moors.

She tipped back her head to look at the heavens. A perfect night. Whisper of leaves, soft as the murmur of gossips behind unfurled fans. Rich fragrance mounting from the earth. The moon a broken silver disc. Shimmering stars thick as spangles on the bouffant skirt of a *première danseuse*. Over and above all an indigo dome, soft as velvet, deep as the universe. Cascading, rippling music of harps and the full mellow harmonies of violins from the radio behind her. The night and the music made one think of dreams and romance, of intent gray eyes, of a deep unsteady voice saying, "Good-by for the present — darling!"

And then he had gone. A modern knight faring forth to slay modern dragons, she had thought, as she watched Peter in gray flannel of impeccable cut and finish go down the sun-dappled path to his roadster with Whiskers, whom he was taking home with him, leaping and yelping at his heels. If she stared hard at the star-studded sky she could see him as he had said, "Carry on, Con. I'll be seeing you!" Could see him turn away, then come back to her. She could see the wave in his dark hair. The set line of red lips in his white face. The twitch of the muscle in his cheek before he said huskily, "Good-by for the present — darling."

He had gone and she had kept on living, gaily, furiously, as if he had not taken her heart with him, as if she were not telling herself over and over that she should be too proud to love a man who had refused to marry her. Eyes on the stars, she lived over the hectic days of preparation for the departure of Angel and Tim and the moment when Angel had caught her tight in her arms and comforted, "It will all come right, dearest, I'm sure it will — try to understand!" which was followed by Tim's gruff, "Come on, Mother, the car is waiting. Con's all right. She has what it takes. Don't forget to come home, gal."

She might have what it took, her thoughts raced on, but she had not had enough of whatever stuff that was to go to the ship to see them off. To see Peter with Lydia clinging to his arm. Why imagine that? She hadn't been there, had she? At the very moment of sailing she had been settling her belongings in this room.

She remembered her grandfather's lined face as that evening at dinner he had looked at her across the expanse of rare lace, between massive silver candelabra with their tall yellow tapers, his tired voice as he said:

"They've gone, Constance."

And she remembered that she had laughed and made a gallant attempt to control the twitching of her lips.

"And left us to carry on, General, to settle down to solid English living. Not too solid. You should see my engagement book. My dates fit together with the snugness of a picture puzzle."

"Would it make it easier for you if we were

to live in town during the season, Constance?"

"It's sweet of you to propose it when you hate the roar of a city. Thanks ever so much but I would rather stay at Trentmere Towers. I adore it. I can go everywhere I want from here."

"Quite so. Quite so." His sigh revealed his relief at her decision. "I hate town and crowds. There are plenty of young bucks hanging round you to act as escorts. Her Grace, the Duchess will present you at Court." He cleared his throat. "Ivor married La— that woman yesterday."

"*Married* her?"

"He lost no time. He knows that never again will he have a cent from me and he owed her money, a great sum. I made it clear to him the night I paid that distressingly cheap person the thousand pounds he had promised her. She wasn't entitled to a shilling but I wanted to get rid of her without scandal. She understands that if she opens her mouth about that scheme of his, she will be imprisoned for her part in the Stag Lane affair. His wife has two large fortunes. One will disappear like dew in the sun if the rightful heirs of Lord Hanford, whom she duped into a mock marriage, find out the truth. I don't feel that it is my duty to inform them. Ivor doesn't know that, though. Lady Hanford, as she called herself, thinks she will in time get another title, but I am not so sure. Not so sure. That leaf is turned over, Constance. We won't refer to it again."

What had he meant by "I am not so sure"? Curious how clearly she remembered each word and inflection of her grandfather's voice. Grief and longing must have made of her memory a sensitized film. Since then with all her strength of mind she had tried to keep that leaf turned over, had tried desperately to erase the memory of that scene in the lounge at Cherrytree Farm. It was growing fainter and fainter. The sting and smart of her heart had eased.

She had had little time to spend dwelling on the past. Every waking moment had been filled and a good many of those which custom decreed should be devoted to sleep. Her ceaseless activity had given her something to write home about. Into her letters to Angel and Tim — she hadn't written to Peter — she had packed gaiety and drama and color. Out of them she had left her longing for the three she loved, her homesickness for Red Maples. Their letters to her were tender and full of affection but they never mentioned her return. One night when she could no longer endure it, she had telephoned across the ocean, but none of the family was at home.

She let her mind drift along on a colorful stream of memories to the accompaniment of muted music. It was like looking at a motion picture done in technicolor with shining fragments holding her attention for an instant. She saw herself in white and nodding plumes and the Duchess, in purple and incredible pearls, preening like a pouter pigeon, as the motor inched along through crowds on its way to Buckingham Palace, saw herself curtsying to the King and Queen in a fairytale setting of scarlet and gold, jewels, music and perfumes. She recalled grand opera at Covent Garden; balls with barons, earls, viscounts, ambassadors in full court regalia, women in enchanting frocks and blazing jewels, Indian princes, foreign royalties, and rows of diamond-encrusted dowagers on the side lines. She remembered the morning she had watched the Guard being changed at Buckingham palace while Big Ben boomed the hour and the Scots Guards in kilts and sporans marched and countermarched to the keening of bagpipes, and how courteous the bobby had been when she had inquired the way to a garage. She thought of the policies of the government she had heard debated in the House of

Lords and of how she had wondered if Peter were addressing a grand jury at that very moment. She remembered a portrait at the Royal Academy from which a boy smiled at her with eyes so like Tim's that her heart had turned completely over. She recalled house parties at great estates and the girls and men who had week-ended at Trentmere Towers. She visualized the packed grandstand at Epsom when the Derby was run and the smartly dressed, likable men with badges and light toppers who had crowded around her and her grandfather.

"Why can't I love one of them instead of a man who doesn't want me, why can't I?" She demanded of the broken moon, but the twist of its half mouth was the only answer.

She rested her arms on the sill of the open window and dropped her head on them. She was so tired of fighting her love for Peter, so very tired.

Into the room burst the swing and splendor of martial music, the high silver notes of trumpets, the singing of flutes, the blare of windy and defiant horns, the beat of drums and almost the rhythm of tramping feet.

She flung up her head. It was like marching with a regiment to hear that, with an army as it tramped on to victory. It was like a great tide sweeping her on. She felt the elixir of courage throb through her veins. "Keep on keeping on," she said aloud. Hadn't that been what she had told herself when night after night she had lain awake thinking of Peter, seeing his white face, with its steady gray eyes, its hard-set mouth as she had seen it last?

From the open window she could see a faint patch of moonlight frosting one of the ivy-covered towers. It tipped a white steeple in the valley with silver, blanched a thatched roof. Across the broken moon sailed a cirrus fleece tempering its light as might a cellophane umbrella. The world was warm, fragrant, hushed, touched with a luminous mist. It was a world in which to conquer, not to go down in defeat. What would the turmoil of mind of these last weeks amount to if she had not grown into a finer person spiritually and mentally, could not control her thoughts?

That meant banishing Peter from them, for the present. She had had his friendship and his tenderness, if not his love. It would be hard to go on without it, but she couldn't go through life clutching at it, could she? She had others to think of besides herself — her grandfather. He had changed in these

last weeks, he no longer indulged in magnificent rages. Was it only his disappointment
at Ivor's treachery, Ivor, who was living
abroad with her moth— the woman he had
married, or was it that he loved Angel and
missed her tragically ?

She looked out into the gossamer beauty
of the night. A runaway star raced across the
heavens, winked farewell and vanished. She
shut off the wireless, flung her filmy lounge
coat over a chair and kicked off her silver
mules. In bed she snapped off the light.
Wide-eyed she gazed at the sky beyond the
open lattice window, watched the bright,
twinkling stars which attended the broken
moon like ladies in waiting as it hung lower
in the heavens, and wondered if humans
ever would solve the interstellar mysteries.

How quiet the night. Only the faint sound
of a cathedral bell stirred the fragrant air.
"Oranges and lemons sing the bells of St.
Clemens." The words her father had taught
her when she was a little girl hummed rhyth-
mically through her memory. He had loved
to hear her chant them. And that other song.
"When I grow rich ring the bells of
Shoreditch. When I grow —" Curious how
the words dodged round the corner of her
mind and hid.

What was that? A bit of cloud outside the

window? Something vaporous! Something opalescent! How still the room was! As if holding its breath. The thing was taking shape! It was a woman! A woman in drifting gossamer that shone. It was as if having left her mortal body far below, she had taken the form of a silver mist to float along a thoroughfare of breeze. A scarf of gauze hid the face. She glided toward the bed. Leaned over it. A faint whisper, "Now and forever." She floated to the door. Vanished.

The Spanish Bride! Con struggled to call out, tried desperately to tear away the veil which separated her from the unseen world from which the phantom had come. If only she had seen the face behind the gauze, if only she could have asked what she meant by the whispered words of Peter's song.

"She returns to remind bride or groom to be true to the loved one," Bunny had said.

The apparition had been so real that she strained her ears to hear the closing of the door.

"Ghosts do not close doors."

Who had spoken? She raised herself on one elbow. Listened. The breeze had strengthened. The casement with the enameled crest swung lightly, leaves on the oak trees rippled with the sound of a running brook. She brushed her hand across her eyes. The moon, a little lower, hung palely in the sky. The stars, not so brilliant now, twinkled steadily.

Had she dreamed it, or had she really seen the Spanish Bride who came to foreshadow the marriage of the heir, to remind bride or groom to be true to the loved one? Her heart shook her with its pounding. She whispered.

"I am the heir. 'Now and forever' the phantom said. What did she mean by that? I love Peter! I've got to talk to him!"

She pulled on her lounge coat. The filmy blue floated behind her like the draperies of the Winged Victory as she ran down the softly lighted marble stairway. The eyes of the portraits on the wall watched her. Her faint shadow stole beside her as she crossed the hall.

A red coal dropped as she entered the Tower room. Something dark scuttled across the floor. A mouse? She tucked her feet under her as she put in the call. Her heart raced against the tick of the old clock as she waited, it seemed for years. A voice came from far across the ocean.

"The Corey residence. The maid speaking."

"Janey!" Con said breathlessly. "This is Miss Connie. I want to speak to Mr. Peter."

"Miss Connie! It ain't possible."

"It is! It is! Call Mr. Peter."

"Mr. Peter ain't here, Miss. He's at Miss Austen's. The engagement dinner. Hadn't you heard?"

"No. I hadn't heard. Good-by." Con cradled the phone. "I hadn't heard," she repeated as she slowly mounted the marble stairs.

XXVII

Morning sunlight get the massive silver dishes on the buffet in the breakfast room at Trentmere Towers a-shimmer, intensified the yellow of the feathery chrysanthemums massed in the Satsuma bowl on the table and daringly flicked one of Lord Gowan's gray eyebrows as he reread a portion of Clive Neale's letter.

"We are almost certain now that your request will be granted. That in recognition of the great and loyal service rendered by you to the Empire, your title will be diverted by Royal License from Hardwick to descend to the son of your granddaughter, who will be given the style, place and precedence to which he would have been entitled had his mother's father survived to inherit."

Lord Gowan dropped the letter and picked up another. He frowned as he read the close.

"So, here is Con's family tree on the distaff side. It has taken time to trace it. It is a shining record of patriotism and self-sacrifice to ideals.

I am sending it to her through you.

Peter Corey."

He slipped the letters into the pocket of his gray tweed coat. Sending it through me, he thought. She is happy as she is. Suppose I don't give it to her? She knows nothing of her mother's people. She doesn't need them.

Mrs. Bunthorne in pale biege linen which accentuated the dried-peach texture of her round face, poured an amber stream of coffee into an egg-shell-thin cup.

"Better drink this while it is hot, my lord." He shot a quick glance at her.

"Why are you doing this, Bunthorne? Serving my breakfast, I mean. Where are the servants?"

"I told Mr. Sacks I would pour your coffee and bring in the mail this morning, my lord." She nodded toward a pile of letters beside a plate. "My lady has two from the States. She will be glad to see them."

"Quite so. Quite so. By Jove, I sometimes think that her heart is across the ocean, not here."

"There is something I would like to say to you, something I think you should hear, my lord," Mrs. Bunthorne declared with the respectful firmness of an old and valued family servant.

"I say, it isn't about Constance? Where is she? She always pours my coffee, always breakfasts with me. Has anything happened?"

"No, no. Nothing has happened to her. Not having heard her run down the stairs — I listen for that young sound every morning — I looked in on her. She was asleep, the bonny child, but she had been crying, my lord, her eyelashes were wet."

"Why should she cry? She has everything. Don't I give her everything, Bunthorne?"

"Everything material, yes, my lord."

"Is she not gay and laughing? Hasn't she a regiment of friends? Isn't she always busy with sports or dancing, dinners, balls? I have noticed that there are as many girls around her as men. I like that. She is interested in the tenants, she will bankrupt me with the improvements she is planning for their farms if I am not watchful. What more can she want, Bunthorne?" There was a note of pleading in his gruff voice.

"She is sad under her gaiety. I am sure she misses her family, my lord."

"I am her family."

"The family with whom she grew up, I mean."

"Quite so, Bunthorne. Quite so. You have lived here so long you know the Trent-Gowan mind and she is a Trent-Gowan. If you are right, what can I do about it?"

"You might suggest that she go to them for a visit, my lord."

He pushed back his chair impatiently and walked to a long window.

"By Jove, I don't dare let her go back. She might stay. She will be obliged to return to renounce her American citizenship. I have postponed her going for fear I may lose her. Come here."

The little woman stood beside him and gazed up into his face with misty, adoring eyes.

"Notice how gray and old and beautiful the chapel looks from here, Bunthorne? Often I stand at this window and picture my granddaughter leaving that door as a bride, smiling and bowing her way to this house between lines of cheering tenants. There has not been a marriage there during my lifetime. It is one of the great desires of my heart to see hers solemnized in that consecrated place."

"Why couldn't it be, my lord, wherever

she decides to make her home? My lady will make a bonny bride."

"Tut! Tut! Don't cry. That is one picture. There is another." He waved his hand toward the acres of woods and fields, distant villages and sun-tipped hills. "Sometimes I wonder who will rule this little kingdom after I am gone. Will it be one of Trent-Gowan blood or will it be a rich man without family background, a brewer, a baker, a mail-order Midas who can afford the taxes and the enormous expense of upkeep? Perhaps in this changing world the patriarchal families have had their day, eh, Bunthorne?"

"I wouldn't be worrying about that, my lord. You have many, many active years before you. Think how hale and hearty your father and grandfather were at ninety. Perhaps in time a man will be happier if he does not own so much. It's a great care and what does it get you but worry and responsibility?"

"Bunthorne, I believe you are turning socialist," Lord Gowan accused with mock severity.

"I wouldn't know about that, my lord, but if you will let Miss Constance go —"

"And just where do you want me to go, Bunny?"

Lord Gowan and the housekeeper turned quickly to face the girl who was smiling at them from the threshold. Her yellow linen frock might have caught and imprisoned the sunshine, her creamy skin was rose-tinted at the cheek bones. Where the light touched the waves her dark hair shone like satin, but her brilliant eyes were shadowed.

"Have you been scolding Bunny because I overslept, General?" Con demanded gaily. "I'm sorry to be late. It took me a long time to get to sleep last night. This morning my mind feels as bleak and bare of ideas and color as a wind-swept hilltop in a snow-storm."

"You don't look as if you had been wakeful. You are bonny this morning, my lady. Shall I pour your coffee?"

"No thanks, Bunny. I want to prowl and investigate the contents of those silver dishes."

"Then I will be going. Good morning, my lord. I hope I gave no offense by my suggestion."

Con's eyes followed the housekeeper as she left the room.

"What has Bunny on her mind? She looked all set to cry. Porridge!" She replaced a silver cover. "Too many calories. Bacon. Smells luscious. Fish cooked to a turn.

Scrambled eggs. We English certainly do ourselves well when it comes to eats. They are a terrible temptation but I must retain my size-sixteen figure. Nobly I will stick to dry toast and orange marmalade. A woman of indomitable courage, I calls myself."

Lord Gowan regarded her with troubled eyes as she sat down at the table and picked up a letter. Was her gaiety forced or was he imagining a hint of tears running through it?

"From Angel! Excuse me if I read it, General?"

"Better drink your coffee while it is hot."

She didn't hear his suggestion. She was skimming the pages eagerly.

"Oh!" she exclaimed, startled. "Listen. Angel writes: 'Peter is so crowded with work he has decided to either live at his Club or take a bachelor apartment in the city this winter.' Bachelor! How can he? I'm sorry. That last isn't in the letter, General. To proceed: 'Commuting will take too much of his time. Tim will be at college, he will get his degree at Mid-year's. I shall close Red Maples when the boys leave, which won't be until October, and then I will be a woman without a family.'

"I can't imagine Angel without a real home to care for," Con said thoughtfully.

"By Jove, she doesn't have to be without

one. If she would come here —" Lord Gowan's gruff voice broke.

"Like her a lot, don't you, General?"

"Liking isn't the word. I asked her to marry me."

"I have an idea, a perfectly *gorgeous* idea. 'There is a tide in the affairs of men, which taken at the flood leads on to fortune.' A man named W. Shakespeare thought of it before I," she disclaimed modestly, "but that doesn't matter. Get the idea? It is your chance with Angel. Why don't you go and get her?"

"I say, that is a great suggestion, Constance. We will go together. Bunthorne fussed round serving breakfast just to advise me to send you back to the Coreys for a visit."

Warm color spread to the girl's hair and faded, leaving her white. Her grandfather regarded her anxiously. He felt the same sinking of the heart, he had felt as a young soldier before going into battle. What was she thinking, feeling, to make her eyes so darkly intent? Was he about to lose her? He hadn't supposed it was possible for him to love a child as he loved her.

"General, I have something to tell you." She drew her breath as if she were about to plunge into icy water. "I called up Red Maples last night. I — I felt that I must talk to Peter. He wasn't there. He was at dinner at Lydia's. She was announcing their engagement. But, before that I had decided that I could not give up my own country."

"But, I say, you said —"

"That I would stay here. I said it when I was hurt, horribly hurt," she confessed passionately. "I had just heard that Angela and Tim had planned to leave me, that Peter had refused to marry —" A brilliant flush stained the pallor of her face.

"What was that sentence you were afraid to finish? Answer." Lord Gowan brought his hand down with a force which shook the table appointments.

The flame in the girl's eyes was a perfect reproduction of the fire in his.

"Why insist upon being told what you already know? You asked Peter to marry me, didn't you? Offered him a fortune and a career if he would, and even with that bribe he politely and firmly declined, didn't he?"

"Who told you that?"

"Don't roar, General, and don't look at me as if I had gone crazy. Ivor Hardwick told me. That's why, after I heard it, I said I would become a British subject. I told myself that I wouldn't go back, I had been too humiliated. Now, I know that while one may give up country and flag for a great cause or a great love, one doesn't give them up because one's pride has been hurt. Last night when I — I — saw —" Better not tell him of the visit of the Spanish Bride, he might think she had been frightened by a ghost. "I realized that I had been a quitter."

She loved Corey, that was why she had been so bitterly hurt, Lord Gowan told himself. Much as he wanted to disbelieve it, he couldn't; love for him was in every word of her passionate explanation. He had known it since the night of the ball when he had seen her dancing but had refused to acknowledge that he knew. His troubled eyes were on her, but they were not seeing her, they were seeing Ivor on the threshold of the Tower room the night he had made the proposition to Corey. He heard his suave voice:

"I say, I'm sorry to interrupt this session, which sounded frightfully stormy as I waited in the corridor."

Ivor, the sneak, had overheard and told. Apparently he hadn't heard Corey's declaration of love. She didn't know that, was eating her heart out because she thought he didn't love her. Maybe never would know if he himself did not tell her, and in time would forget the man she thought she loved

384

and marry in England. Would a day come, now hid in the hazy future, when he would say proudly of a straight noble lad, "This is my great-grandson, the next Lord Gowan"?

If he told of his vision would it hold her? Few girls married their first love. She believed now that Peter Corey had renewed his engagement. She had been gay and happy here. She was hurt now but she would be gayer and happier as the days went on. The memory of the Coreys would dim. Would they? Would he himself ever forget the charm and sweetness of Angela? Ever get over the desire to have her with him always? He rose abruptly and Con, looking at him, wondering, stood up.

"Constance," he said gruffly. "I don't know who told you of Peter's engagement, but I am sure it is not true. Has it ever occurred to you that the Coreys left you in the unselfish belief that you could come to a decision as to your choice of country more quickly without them? That Peter would not tell you he loved you devotedly, passionately, for fear you might marry him and afterward regret this family home you had given up?"

"Peter! Loves *me!*"

The radiance of her face, the shaken incredulity of her voice were like a steel band

about Lord Gowan's heart, but he managed
to say with an unsteady attempt at joviality:

"Quite so. Quite so. It is my turn to quote:
'To make the time between thought and action as short as possible is the secret of success.' Shall we sail for the United States on
Saturday, Miss Trent?"

XXVIII

Con saw Sniper Blake's eyes bulge like china-blue marbles in his fat red face as she stepped from the train.

"Well, look who's here! Lady Trent. I say, what's happened? Weren't you the lord's granddaughter after all?"

Her burning face was the shade of her rose-red tweed suit as his greeting focused the eyes of the other persons on the platform on her. She was in luck that it wasn't the train upon which the business portion of the community came from town. She tried to smile though her face was stiff from annoyance.

"You might soft-pedal the loud-speaker, Sniper, and call one of your men to drive me to Red Maples. Gorgeous afternoon, isn't it? The sky's a Maxfield Parrish blue. The air is like wine. Nothing like New England air."

"Guess you've forgotten our winters when we roast in flannels one day and freeze the next. Pretty good place to live, though.

I'll take you up myself. Don't do it usually. I'm here to check up on my men. But it isn't every day I have a chance to drive a countess or 'my lady.' Got any trunks?"

"They are coming by express." She indicated the tan suitcases and hat boxes striped with red behind her. "Those are mine."

"Okay. Looks like you've picked up some clothes while you've been hitting the high spots. I've heard that that grandfather of yours is lousy with money. Hop into that swell sedan. Bart, put in those bags."

He sounded like a superdictator, he looked like candidate No. 1 for a high-blood-pressure clinic, Con thought, as from the seclusion of the back seat she watched him direct the stowing of her bags by a man with a shock of coarse, stringy red hair. Sniper was still the overbearing bully of dancing-school days. As the car started he twisted halfway round to converse.

"Guess the family isn't expecting you, is it? Saw Mrs. Corey in the big car with the chauffeur all dolled up, heading for the city."

Angel away. The radiance of Con's happiness in her homecoming was slightly dimmed. The General had told her she should let the Coreys know they were coming but she had insisted on surprising

388

them. In that case, he had assured her, he would remain in New York with Clive Neale and his orderly-valet until he heard from her that he would be welcome at Red Maples. Lucky he hadn't come with her, she thought, and tried to concentrate on the driver's conversation, if a ceaseless monologue could be called conversation.

"Tim's playing off the tennis finals at the Country Club, this P.M. He seems okay now; there was a time last winter when I thought he was through. Pete's a busy boy. Guess he's working day and night. Looks as bad as Tim did last winter, but he's round more or less. When you want him in this town page Lydia Austen. I heard she gave a swell engagement dinner the other night."

Con avoided his bulging eyes by looking from the sedan window. Had Janey been right? Were Peter and Lydia together again? Why, why had she come back? Don't be a quitter, she told herself fiercely, you were coming home, weren't you, before the General told you Peter loved you? Only watch your step, lady, when you see him. Watch your step. Be cool and remote as a snowy cloud. Aloud she said:

"Looks as if I would dine with myself to-night, doesn't it, Sniper?"

"Say cut out that 'Sniper' stuff. That went

for dancing school but now I'm Dexter Blake, a selectman and a director of the bank. My family has lived in this town as long and been as prominent as the Coreys."

It had, Con admitted to herself, but what a difference in the quality of the representatives of this generation.

"Sorry, Sni— Mr. Dexter Blake. Here we are at Red Maples. I had forgotten it was so beautiful. So —"

Her tightened throat cut off the sentence. Through misty eyes she looked at the clapboarded house with its two balanced wings of whitewashed brick and its colonnade porch which seemed to be holding out welcoming arms. The delicate ironwork of the balconies was like an etching against the whiteness of the building. The shutters were the shade of the hedges of the old box which bordered the lawns. Massive oaks, lindens and birches framed it and high above a chimney flamed the tip of a maple like a red torch heralding the advance of autumn.

She was out of the sedan before it stopped. "Thanks no end for getting me here so quickly, Sni— Dexter. How much?"

"Nothing. I guess I can take you to drive without charging, can't I? Perhaps it isn't done in England, but it is here. Where'll I dump these bags?"

"Leave them on the porch. The maid will take them in. Thanks again, Dexter."

As she waited for her ring to be answered she watched him lumber down the walk and wondered how a person could lose all the charm, all the male fascination he had had in dancing-school days. The door opened.

"Miss Connie! Is it you, or am I seeing things?" The yellow-haired maid caught her in an ecstatic hug.

Con had a flash-back with sound effects of a footman in maroon livery, bending almost to the floor:

"His lordship is waiting for you in the hall, my lady." The "my lady" era was over. What next?

"It is I. It's grand to see you, Janey." She stepped into the hall. "Mrs. Corey has gone to town, Dexter Blake told me."

"Now how did that Blake fella know that? She's gone to the city, Miss, but she'll be back soon. She's bringing home guests for dinner."

"Guests! Then I will make an odd number."

"Sure an' what if you do, Miss Connie. I guess they'll be crazy to have you. You know the Madam, there'll be plenty to eat."

"Take my bags up, will you? I would like to look around downstairs for a minute."

"Sure, I'll take them up. We've made lots of changes since you've been gone. I told the Madam, looks as if the house was being done over for a bride."

A bride! Lydia? Con swallowed something in her throat which seemed as large as the remains of Plymouth rock before she said:

"A bride! How exciting."

"Madam just smiled so I guess there's nothing in it. Your room's ready. Gee, you're prettier than ever, Miss Connie! The Madam said she wanted it perfect so you could step in any minute. Mr. Peter'll be glad he's coming home for dinner tonight. He thought he'd be too busy but I heard the Madam tell him that this was a special occasion, so he said he'd try to get here. Here's the powder room all done over. Ain't it a dream? Madam had it red, she said you would look so lovely against the background."

The lump was back in Con's throat as she stepped into the small room. Angel must have been sure that sometime she would return. Chinese red paper with an etching of silver covered all but one wall, which was a huge mirror. Below it a mirror shelf held silver toilet appointments and boxes with red knobs. A stool covered in silvery-gray satin was the last perfect touch.

"It's marvelous, Janey. And devastatingly becoming. I could spend my life here."

"Sure, and it's your same old joking self that's come back. Bein' a princess hasn't spoiled you, Miss Connie."

"I wasn't *quite* a princess, Janey. Please don't tell anyone I have arrived. Let's surprise them. Set a place for me at dinner and when they are all here, knock on my door twice and I'll come down."

The maid's eyes sparkled like brown diamonds. She paused halfway up the stairs.

"Sure I'll do that very thing, Miss. Sounds like a movie, don't it? I won't even tell cook. If you don't want the Madam to suspect though, you'd better dress in one of the back bedrooms, the green one. She goes into your room every day."

"Put the bags in the green room. I'll be up in a minute."

She walked slowly about the rooms she hadn't seen for almost six months. The blue paneled walls of the living room, the books in recessed alcoves, the hangings patterned in lavender, purple and white lilacs, the small sofas smooth and soft in their summer slip covers of matching chintz, the pale yellow crysanthemums in crystal bowls, the eighteenth-century pieces which Angel treasured, made a perfect ensemble.

Through the windows at the end of the room, which seemed all glass, she could see the broad terrace, with white furnishings, the blaze of color in the garden and far away the sparkle of the rippling water of the lake. She felt like a stranger as she went slowly up the curving stairway, as if the gap in the household made by her departure for England had closed up, that there was now no place for her.

She stopped at the door of her old room. That had been freshened too. Shell-pink walls, curtains of thin creamy stuff, hangings with wide alternate stripes of pink, pale yellow and turquoise blue at the groups of windows. Flowers, two perfect pink Perfections, in a slim silver vase and half a dozen pale yellow roses in a crystal holder.

That didn't look as if the gap had closed. The room was holding out its arms to her, as the house had seemed to do. She had never felt that way about her grandfather's home. As on a screen she saw the gloomy ivy-covered towers, the rooks circling above them, and she saw the Spanish Bride's room, with the family crest woven into the brocade on its walls. She thought she could hear that phantom whisper, "Now and forever."

The room she entered was cool and inviting, all soft green and white. Janey had lowered the Venetian blinds to shut out the strong sunlight, had unpacked her frocks and hung them in the closet. She glanced at the enameled clock ticking off the minutes. She had time for a rest after her shower; she needed it, she had been so excited last night at her nearness to home that she hadn't closed her eyes.

Later, refreshed, she slipped into a pale gold negligee and stretched out on the chaise longue. She listened dreamily to the house sounds. A car in the service drive. That would be the express delivering the ices for dinner. Someone driving into the garage. A whistle! Tim, coming from his tournament. Whiskers yelping. The bang of the side door. She would recognize that sound if she heard it in Timbuktu. They were running up the stairs. The dog was yelping and sniffling and whining.

"What's the matter, young fella? What are you snuffling round Con's room for?" Tim's voice.

She had forgotten the terrier. Would he spoil her surprise? He was scratching at the outside of the door as if he were frantic. It was flung open.

"Stop clawing, you idiot. Who do you think's — *Slim!*"

She met him halfway across the room. He caught her shoulders. Whiskers, bright eyes snapping, jumped on her in frenzied welcome.

"Why you — you — if this isn't the darndest —"

Tim's voice caught. He shook her slightly. "What do you mean walking in on us like this? Does Mother know?"

Con shook her head as she looked at him through pools of tears.

"She doesn't. No one knows. I — I thought I'd just surprise you."

"You've done it, all right. You shouldn't do such things, my heart won't stand it."

"Tim! Is your heart weak?"

"Don't be foolish, you ought to know a figure of speech when you hear it. Do you think I could win the Country Club championship if I had a weak heart?"

"You did win? How grand! I was sure you would."

"How did you know I was playing today?"

"Dexter Blake, Sniper to you, told me when he brought me from the station."

"He did. I'll bet he reeled off a lot of gossip too, didn't he?"

"He talked all the way, he had to say something. Whiskers, don't eat me up."

"Come here, young fella. When do you

intend to spring this surprise, Slim? I think it's wrong but I suppose I can't give you away."

"Don't look as if I were about to commit highway robbery, Timothy, my lad. Janey and I have it beautifully planned. When the guests have arrived she will knock on this door twice and I will run down the stairs. Believe me, it will prove a smash-hit at the box office."

"Have it your own way, 'I'm allus willin' to oblige.' It doesn't seem fair to — Well, it doesn't seem fair, that's all. Come on, Whiskers, we'll let our surprise package dress, unless she's planning to add the last perfect touch by appearing in that nightgownish thing."

"It isn't a nightgown, Tim Corey. It's a negligee. Gay Paree. You'd better do a little changing yourself unless you intend to dine in a green cardigan and slacks — that would please Angel."

Tim's grin was broad and indulgent.

"Off to a good start, aren't we? Lucky you're not the *femme* lead in my young life, we'd have a monkey and parrot time. I'm going. *Prenez garde, Mademoiselle.* Look out for the stick after you shoot your rocket."

Dressed in white dinner clothes Tim perched on the arm of a deep chair in his brother's room as Peter was bowing his black tie. Their eyes met in the mirror.

"What's on your mind, kid?" Peter asked. "You ought to be all smiles and blushes — I heard you played a corking game this afternoon — instead you look as if you'd had the world dropped on your shoulders."

"It isn't the world, it's a little matter of loyalty. I don't know whether to warn a pal about something that's likely to happen to him — her — or just let nature take its course."

Peter laughed as he slipped on his white coat.

"Better let nature take its course. Keep hands off other people's affairs, fella. 'Him-or her' — you don't seem sure of the gender of your 'pal' — won't thank you for interfering."

"I'm not out for thanks." He stepped into the hall. Poked his head back into the room. "I almost forgot. When you're ready to go down Mother wants you to knock twice at the door of the green room and tell one of her guests who is dressing there that dinner is served."

"What the dickens has happened to Janey? That's her job. Why am I to —"

Realizing that he was protesting to space Peter stopped. What had Tim meant by his talk of loyalty and pals? What had the boy on his mind, he wondered, as he tucked a handkerchief into his breast pocket and left the room.

He stopped at the door of Con's boudoir as he stopped each time he passed it, seeing her against the background of her books and photographs and treasures as he had seen her countless times before she left Red Maples; thinking of her in England, thinking that he had been mad not to tell her he loved her before she had made her decision to remain — her wistful eyes as she had said good-by had haunted him; knowing that if he had it to do over again he would do the same. It was hard to live without her, but it would be harder to live with her feeling that it had been unfair to marry her until she had had time to consider and decide if she would carry on the great traditions of her father's family.

She had decided. Perhaps she was already engaged to an embryo earl or baron. She would have to come to the United States to renounce her citizenship. It was a wonder Lord Gowan hadn't insisted upon that before this. Well, he had his work to help him forget her.

The white-capped maid hurried through the hall.

"Did Mrs. Corey send you to round me up, Janey?" he asked. "Tell her I'm on the way."

"Oh, no, Mr. Peter, it wasn't for you. I — I was coming to knock on the green-r—oom door, sir."

"Does even the idea of knocking on a door make you red in the face and breathless? I'll do it and save you from a nervous break-down. Run along."

"If you think you — you'd better, sir." She swallowed audibly and visibly. "It's the green-room door, Mr. Peter. K-knock t-twice."

What the dickens is she giggling about? Peter asked himself as she disappeared. There's something cockeyed about this whole business. Who is this mysterious guest? I'll bite. He knocked on the door. It was flung open.

"All right, Janey. I — Peter!"

Peter's heart stopped, raced on like a thousand-horsepower motor. It was Con staring at him, Con in something white splashed with gigantic pink roses. Why was she here? Had she come to renounce —

"Peter! I'm sorry! Don't, please don't look so — so — stricken. Tim said it was wrong but I did so want to surprise you."

She was clutching his arms, raising her lovely face with its dark, drenched eyes, its vivid scarlet lips to his.

"Aren't you glad I'm here, Peter?"

"Glad!" His lips set in a hard line. "That depends upon what you came for. They're waiting dinner for us. Come on. Does Mother know you're here?"

She shook her head, bit her lips to steady them. Tim had warned her to look out for the stick from her rocket. It had come down and plunged straight through her heart.

"Stay in the hall until I tell her," she heard Peter say, then his exclamation, "Lord Gowan! Mother. You knew?"

"Yes. Peter. Come in Connie, dearest." Angela Corey put her arm around the girl and kissed her tenderly.

"Your grandfather wrote me you and he were sailing and I motored to town for him this afternoon." Her voice was shaken. "Dinner is served. We will feel less jittery after we've had something to eat."

Con felt as if she were in a dream as she looked across the table at her grandfather. He appeared years younger than when she had left him in the city, was it only this morning? She was glad he could see her in the home in which she had grown up. This room with its white walls and finish, its white damask hangings, was a perfect background for Angel in her orchid frock. There was nothing finer at Trentmere Towers than the glistening silver and fine china on the table and as for that feathery mass of stephanotis and yellow mimosa in the center, nothing the liveried servants arranged could equal that in artistic beauty.

"Well, did the rocket boom to suit you?" Tim, beside her, inquired.

"You told," she accused. "You said you wouldn't."

"Better a pale pink lie than a tragedy. I was afraid of the effect of the surprise on Pete. He's been working hard. Bad Boy Dafter won't have to worry about bed and board for the next forty years. He's all set. Pete's going through pretty deep water," there was a hint of mystery in his low voice.

"Deep water!" Con looked at Peter seated at the head of the oblong table. Even his lips were colorless. Was he sorry she was here?

"Is — is it Lydia again?" she whispered. Better get it over, plunge the dagger of loss into her heart to the hilt, she told herself.

"Lydia — didn't you know she was engaged? Picked up an Englishman on the ship coming home, he's something big in the City, after Peter had snubbed her unmercifully. Honest, I was sorry for her. Forget her. Great stuff, that family tree of yours, isn't it?"

"Tim, it's wonderful! It makes up for —"

"I know, let's forget that, too. It appears that your grandfather is about to make a speech. He has dropped and replaced his monocle three times."

Lord Gowan rose and lifted his wineglass. "I give you Angela, the future Lady Gowan," he proposed.

Half an hour later Con retreated to a swinging seat on the dusky terrace. She wouldn't be missed inside. Her heart was racing, her face burning. Angel at Trentmere Towers. It would be heavenly to have her there but just what would she herself do, when Red Maples was closed? Silly, you couldn't live here anyway without her, could you? she flouted herself. Would you stay in this town if Peter married?

"You've chosen a dark corner, but not quite dark enough." It was Peter's voice. He swept aside her bouffant skirt and sat beside her.

"What's all the shootin' about, Con? I saw you dash out of the room as if afraid you would cry. Not sorry Mother is to marry Lord Van, are you?"

"Sorry! Petey, it's the greatest thing that ever happened. Don't you see, when I go back to visit —"

"Then you are not planning to live in

England? The last I heard you were cheering for your King."

"I know, Peter. I was frightfully hurt when the General announced that you were all walking out on me. For a minute I thought it — it was because —"

"You needn't tell me what you thought. You slashed my heart to ribbons. Do you know what I thought when you opened that door upstairs?" His low, vibrant voice set her pulses racing. Could he hear them thrumming?

"I hope you thought I hadn't aged frightfully in the years and *years* since you left Cherrytree Farm."

"I thought you had come to renounce your American citizenship."

"Would — would you have cared, Peter?"

He bent his head to hear the whispered question. As her dark eyes met his, he caught her in his arms and pressed his lips hard on hers. "That's how much I would have cared. Going to marry me? Love me?"

"Now and forever, Peter."

Later she tipped her head back against his shoulder and looked up earnestly into his eyes.

"I saw her, Peter. I knew this would happen."

"Have I ever told you that you have the

loveliest smile in the world? The most gorgeous eyes? Whom did you see? What did you know would happen?"

"She floated in through the window. I love your eyes when they are full of little sparks of laughter, but don't laugh at that."

"I'll try not to, darling, but ladies who float in through open windows are a trifle out of my line. Who was she?"

"The ghost of Trentmere Towers. The Spanish Bride who appears only before the marriage of the heir. I was sure I would be married but I didn't know it would be you."

He kissed her warmly, tenderly, thoroughly.

"After that dare tell me you didn't know it would be I. Speaking of marriage —"

"The General was speaking of it to me only yesterday. He said if I married —"

"When. Not if."

"You are as much of a dictator as he. All right then, 'when,' he wants the ceremony to be at the Towers' chapel." She clasped her hands about his arm. "Oh, Peter, could we? I would love it."

His brows knit above his intent eyes. After a moment he asked:

"Willing to sail for England next week?"

"Tomorrow, if necessary."

He caught her close.

"Then, you sweet soul, we could."

The employees of Thorndike Press hope you have enjoyed this Large Print book. All our Large Print titles are designed for easy reading, and all our books are made to last. Other Thorndike Press Large Print books are available at your library, through selected bookstores, or directly from us.

For information about titles, please call:

(800) 223-1244
(800) 223-6121

To share your comments, please write:

Publisher
Thorndike Press
P.O. Box 159
Thorndike, Maine 04986